Praise for *Redheads*

"*Redheads* is a terrific book about apes and people, do-gooders and do-badders, science and superstition, ecology and psychology, nature and nurture, and how we all fit together in this old world. Sochaczewski casts an unflinching eye on the foibles of man and beasts alike and no one comes out unscathed. Now I know what Paul was doing all those years in Southeast Asia, and it's sure paid off!"

– Mark Olshaker,
Author of *The Edge*, co-author of *Mindhunter*.

"A ribald, engrossing novel with a deeper message regarding the clash of cultures and our relation to the environment."

– Edwin Bernbaum,
Author of *Sacred Mountains of the World*

"*Redheads* combines the witty insights of George MacDonald Fraser with the realism of Thomas Hardy – a real Asian treat"

– Jeffrey A. McNeely,
Chief scientist, IUCN-The World Conservation Union

"*Redheads* pits the ideals of science and biodiversity conservation against the real world of nasty politics, reductionist thinking, and economic 'imperatives'. The engaging spell of the author weaves the impression that indigenous peoples and other primate inhabitants of the forest are the only hope we have left of saving the tropical ecosystems of the world."

– Darrell Addison Posey, Ph.D.
Oxford Centre for the Environment, Ethics & Society

"Sochaczewski, author of *Soul of the Tiger* and an 'old Asia hand', displays both his extensive knowledge of rainforest politics and a real ability to tell an entertaining story."

– Chris Elliott, Ph.D.
Director, Forests for Life Campaign, WWF-World Wide Fund for Nature

More praise for *Redheads*

"With the trained eyes and the sensitivity of someone who lived among the orangutans in the wilds of Borneo, Sochaczewski tells a captivating story of the struggle to save the rainforests. *Redheads* reads like a fast-paced, high-powered movie script that makes the issue of environmental devastation come alive and demand reforms."

– Robert A. Pastor,
Professor, Emory University and former National Security Council Staff

"A great read. *Redheads* accurately and entertainingly captures the cynical reality of today's conservation conflicts. This entertaining book is a must for anyone interested in learning how the global environment movement really works."

– Daniel Navid,
Director, Environmental Law Training Programme of the United Nations

"*Redheads* is the perfect example of a new genre, an eco-thriller so suspenseful that you learn about this strange world while sitting on the edge of your seat. *Redheads* is a roaring tale of tropical suspense. It is witty and smart and altogether a wonderful treat."

– Thomas Bass,
Author of *The Predictors* and
Camping with the Prince and Other Tales of Science in Asia.

"This rambunctious romp through the Borneo jungles is both fun and deceptively insightful. If this is how the world REALLY works in the realm of nature protection, then where do we go from here? The story reveals important realities about the way things can be in the hurley-burley world of nature protection and environment-alism. Noble-intentioned jetsetting environmentalists: Take Heed!"

– Sir Russell Betts, Ph.D.
Former director of WWF-World Wide Fund for Nature's Indonesia program.

REDHEADS

PAUL SPENCER
SOCHACZEWSKI

Sid Harta Publishers
2000

Published by Sid Harta Publishers (Australia)
P.O. Box 1102
Hartwell
Victoria 3125
Australia

Telephone: 61 3 9560 9920
Facsimile: 61 3 9560 9921
E-mail: author@sidharta.com.au

First published: April, 2000.
Copyright: Paul Spencer Sochaczewski.
Design, Typesetting, Graphics: Design Plus.
Cover photograph: Jeffrey A. McNeely.
Illustrations for chapter headings courtesy of
Editions Didier Millet - *The Encyclopedia of Malaysia*, 1998 (Vol.3).
Proofreading: Dr. John Quigley; Mollymook Manuscripts.

This book is a work of fiction. Among the fictional characters, any
resemblance to persons, living or dead, is coincidental. Similarly, the
Sultanate of Manusia is a fictional nation. In the few instances where
real people are mentioned, it is not claimed, nor should it be assumed,
that their lives bear any resemblance to the events in this book.

A portion of the income earned from *Redheads* will be donated to
support nature conservation efforts in Borneo.

Sochaczewski, Paul Spencer
ISBN 0-9587448-9-0 (paperback); 0-9587448-8-2 (hardcover)
Printed by Australian Print Group, Maryborough, Victoria, Australia

The Author

PAUL SPENCER SOCHACZEWSKI has spent more than 30 years on the conservation front lines. He served in the Peace Corps for two years in remote parts of Sarawak, a Malaysian state on the island of Borneo, and was creative director of J. Walter Thompson, advertising affiliates, in Singapore and Indonesia for another ten. He ran World Wildlife Fund International's global public awareness campaigns to protect tropical rainforests and biodiversity and is now a consultant for IUCN – the World Conservation Union and the International Osteoporosis Foundation. While on sabbatical in Hawaii in 1992, Paul changed his family name from Wachtel to the original vowel-challenging name of his Polish-born father, explaining why some of his titles are still listed under Paul Spencer Wachtel. He is co-author (with Jeff McNeely) of *Soul of the Tiger – Searching for Nature's Answers in Southeast Asia* (Doubleday, Paragon, Oxford University Press, University of Hawaii Press, Sho Koh Na) and *EcoBluff Your Way to Greenism – The Guide to Instant Environmental Credibility* (Bonus Books). He has written more than 500 by-lined articles for many publications, including *International Herald Tribune, Wall Street Journal, International Wildlife, BBC Wildlife, Earth Times, E: The Environmental Magazine* and *GQ Active*. He is on the editorial advisory board of the *Indonesian Heritage Encyclopedia* and the *Encyclopedia of Malaysia* (Archipelago Press).

Author's note

Some projects happen with a burst of fireworks. Other endeavors, and I include *Redheads* in this list, need years to gestate and evolve.

I was first introduced to the tropical rainforest when I worked in Borneo in the Peace Corps, an experience I'd recommend for everyone with more than a pinch of curiosity in their souls. The Sarawak rainforest, and the people who live in or near it, created an other-worldly stage for my modest adventures. I was blessed to be able to experience life from a new perspective, enjoying gee-whiz boys' adventures – hunting wild pigs, burning leeches off my legs, pulling longboats up shallow rapids, getting drunk on rice wine in longhouses on the upper Baram River while listening to Kayans reminisce about the good old days and speculate on the future. So my first acknowledgement goes to the countless people of Southeast Asia for letting me into their homes, and sometimes, their hearts.

My colleagues in the diverse, and not always pretty, world of international nature conservation have helped me understand that, like the song says, the job of protecting the environment "don't come easy." There are no quick fixes to saving orangutans and the forests while respecting the needs of people. The biology of the rainforest is complicated, to be sure, the diverse range of social needs and private greeds can make a sane man weep, and the available options are often Byzantine in their complexities. I've learned from innumerable conservation professionals. Colleagues in Asia include Professor Emil Salim, Julius Tahija, Harrison Ngau, Effendy Sumardja, Setiati Sastrapradja, a game warden whom I know only as Fata who risked his life in an attempt to catch turtle poachers in Aru, and many other people who don't accept the realpolitik compromises that so often lead to destruction of nature. And in the international arena, special thanks to Jeff McNeely, Dan Navid, John MacKinnon, George Schaller, Russ Mittermeier, Edward O. Wilson, Richard Evans Schultes, Peter Raven, Bruno Manser, Andrew Mitchell, Javed Ahmad, Jeff Sayer, Jim Thorsell among dozens of other insightful and effective conservationists.

My writing support has come from many quarters. Annelies and the Sunday Morning Breakfast Group, over a decade ago, helped play the 'what if' game. Gary Provost never stopped admonishing my colleagues and me at the Writers' Retreat Workshop to 'tell the story.' Jim Clad provided a journalist's rigor. Kerry Collison has been gracious and generous with his support. Mark Olshaker has been a literary role model. Didier Millet provided the illustrations in the book and fine companionship on the trail. David Hallmark and Bill Stone have been with me on various Borneo adventures.

Finally, when your eyesight is going gonzo from staring at your screen for too long it's essential to have a bit of love floating around. Special thanks for my son David for giving me huge energy and happiness, Monique for helping me see life through joyous eyes, Mathilde (travel well) and Bernie for love and ice cream.

While *Redheads* is fiction, the destruction of Southeast Asia's rainforests is real. Nobody said doing the right thing should be simple. But the encouraging news is that there are good folks fighting for the rainforest and its people. Use your common sense and support the people and organizations that strike you as having integrity and guts.

Paul Spencer Sochaczewski

For Aunt Sarah.
I wish you peace.

PART I

RAPE
AND
PILLAGE

CHAPTER 1

1 January. 09:00.

Mount Malu National Park

Urs Gerhard smiled. You guys might be the first people in loincloths to make the cover of *Time*.

Urs stood with his companions at the crest of the hill. They watched a dirty, yellow timber truck accelerate as it free-wheeled down the dirt road into the deep valley. At the lowest point, the driver madly downshifted, straining to keep the momentum as the truck reached maximum speed and started uphill.

A cloud of heavy, red dust, which had been following the Komatsu truck like an obedient specter, engulfed the vehicle as it slowed on the incline, obliterating it from view as effectively as if it had been hit by a Stinger missile.

If we pull this off, those government guys will really be after my ass, Urs thought. He would have laughed out loud, but kept his peace. His Penan friends seemed uncomfortable when the Swiss chuckled privately.

He settled for scholarship. "What is the word for dirt in the air?" Urs asked the Penan tribesman at his side.

"*Tana marang*," the smaller man replied in the Penan language. Flying earth.

Urs Gerhard reached into his woven backpack for his journal and carefully noted the phonetic pronunciation. He wrote on the back of a page that he had decorated with a detailed botanical illustration of the *Comaphora mukul* plant, which the Penan brewed in a tea to fight fever.

The red dust, Urs thought, was the second most obscene aspect

3

of the loggers' invasion. It created dirt in a place that ought to be clean; it represented barrenness where there ought to be fertility. The hot dust, which he estimated would reach him in about thirty seconds, was almost as bad as the whine of the chain saw and the shocking quiet that came immediately after the felling of the huge rainforest trees. The Penan called the one 100-foot-tall trees the 'pillars of the sky.' When the trees crashed to the ground, the birds, monkeys and insects went silent in a communion that recognized something terribly unnatural had occurred.

The loggers were invading the Penan homeland. The tribesmen, ill at ease in a world run by power and money, had tried to explain their problem to a government representative, had asked that the logging be stopped. The officials smiled and sold more timber concessions. No, talking didn't work, Urs thought regretfully. Something more dramatic was called for.

The overloaded truck snailed its way up the hill. The six Penan and the Swiss stood quietly. The single female Penan wore only a faded blue sarong wrapped around her waist. She suckled an infant. The male Penan wore dark blue loincloths that crossed under their crotches before ending in front and back flaps which hung halfway down their thighs. Each man's black hair was cut in straight bangs in the front while the back portion was left to grow long down the neck. Just above their knees, the men wore bracelets woven from monkey hair. They were barefoot and had been all their lives. On each foot the callused big and little toes spread to a width that could never be accommodated by store-bought shoes.

Urs was similarly dressed. A leaf containing a poultice of medicinal plants was tied around his ankle, healing a gash received when he had trodden on a sharp root. A six-foot-long blowpipe leaned against his shoulder.

The Penan knew the purpose of the truck, but it had no place in their scheme of things. It was as alien as a microwave oven would have been.

The owners of the truck would have disagreed. It was, Urs had learned, one of a fleet of 23 owned by the Hong Neiyi Timber Company. Hong Neiyi was the most visible element of an international, multiracial conglomerate. It was owned by Manusians, managed by a Korean and Manusian joint venture, and sold logs to Japan, which consumed the vast majority of Manusia's export. Like most of the 56 timber companies operating in the Sultanate of Manusia, the official owner of Hong Neiyi was a Manusian-born Chinese. It was a scam which provided marginal deniability to the real owner – Aminah binte Sjam, the wife of Mustafa bin Kayu, the Manusian Minister of the Environment. She did not think it would be productive for it to be widely known that she was profiting from the destruction of the same rainforests which her husband, during a speech at the United Nations, had sworn "to hold in trust for the world".

The Penan had been coached. However, Urs, like a conscientious schoolteacher, wondered whether they would remember their lines. He wasn't certain this little gambit would work, but it was all he could think of.

The truck, carrying seven 20-yard-long tree trunks, each a yard and a half in diameter and weighing as much as 200 men, groaned up the hill. The Penan walked into the center of the sun-baked dirt track which the timber *kampeni* had hacked out of the jungle. Urs slipped ten feet into the foliage and virtually disappeared. He did not want to be visibly part of this operation. His pet macaque, an infant whose mother had been barbecued for dinner three weeks before, nibbled on Urs' ear and then climbed onto Urs' head to groom the man. The tiny monkey, which he called Liebchen, worked her way carefully through her master's light brown hair, which gleamed reddish in the dust-diffused light. She picked out more than a few lice and ate excitedly.

The issue seemed so simple: forbid logging and let the Penan keep their forest. Urs understood simple issues. He had always considered himself a simple man, like the uncomplicated Penan he had befriended. But his mother had told him that a simple man with a passionate cause equals a dangerous creature, not unlike the European brown bear from which Urs got his name.

Urs watched the truck climb. The last time he had been in a car or truck had been two years earlier, when he had taken the bus from the Anjing International Airport to the port, where he had boarded a coastal steamer to Bohong, the first stop on his return trip to Mount Malu. Since then the Manusian security forces had been chasing him; angry that a foreigner had scoffed at their immigration laws, furious that he had been able to survive in the rainforest and apoplectic that he had befriended the disenfranchised, Penan tribesmen on the bottom of the Manusian pecking order.

Soon they'll have a real reason to want my head, Urs thought, when he watched six of his Penan friends stand at attention directly in front of the chugging truck.

"Shit," the young Chinese driver said in English as he braked.

"What the fuck is this?" he mumbled in Hokkien as the truck skidded to a stop just before flattening Urs' nearly-naked friends. Everyone was quickly engulfed in a red cloud. The driver jumped down from the truck's cabin.

The tiny monkey found a particularly juicy louse and offered it to her master. Urs allowed the monkey to put the gift in his mouth and he chewed mechanically, not taking his eyes off the confrontation.

A teenage Penan named Avalon approached the driver. Avalon, who had received his name from classmates at a government primary school he had attended for four years, spoke a little Malay. The driver spoke a little Malay. They had a short conversation in which the Penan explained, politely, that the driver was cutting down their home forests, asked he be so kind as to please stop and requested that he tell his colleagues to stop as well.

"What the hell," the driver shouted. "I've got a job to do. Who are you, anyway?"

"Avalon."

"No! Who *are* you?" he asked exasperated. "You're Penan," he said immediately, answering his own question. "No Penan is going to tell me I can't drive along this road. It isn't your road. It belongs to the *kampeni*," he shouted as he stormed back to the cab and started the engine.

Five Penan remained in place blocking his progress. The sixth, acting on a signal from Urs, mounted the truck's mudguard. The driver turned off the engine when he saw that the end of Laki's blowpipe was two feet from his neck.

Grumbling, but too terrified to protest, the driver climbed out of the truck. Standing with his hands on his hips, he asked: "What now?"

"You walk," Avalon answered. The Penan gave the acne-faced young driver a gourd of water and some smoked squirrel meat to ease his 20-mile trudge back to the timber company's base camp.

He had gone no more than 200 yards when Avalon, suddenly

remembering his instructions, ran after the terrified Chinese.

"Excuse me," Avalon said breathlessly.

"What?"

"I forgot to ask you for the keys."

The Chinese thought of slugging the guy but noticed that he was still within sight of the Penan, who could catch him with little effort. He slammed the keys to the ground. "Jungle bunny. Probably can't even drive," he mumbled in English, as he slunk off.

Urs joined his colleagues and showed them how to pry off the oil sump and put sand inside. He watched with satisfaction as his students sliced the worn tires with their machete-like *parangs*. Urs showed them how to start the engine, how to release the emergency brake, how to put the vehicle into reverse and, most importantly, how to jump out of the cab just as the behemoth started rolling backward. It made a spectacular sight as it gained speed, rammed into an embankment and jackknifed as the cab plunged into the forest. The truck fell on its side, blocking the road and littering ten ton logs like pick-up-sticks. Urs took out his sketchpad and pencils to record the scene of his first battle. His friends were calm, but not entirely joyful. The monkey Liebchen whined as the red dust stung her eyes.

* * * * *

Calves, thought Gilda. Maybe those are Bujang's best attributes. Hard, knobby calves like tree roots.

"Figs, Madame Doctor Gilda," Bujang said, as he pointed up into a tree that, from the ground at least, looked to Gilda to be identical to the billion other trees in the national park. Near the base, Bujang pointed out orangutan feces, perhaps two hours old. They were covered with flies, beetles and ants.

Gilda took out her *parang*, sliced a chunk off the tree at head height and, after checking her notes, marked the number 89 on the raw wood. Bujang would come back later to carve the number deep into the trunk.

Gilda was satisfied. She had found another tree which produces orangutan food, another small achievement in her efforts to document the lives of the red apes. Her plan was to map all the orangutan fruit trees in her study area and see whether there was a correlation between the visits of certain orangutans and the time when the fruit was ripe, or between the rainy season and the orangutan breeding cycle. She hadn't quite worked it out. But there was sure to be a correlation.

Gilda was proud that her methodology, like that of the best scientific experiments, was simple. Find evidence of orangutan feeding. Try to identify the tree and which animals were present. Write it all down. "Must make a note to work on the notebooks," she mumbled to herself. Just half an hour earlier, she and Bujang had come across tree number 7, which she had marked many years ago. Bujang reminded her that it was a wild mango. She puzzled over which orangutan was last seen feeding there and when? Those notes were somewhere in a pile back at camp. Must sort that out.

Bujang led the way, as usual. Gilda admired the unselfconscious way her camp foreman moved. A case could certainly be made for his hips, she thought.

"Bujang, why do you think there are so many different plants and animals in this forest?" Gilda asked the Kayan tribesman in her broken Malay sprinkled with kitchen-Indonesian, the only language they shared except for a few English phrases like "Madame Doctor". Language was not important to Gilda, since she considered herself a pilgrim in search of unspoken truths. But sometimes language was necessary – to tell the cook what to make for supper, to seduce the Minister of the Environment in order to renew her work permit, to write a letter to her husband and her son. Sometimes she wanted to talk to Bujang about something more complex than whether orangutans defecate in their nests. But a scientist has to make sacrifices. Gilda and Bujang talked at each other. They got by.

Gilda's world was that of the orangutan and the three-foot tall animals had their own communication. But what if I *could* talk to them, Gilda often wondered. What could they tell me about life in the forest? Are they angry when the more agile gibbons get the best fruit, when the poachers shoot the females and capture the babies, when the males have sex with the females and then shuffle off into the jungle? Maybe Gerry will be able to teach them enough so we can chat – the first true inter-species dialogue.

After ten years in the forest, Gilda had learned to spot a ruffle in the treetops that indicated orangutans. Gilda and Bujang found their quarry some thirty minutes due west of Camp Trinil: four orangutans – two adult females, one juvenile about six years old and a nursing infant.

"Why do you think they call them orangutans, Bujang?" Gilda asked after she was reasonably sure she wouldn't get a reply from her earlier question.

"Because they act just like people and they live in the forest," Bujang answered sensibly, providing a literal explanation of the Malay word orangutan, which means 'man of the forest'.

"That's a cop-out. What do you call real people who live in the forest?"

"Penan," Bujang joked.

"You really don't like them, do you?" she said, referring to the slight, pale nomads.

"They're not civilized, like us," Bujang replied, haughtily. Gilda was not certain whether "us" included female Hungarian-American expatriates risking malaria to study orangutan family development patterns.

Bujang explained. "The Penan, they don't live in proper long-houses, like we Kayans do. They don't bathe as often. They marry their cousins. They hardly wear clothes. They ..."

Gilda reconsidered. His back. Definitely his back, she thought, watching his shoulders glisten with mid-morning sweat.

The extended orangutan family group descended a steep ravine. Gilda didn't have the energy to follow them, but she did anyway – not wanting Bujang to think she was weak. It was only 9 a.m. and she was already well into her second (and last) quart bottle of water. After feeding for an hour, the animals then climbed, taking the high road through the trees. Bujang's wide, callused feet took him directly beneath the arboreal orangutan highway. Gilda stumbled after him, her feet slipping on the glistening, wet clay as she puffed across a stream, scrambled up a 30-foot hill, slid down the far side, winding up in the same stream but on a distant curve in the large S-bend the water described here. "This is stuff for Sisyphus," Gilda muttered and they crawled up yet another steep hill. Half an hour later, they arrived at a ridge that paralleled the Hotut River, which bisected the Mount Malu National Park. The orangutans seemed to be napping.

"Bujang, what would you do if I wasn't here?" Gilda asked in staccato baby-Malay.

"I don't understand. You are here."

"Yes, but what if I had to leave Manusia? What would you do?"

Bujang thought for a moment before answering. Gilda took this as a good sign. Maybe he really does like me, she thought. Maybe I'm more than an easy lay and a regular paycheck.

"I would be very sad, Madame Doctor Gilda," Bujang replied. "*Sedih, sedih, sedih.*"

"You know, if I left the country, then the orangutan research project would stop," Gilda said.

"Yes. I know."

"And then you wouldn't have a job."

"Yes, you're right."

Good so far, Gilda thought. Dare I risk the next question? What the hell. Damn this language. It's so infantile that I can't even say anything in the conditional. "And if I went, you would marry one of the longhouse girls?"

Gilda turned to watch Bujang's reaction. Blank.

"But you are not going away, are you?" Bujang finally asked.

"No, not as long as the authorities keep on renewing my work permit. But they're getting more and more nervous about foreigners in this area, ever since that madman Urs escaped into the forest."

Bujang stopped and turned. "Do you know this Urs man?" he asked.

"No. But I wish I did. I would tell him to get the hell out of my forest. It was calm before he came. Now the government people are nervous, the longhouse people are nervous, even the orangutans are nervous."

A sharp metallic clack screamed through the air.

"What's that, Bujang?"

"*Pangkas*, Madame Doctor Gilda."

"*Pangkas*. Must look that one up. I don't suppose that bird has any religious significance?"

"Sometimes," Bujang answered.

Damn these woggiepoos. Sometimes this, sometimes that. Can't a girl ever get an empirical yes or no?

"Bujang, hold still. There's a leech on your back." Gilda took her *parang* from its wooden sheath and scraped the blood-sucking

10

worm from his skin. I wonder if this *parang* really has magic like that old man said, she thought idly.

Gilda and Bujang followed a deer trail into a valley and squelched across a muddy stream.

"Bujang, are you happy when we are together?" As soon as Gilda asked the question she realized how ridiculous it sounded. What's happiness to this man? Well-cooked rice? Good wild boar hunting?

"Yes, Madame Doctor Gilda." Well, she thought, I got the answer I deserved.

"Bujang, I have an idea. You like being with me and I like being with you. We have dynamite sex together. And it's in your interest to make sure that I stay here. Why don't the two of us, like, ..."

Gilda's marriage proposal was interrupted by a screech from the middle branches of a durian tree.

"What's that?"

"Orangutans, Madame Doctor Gilda."

"I *know* that. What's going on?"

"*Perkosaan*," he replied. Rape.

Gilda was delighted. She had read MacKinnon's reports about orangutan rape, but in her fifteen years at Camp Trinil had never witnessed it herself. Unfortunately, all she could see that morning was an occasional flash of red-orange fur and bouncing branches. Forty feet above Gilda and Bujang, Leonardo, a 13-year-old sub-adult orangutan, raped Delilah, an adult female.

"I can't really see what's going on, Bujang. Can you?"

"Not too well, but I've seen it before," Bujang answered, pleased to be able to help Gilda in her research. "Leonardo is afraid of the big male who controls this territory, but he needs sex – so he takes it quickly and leaves."

"What do you mean, 'he takes it quickly'? What does he do?"

"Well, he just approaches her and does it."

"How so, Bujang? Show me." Gilda unbuttoned the front of her field dress. "It's important that I get this right. This is important social behavior we're witnessing. I might even get a scientific paper out of this. So, let's say that I'm Delilah. Let's pretend that this log is the branch of a tree. Now, I'm just sitting here, eating some fruit." She took a Mars bar from her pack and started to nibble. "Show me what happens."

Bujang approached Gilda quickly, from the rear. He pushed her down hard so her stomach crushed the rotting log, sending a stream of termites scurrying. Gilda's upper body and legs were raised off the ground, balanced like the ends of a seesaw. Bujang yanked her skirt back over her head, ripped off her white cotton panties, and took her from behind.

In the trees, Leonardo stopped pumping to look down at the strange sight. He growled a muted orangutan hiss.

Gilda wriggled. She saw a lizard scurry under the log, two feet from her nose. "Try to time it accurately, Bujang," she gasped. "This is science. Take as much time as the apes do." She heard him start the stopwatch function of his Casio watch, a present she had given him on his last birthday.

"I'm not sure how long it lasts, Madame Doctor Gilda," Bujang said when he paused after a minute. "Leonardo's stopped, too."

"Don't stop damnit. Keep going. Improvise."

"Oh, OK. Leonardo's starting again." In the trees, Delilah bared her teeth and screamed.

"That's good," Gilda whispered.

"Now he's stopped again."

"Don't stop. Oh, don't stop."

"One minute, forty-five seconds," Bujang said when both he and Leonardo had finished.

Gilda took a deep breath. While she lay prone on the rotting wood, catching her breath, Bujang cleaned himself with some leaves and the remaining water from Gilda's bottle. Gilda stirred when she felt the ants move up the inside of her thigh. By then, Bujang had already put on his faded red basketball shorts and was climbing the tree to collect some of the odiferous durian for lunch.

Gilda fixed her dress and reached into her pack for her notebook. I wonder what old Jaap Van der Kamp would make of all this, she thought. The things I do for science.

Chapter 2

10 May. 11:00.

Nirvana

Early in his teaching career at Camp Trinil, Gerry realized that he needed a quiet place where he could escape from his orangutan students and not be bothered by the frustrations of trying to teach sign language to a bunch of delinquent apes.

Gerry had created his private place near a waterfall that fell into a pool as big as a Californian hot-tub. The water then dripped downhill into a clear stream that eventually trickled into the Hotut River which flowed by Camp Trinil, eventually flowing into the South China Sea.

Although part of the location's appeal lay in its physical beauty, Gerry admitted that what he really liked about it was that it was so difficult to get to. There was no direct path to the spot and every time Gerry made the hour's journey he took pride in stumbling uphill through thorny rattan patches and then down small, but dangerous, escarpments.

His original idea, when he first discovered the waterfall, was to build a retreat by himself. For Gerry, the construction of his hideaway was not merely a civil engineering project, but part of a serious ritual – a test of his manhood. First, he had assembled a survival pack to strap onto his thigh. He had worn this pack during his first weeks at Camp Trinil whenever he left the security of base camp. The small canvas pack, with velcro attachments, contained emergency fish hooks, a red plastic worm, waterproof matches, a mirror, a compass and water purification tablets. It also contained a tiny spool of 20 yards of parachute cord, which the owner of the

Chapel Hill Adventure Travel and Tennis Shop assured him was used by all the great explorers. Gerry wasn't too sure exactly what he would use it for, but thought that in a pinch he would be able to weave a hammock or make a snare to catch dinner. He strapped on his slightly rusty parang and set to work.

The afternoon was not a success. He realized, after an hour of hacking and cursing, that it was not all that easy to construct a pleasure dome, however modest, if one was not to the parang born.

"*Ikut saya nanti petang*," he had instructed Bujang in his beginner's Malay – come with me this afternoon. On a level spot near the waterfall, Gerry pulled out the simplistic architectural plans he had worked on for days. Bujang was a skilled carpenter and, after raiding the camp's stockpile for planks and nails, in three afternoons constructed an open-air lean-to structure on a raised platform. It was in the shadow of a towering durian tree which created a spangled half-sun half-shadow that was favored by iridescent blue and red butterflies which found the area a congenial place to spend their short lives.

"Here, Bujang, thanks for helping," Gerry said in Malay, as he offered the sweaty Kayan the equivalent of five US dollars, a healthy sum. "And, seriously, you've got to promise not to tell anyone about this place. Particularly not Doctor Gilda. Let's just keep this between us guys." Then, to bring home the point, he added, squeezing Bujang's hard shoulder, "Don't disappoint me or there could be, you know, real unpleasantness."

Whether Gerry's subtle message, conveyed in stumbling Malay, was misunderstood, or whether Europeans in Asia are doomed to have no secrets even though they may wish to think they have, the entire camp knew about Gerry's hideaway by dinner. When told where it was, few felt sufficiently curious to traipse up and down hills to view the construction and most wondered why Gerry had chosen that isolated spot when he had all the comforts of the camp to enjoy.

"I'm off to do some bird-watching," he would call cheerfully to Gilda as he set off most afternoons, waving his King and Dickinson Field Guide to the Birds of South-East Asia. "See you at dinner."

Once ensconced in his shelter, Gerry came alive. He stripped naked and lay under the waterfall for the best part of an hour, washing away the sweat and grime and pressure of trying to teach sign language to animals who were brutishly clever but who didn't really want to spend time in school.

Prior to bathing, he always lit a dozen incense sticks and a few Double Rabbit-brand mosquito coils, while whistling the Malay-language jingle for the circular coils that he heard constantly on the radio – *"membunoh nyamuk sampai mati"* – kills mosquitoes till they're dead. It was catchy and it was the first advertising slogan he had translated all on his own.

Any intrusive insects that were silly enough to brave the smoke-screen had another surprise. Gerry sprayed the stilts and floorboards with great doses of ant and roach insecticide ("as powerful as an angry elephant", the pack's label claimed). Just let them try to climb up to his private place.

Just before Gerry settled down on the folding chaise lounge he had purchased in Anjing, he added the final touch – he spiced the already-lethal fumes with a liberal dose of flying insect killer. Together, his precautions usually ensured him half an hour of insect-free peace.

On this particular, sweaty afternoon, Gerry, the acting head of Camp Trinil, unlocked the metal ammunition cases that he had told Gilda contained his photographic equipment. He took out his real survival kit. First the Hawaiian Fantasy sun-tan oil, which smelled like a coconut ice cream sundae. He smeared himself with the oil, while facing one of life's basic dilemmas. When he had first returned to Chapel Hill after a year in the forest, some of his friends were surprised that he was not tanned, but only vaguely less pallid than usual. They made him feel somehow unsuccessful. After all, he was in the tropics, wasn't he? His friends could barely scrape together enough money to go to the beach for a long weekend to get some color and here Gerry was, actually living on the equator. However, on the other hand, the locals of Manusia abhorred the sun and did everything they could to keep out of it – sunbathing was akin to public expression of emotion, being in the category of behavior that was just not practiced by respectable, sensible folk. Gerry was divided on the issue. Should he cultivate a sickly pallor like Gilda, thereby showing that he spent most of his time in the deep forest where only five percent of the sun reaches the ground? Or should he add some color to his cheeks since, after all, what was the point of being in the tropics if you couldn't catch some rays?

Today Gerry rolled back the canvas roof and opted for fashionable melanoma. He lay in the sun, listening to the Stones on his Walkman.

There were other marvels in his metal boxes – several issues of *Playboy*, *Penthouse*, and *Hustler* that he had picked up the last time he was home and which he had refused to even glance at until he was firmly established in his refuge. He lay back in the sun, humming to 'Gimme Shelter', turning a stained page every once in a while, languorously rubbing himself with essence of Waikiki, oblivious to the distant glances of Bujang, who, during Gerry's frequent absences, had managed to pick the locks of the ammunition boxes and enjoy the pictures of blondes with big tits.

Gerry felt obligated to pursue some intellectual pursuit when he was at Nirvana, as he had named his simple paradise.

"Now, what shall it be today?" he murmured to himself. He mentally rummaged through the list of conundrum options: Why do the gentlest of Asians kick dogs? Why is the food so hot? Why don't Asians sweat? Why is there so little respect for privacy? Why do Europeans need so much stuff? Why are white women so attractive to brown men? Why is the opposite also true?

Each day Gerry would roll a joint and consider one of these problems and try to come up with a sensible answer. It was evidence, he felt, of his disciplined mind grappling with some of life's bigger issues. At the end of his stay in Manusia he would publish the results of his internal dialogues and be acclaimed as both a great linguistic explorer and a truly big thinker on truly big issues.

Gerry decided to explore the thorny question of why Asians like noise so much when they are generally pictured as quiet, placid people. Having decided that this was the issue of the day, he put it aside in his mind to mellow – fully intending to come back to it later, like a fine wine. However, first he had other business to attend to. The *Penthouse* letters column. Were they real letters? he wondered. Perhaps he should write to the editor about his après-class sessions with Queenie. Would readers in Portland be able to relate to an orangutan performing oral sex on a Jewish psychology student and amateur basketball player from Chicago? He sneaked a peak at the Pet of the Month, a German brunette named Helga, who was in the process of disentangling herself from a fringed pair of western cowboy chaps while fiddling with a Colt 45.

He decided to keep Helga waiting and felt proud that he was sufficiently in control of his desires to plow through a Ray Bradbury story about telepathy in the 23rd century before turning back to Helga to have a closer look at the intricate leather etchings on her holster. On turning the page, he was bemused to see her crouched down while wearing her spurs. Gerry was wondering whether young Helga really wore spurs to bed, when a shadow suddenly descended over the centerfold. Gerry looked up, trying to figure out what creature loomed above him.

"*Siapa* ... who ... what are you?" Gerry stuttered, not sure what language to use. For he was confronted by a six-foot tall gangly white man, wearing nothing but a loincloth, round granny glasses and a grin. A monkey sat on his right shoulder. He looked like a European lost in time.

The visitor remained quiet.

"Yes, what can I do for you?" Gerry asked again, after covering his fast-fading erection with the November issue.

"My name is Urs," the stranger finally answered. "Perhaps you have known of me?"

"Urs. Of course. Hi, guy. Glad to meet you. Of course I've heard of you," Gerry rambled.

Urs refused the extended, oily hand.

"We need to talk."

"Sure, have a seat. Some dried fruit?" Gerry offered as he slid off the sun chair to slip on his khaki Eddie Bauer bush shorts. Urs was amused by the American's sheepish gestures.

"*Ja*. It's good." Urs munched contentedly. Gerry smiled awkwardly at the visitor and sat back on the chair, instantly realizing that he had given away an advantage to the Swiss, who had remained standing, towering above the American.

Urs reached for another wrinkled apricot and chewed it noisily, before continuing.

"You know what I do?"

"Yes. Well, sort of. I mean, sure I've heard about you."

"You have heard what?"

"Hey, lighten up, Urs. I'm on your side. I've heard you are helping the natives fight against the timber operations. Doing a Robin Hood trip, trying to help the little guys. That kind of stuff."

Urs took off his glasses and cleaned them on his loincloth. Before replacing them, he rubbed the bridge of his nose. Gerry noticed a large, septic mosquito bite just under the Swiss man's left eye.

"I have a favor to ask you," Urs said with a half smile, his eyes hooded with fatigue.

Uh, oh, Gerry thought. He wants to borrow a magazine. He'll wander off with it and I'll never see it again.

"I need a, how you say it, an intermediate," the Swiss said. "Someone to send out mail for me and get mail for me without the government people about it knowing."

Gerry thought a moment and wondered why in the world this semi-human character needed mail. Playboy was banned by the Islamic Sultanate's postal authorities, so Urs couldn't expect to get a subscription through. Maybe he has a girl back home who writes him "Dear Urs" letters.

"It is important for our fight that people all over the world know what is happening to the forests, so they can put pressure on the government in Anjing," Urs explained. "But, as you can see, it is difficult for me to have my own mailbox."

"And you want me to be that mailbox?"

"Ja, that is right."

"Wow, that's a pretty heavy request. Why me?" Gerry asked.

"You mumble, I do not understand you," Urs said quietly, rummaging through the dried fruits to find the white pear slices, which reminded him of home. He ate three, and passed a wrinkled prune to Liebchen, who chewed wetly.

Gerry had learned from a girlfriend, who was studying for her MBA, that if you want to take command of a situation you should never let other people see your teeth. Monkeys showed their teeth when they were afraid, she explained. Gerry thought it was good advice and, whenever he remembered, he tried to speak with his mouth half closed. He did not mind doing so, since he had broken two incisors when he had fallen down an escalator the year before at Bloomingdales. He generally explained it as an old lacrosse injury. Few people were as direct as Urs in pointing out that his behavioral tic made his speech virtually unintelligible.

"How did you find me?" Gerry asked, speaking a bit more clearly. He was uncomfortable that someone knew more about him

18

than he knew about that someone. Gerry had heard about Urs, of course. Urs Gerhard was the new celebrity of Manusia, an outlaw from somewhere in the Swiss alps. Half the police in Manusia were looking for him since the timber truck hijackings had started.

"You are not difficult to find," Urs declared. "My friends and I can find almost anyone."

"I'm going to have to think about this for a while, Urs," Gerry said.

"I understand," Urs replied, not moving.

"Good. So, why don't we meet, say, here, in, say, a couple of weeks and we can talk some more."

"The sky could fall in during a couple of weeks," Urs said, attempting a Swiss joke. "You think, that is good. I will wait. Here."

Gerry switched into logic mode. Urs was helping the local peoples in the fight to keep their forest homeland. During the past few months the Penan had blockaded roads throughout the region, had sabotaged timber trucks. The police were after the Swiss. Conclusion: Urs was big trouble; Gerry could be thrown out of the country if anyone found out that they had even met. Gerry couldn't afford to be thrown out, at least not yet. He didn't have all the data he needed for his Ph. D. dissertation on orangutan communication skills. Shit, why did this guy have to show up?

Urs stood by quietly. He flicked through a copy of *Hustler* and smiled at the ads for satin bed sheets, hydroponic marijuana growing systems and electronic keyboards. Gerry noted that the Swiss, with scarred legs from constantly scraping leeches off his skin, arms with odd gray and brown patches that reminded Gerry of the fungus that attacked all his camera lenses, was not such a revolutionary to the native cause that he did not require some contact with the outside world.

While Urs glanced at the nude photos of women that their boyfriends and husbands had taken and sent to the magazine, Gerry thought about the implications. Maybe Urs could be useful to me.

"Urs, I've got a question for you," Gerry said, hoping to change the subject away from revolution. "You're an old Asia hand. One thing I can't figure out is why wrestling is the favorite television program in Manusia." It was a question that had been nagging Gerry for weeks. It seemed that Manusians were placid, polite people, but they just loved watching large, hairy white men bash each other.

Urs looked at Gerry as if the American had skied down the Matterhorn on a skateboard. "I do not watch too much television."

"Right. But you *have* seen TV. I mean, TV here. In Manusia."

"I have."

"And didn't you find it unusual that they like wrestling so much?"

"You have decided?" Urs asked bluntly, tiring of the conversation.

"If I agree, Urs, what's in it for me? I mean, what's the bottom line?"

Urs smiled his nothing smile. He resembled a zen holy man nearing the end of a traveling salesman joke and not worried that he had forgotten the punch line. "You will help a lot of people," he said finally.

This Urs is one strange dude, Gerry thought. He had read an interview the Swiss man had granted to Jonathan Goh, a bright young reporter with the *Singapore Straits Times* who had evaded Manusian police to meet with Urs in the forest. Goh had done his homework. Never before had a newspaper carried such a damning story about greed and corruption in the Sultanate. The edition of the newspaper carrying the story was promptly banned by the Manusian security service, which meant that most people in the country with friends overseas were certain to have had a copy of the article sent to them.

Gerry was dying to ask Urs whether the Penan girls were good in bed. Instead, Gerry stalled and talked politics.

"Do you think you have a chance, Urs? To get rid of the timber people, I mean."

"Yes, we have a chance. If people know about us."

"What if they catch you?"

"If they catch me, they catch me. The Penan don't need me. They will continue to fight."

"What if I refuse to be your conduit?"

Urs frowned at the unfamiliar word, but put it in context and added it to his vocabulary. "Yes, you could refuse."

"Right. Well, I'm sorry, old buddy. I'd really love to, really would, but, you see, I'm here as a guest of the Government – the

Ministry of the Environment, to be exact – and they distinctly told me to keep out of political activity. So, I'm afraid I can't help you. Sorry."

Urs remained standing. Quietly. He stared at Gerry. Liebchen leapt down to Gerry's lap and began licking his stomach. It was the first time she had tasted Hawaiian Tropic. It was good.

"That is too bad, Gerry. I was hoping you would agree."

"Well, sorry. But we can still be friends. You'll manage without me."

"No, I meant I was sorry for you."

Gerry didn't like the tone in Urs' voice. He picked up the monkey and placed her on the cot next to him. "Pardon me?"

"If we are friends, then I can tell you. If you cannot help me, then it might be embarrassing for you."

"Embarrassing. How so?" Gerry asked with a bravado that belied his sweaty palms.

"Gerry, I need someone I can trust. The police would love me to find. You will help?" Gerry wasn't sure if it was a statement or a question.

"No, please answer my question. What do you mean embarrassing?"

"I've already given your name to some of my foreign contacts: Jerry Schwartz. Spelled with a 'J' so you'll know it's for me. Bohong Post Office. PO Box 2837. Camp Trinil. Mount Malu National Park. Manusia."

Gerry's bravado was as limp as his dick. The bastard had his correct mailing address.

"Shit."

Urs found a dried apple slice lurking in the bottom of the bag. He bit into it and spat half to Liebchen. "You should be getting some mail any day now," he said, finally.

"I guess that makes it a *fait accompli*. You speak French, don't you?"

"I am from the Wallis. We speak German. We speak French. We get by."

"I guess you've got yourself a new partner, Urs," Gerry said, checkmated.

The two men chatted for a while about logistics, mail drops and codes, a conversation Gerry found simultaneously disturbing and exciting. The more he thought about it, however, the more interesting it became. This was as close to espionage as he was ever likely to get.

"Well, nice to meet you. I must go back down to camp," Gerry said, fifteen minutes later. He thought that excuse sounded better than saying that he was afraid to return in the dim twilight.

"Be careful, it's getting dark," Urs advised, brotherly. "If you like, one of my friends can escort you down," he said, waving his hand toward the surrounding forest that Gerry knew contained several pairs of silent, watching Penan eyes.

"No thanks. I know the way like my backyard."

"I'd like to give you a present," Urs said quietly. He walked a few yards into the forest and came back with a foot long dart fashioned from a thin, rigid frond of rattan. One end was encased in a funnel-shaped cork buttress. The working end was crusty with a strychnine-relative, *Antiaris toxicaria*, a black, tar-like plant extract that would help your digestion if you ate it, and kill you quickly if it entered your bloodstream. "This is a poison dart. Kills within minutes, you know. I don't think there's an antidote. But you're a scientist – maybe you know of one. Anyway, it's yours to keep. All my friends carry them and they go wherever I go. Funny, they're very protective of me and get very angry when someone tries to, how you say, cross double me."

PART II

NEGOTIATIONS

CHAPTER 3

23 July. 15:00.

Camp Trinil

"Squark, squelch urgent glurk Doctor Gilda mgrunch ..."

Gilda lurched across the small room and reached for the field radio, stumbled on her backpack and sent the radio clattering across the rough wooden floor, frightening Ringo, who had been asleep under her bed. The red ape groggily opened his eyes and lazily reached out his long arm to haul in the offending Motorola. Gilda retrieved it just after he had begun chewing on the mouthpiece.

Which of these damn buttons do you push? Gilda tried them all.

"*Ja*? Hello? *Apa khabar*?" she asked, never sure what language to use when receiving a call that might be a Stuttgart hell-and-brimstone missionary or a Baton Rouge herpetologist.

Through the glurgglum squrecha squawrks Gilda heard Tusau Padan, Mustafa bin Kayu's Princeton-educated administrative assistant calling with a "red alert". Gilda was instructed to meet the Minister in Bohong the following day to "discuss urgent business."

"Shit goddamnit."

It wasn't that Gilda didn't want to see the Minister of the Environment. She quite enjoyed the time they spent together. He was bright, sophisticated and offered her a chance to discuss things other than life at Camp Trinil. He was also responsible for her future in Manusia. One word from him to his colleagues in the Immigration Department and Gilda would get to keep her work permit for another year.

No, she wanted to see Mustafa bin Kayu. She just didn't want to see him now. There was too much going on. Francine, an orangutan Gilda had 'rehabilitated' to live in the wild, was about to give birth. Gilda was ready to start sorting out her backlog of notes and she felt that the time was almost ripe to pop the question again to Bujang.

Where are those bras and panties Taffy likes so much? Gilda sifted through her underwear box and confirmed that her dressup red underwear hadn't been too badly savaged by silk-eating lingerie monsters. Gilda regretted the day that she had told the Minister the frequency of the clandestine short-wave radio link-up that connected all the expatriates in Manusia's isolated corners. He had used unfair tactics to obtain the information, Gilda complained. Taffy, as she called him, had been nibbling on her nipple while cradling an ice cube in his mouth. Oh well, *apa boleh buat*, never mind, she sighed as she inspected her lacey bra – a bit musty, but still in pretty good shape.

Where the hell was Bujang? she wondered, before remembering that she had sent him off before sunrise to check on the movements of Jessica and Tuffy – the orangutan mother and son she had been observing for two months. It was so useful to have him around.

Her glow was machine-gunned by another burst of static.

"Squawk," the radio said.

"Hello," Gilda replied.

"Screech."

"Hello, damnit. Stop that awful screeching and say something."

"Awrk." It sounded like a strangled hornbill.

"Camp Trinil here."

"Hello, Madame Doctor Gilda. Do you screech me?"

It was the office manager of the International Nature Federation calling from the office in the Manusian capital of Anjing.

"Scrark."

Gilda picked up maddening snatches of what was being spoken, some acronyms, such as INF, she recognized – some code words, such as Baby Derek, forced Gilda Korda Brekenridge to sense that this was going to be a really tough day.

Gilda inspected her rapidly evaporating bottle of Poison cologne and sprayed a few expensive droplets under her arms. Just in case Bujang got home early, she also sprayed her inner thighs. He

26

probably won't even notice, she thought with regret, since he generally kept his nose well away from her netherworld – as she called that swampy region. Who knows? One of these days a girl might get lucky, and Pasteur (or was it Curie?) always said that chance favors the prepared body.

She refused to glance at the small mirror on the wall, terrified that the age lines around her mouth that she first noticed two weeks ago might still be there. Gilda reached into the makeshift closet – nothing more than a corner of the room demarcated by an old sheet.

"Squark," cried the radio.

She grabbed one of her khaki field dresses ("hello visit next squirch"), the outfits she had had tailored for her in Anjing ("possibly accompanied by the screuch ambassador, do you read me?"). They were modeled after a Banana Republic dress purchased in Palo Alto while she was back in the States for a speaking tour three years ago. She had always liked the batik collar.

"No, I do not read you, you incompetent turkey of a radio operator," she cried. "Repeat. Repeat your message," she yelled, as she reached further into the closet, accidentally pulling the wires off the car battery which powered the radio.

"I suppose they'll call back," she said out loud as she inspected her dress. Of all her batik-collared khaki dresses, she liked this one the best. She had picked out the design herself – golden Hindu Garudas on a pale blue background that the Chinese tailor had graciously told her was appropriate for the 'orangutan queen'.

In a way, it was true. Gilda was queen of all she could see. But Camp Trinil comprised a modest queendom. Seven roughly constructed wooden structures set back from the shallow Hotut River in the middle of a national park the size of Connecticut. Gilda's wooden two-room house. Gerry's single-room shack. A similar-sized 'guest house'. An open-sided communal dining room with attached simple kitchen. A couple of dorms for the laborers, a shack for tools and the generator. A row of latrines out back. A stuffy herbarium filled with uncatalogued tinder. A feeding platform for rehabilitating orangutans. Most of it connected by elevated walkways three feet above the mud. Not exactly Versailles. But Gilda's riches were not in material goods. She had power over sentient beings. Never mind that only 12 of them were human and the other 40 were apes. They all needed her.

"So, let's get this act together," she mumbled to herself. "Ringo, wake up," she shouted. "Ringo-I'm-hungry. Why-don't-you-run-out-and-see-if-you-can't-find-some-wild-mangoes," Gilda said, deliberately.

The ape shuffled over to Gilda's backpack and rummaged for her garter belt, which he wrapped around his forehead like a headband.

"Put that down, Ringo. Right now."

Then, enunciating clearly and making eating gestures by putting her fingers to her mouth, she said very slowly, in the same tone of voice with which she instructed the kitchen staff to boil the drinking water for a full twenty minutes: "Ringo, get fruit." She used her own signs – pointing at the ape, herself and her stomach, mimicking the climbing an imaginary tree and the plucking of its mangoes, using her mouth to pretend eating and, finally, smiling.

The sixty-pound orange ape saluted and shuffled off into the late afternoon heat. He'll probably bring back durians instead, Gilda mused. Never mind. I can give them to Taffy. He likes those woggie-poo fruits.

Gilda had to get out of the stuffy two-room house. But she had to finish packing first. She had to make notes for her meeting the following day with the Minister. She knew how paranoid he was about foreigners. He was always threatening to throw her out. She had always thought he was kidding. Was he? Should she tell him that one of the laborers had seen Urs Gerhard on the far side of the national park – a four day walk away? Would that win her points? She had to make sure Hassan had the boat ready for the trip downriver. She had to plan an itinerary for those blasted visitors, whenever they might arrive (and whoever they might be). She had so much to do and so little time. Her six-monthly report to the INF was overdue; maybe that's why they're sending this Baby person out here? She had to ask Wanita, the cook, what supplies she needed from Bohong and Gilda was a little behind in writing up her field notes. Well, actually, she was four years behind. However, surely her job was to make field observations? Not slave over a dilapidated laptop, like a secretary. Anyway, what kind of name was Baby? Are they sending me a mindless Filipina?

Okay. Calm down. First things first. I'm leaving tomorrow. Have to tell Gerry. Maybe hand over power in the *parang* ceremony.

Do I bring Bujang with me? No, better not. Leave him here. Taffy might get jealous. Definitely tell Gerry. Now, where was that lipstick? If that beast Ringo ate it again, he's going to be sorry.

Penan encampment

Urs took off his glasses – the second of three pairs he had brought with him – and carefully wiped them clean on his loincloth. One lens was cracked. This affected his vision less than his peace of mind – without his glasses he was functionally blind. He accepted the photocopy handed to him by the journalist. Urs had learned English in school, but he had had little practice in the intervening years. He read carefully and slowly, trying to take in each word in the coded cable that had been sent to the US State Department in Washington by Richard Fangar, United States Ambassador to Manusia.

"The so-called native people together form a numerical majority, but their tribal factions have never unified into a single political force. They are increasingly annoyed by what they perceive as high-handed attitudes of officials in Anjing. They perceive the country's leaders to be prejudiced against 'upriver' people and complain that the central government is exploiting natural resources found in traditional tribal homelands to cover the country's expanding foreign debt.

"The natives have several grievances:

"First, they feel they are being left out of the preferential treatment accorded to Malays as 'sons of the soil.' The natives feel that they, too, are 'sons of the soil', but are being treated like 'bastards of the dirt'.

"Second, they argue that a proposed dam on the Jerang River, with proposed World Bank funding, would force thousands of people to evacuate their traditional homelands.

"Third, they complain that avaricious timber operators and greedy politicians are indiscriminately cutting trees on their land, resulting in erosion, poor hunting, no fish, dangerous passage on the river due to debris and disruption of cultural patterns.

29

"Fourth, they would complain less about the third point if they were earning some money from the exercise. They aren't.

"The native campaign is being backed by (some say master-minded by) a renegade Swiss named Urs Gerhard, who lives with a band of nomadic Penan – a tiny, generally disenfranchised group which is annoying the power elite in Anjing. Up to now, the Penan actions are no more than a minor wound to the body – but left to fester, they could threaten the stability of the nation as a whole.

"What is this word 'RAY-NEE-GAHD'?" Urs asked the visitor to the Penan camp.
"An outlaw. Somebody who breaks laws."
"Ah. Like in the movies – a cowboy?"
"More like an Indian."
Urs was pleased. The Penan fight was getting attention.
Laki walked around the small fire and offered the men some tiny grilled fish. Robert Hallmark, journalist with the *Sacramento Bee*, tried to pick the flesh off the bones of the minnow-sized fish until he saw that Urs simply popped the whole thing into his mouth and chewed heartily. Hallmark did the same. The fish tasted like burnt mud. He did not mind, though. He was the first western journalist to interview Urs Gerhard and he was willing to put up with tougher hardships than lousy food. He sat back against a tree and restlessly rubbed his back against the trunk, trying to relax his stiff muscles. His limbs ached from the five-day walk in from Brunei and he could feel insects crawling underneath his trousers towards his crotch. But it was exciting just to be in Borneo, he thought. Land of headhunters …
Good thing I've done my homework, Hallmark reflected. A few hours on the net and he got the info to put this renegade into geopolitical perspective. The island of Borneo, the third largest in the world, occupied a strategic position in the modern world that greatly exceeded its anthropological importance as the place where decapitation had been elevated to its apotheosis.
Four countries – the Sultanate of Manusia, the Sultanate of Brunei, the Indonesian provinces of West, Central, South and East Kalimantan and the Malaysian states of Sarawak and Sabah, shared an island bigger than Texas. Every twenty years or so, one of the

countries would decide that the chunk that another country was sitting on was rightfully its. The result: histrionics and, occasionally, guerrilla warfare – during which local populations were quietly told that the generation-old ban on headhunting had temporarily been lifted, provided it was done across the enemy's border. This was great fun, since the rivalries between warring tribes had the fire of the Oxford-Cambridge race or the annual Michigan-Ohio State game – but with far more ancient histories. In recent years, people had sublimated the desire to decapitate their neighbors and instead engaged in displacement activities like longboat regattas, athletic contests and cockfights. In the past, a young man who returned from a distant battle with a human head was made a hero in the village. Today, he might come back from his travels with other evidence of his manhood – a Sony television from Anjing or a fistful of dollars and a custom-engraved construction worker's helmet reading "Bechtel Saudi".

Anjing, Manusia's capital, was a pleasant, small city of half a million. It boasted four international hotels, several charming restaurants, and a pleasant riverfront esplanade which fronted a recently-renovated row of Chinese shophouses constructed during the British colonial period. Chinese temples sat comfortably within a stone's throw of Muslim mosques and Anglican churches. It was a small capital, but infinitely more pleasant than the huge metropolises of Jakarta, Manila or Kuala Lumpur.

Bohong was one of three upriver towns, each with about 50,000 people, which were accessible from Anjing only by air or express boats which plied the wide, silt-laden rivers of the Sultanate.

The four Borneo nations held an important corner of the world. Fate had put them within a six-hour plane ride from half of the world's population. They contained vast oil and mineral resources. They were independent, generally with sophisticated leaders who were able to manipulate less-sophisticated upcountry populations. Strategically, Borneo was the "pulsating free nucleus of South-East Asia", as Ambassador Fangar had explained when he had addressed the National Press Club in Washington, DC, since the country sits in the midst of the former communist states of Indo-China on the north, the topsy-turvy democratic/military-ruled Philippines on the northeast and Australia on the south, a beer-soaked giant which nevertheless regularly managed to infuriate the region's national governments by asking impertinent questions about human rights and presidential finances.

"You are with a big newspaper, *ja*?" Urs asked, hopefully.

"Not that big. But important."

Urs looked disappointed.

"Look, Urs, it's not the *Washington Post*. But you and I, we're both starting small. We've both got big careers ahead of us."

"You think the Penan story is a good story?"

"Boy, is it ever," Hallmark answered. He had taken pages and pages of notes, hundreds of pictures. "Urs, I have a present for you." Hallmark reached into his pack and handed the Swiss a pocket-sized Olympus Infinity camera and ten rolls of Ektachrome. "Take some photos next time you wipe out a timber truck. It makes for a better story."

Hallmark started to show him how to use the automatic-everything camera, but could see that Urs' mind was elsewhere. Urs admitted to the American that he had never thought that he would be leading a rebellion. The only previous civil uprising he had taken part in had been the Zurich Opera House riots, which pitted the students of that rich city against the banking establishment over control of the Opera Annex. The students wanted the government to transform a downtown building into badly needed low-income apartments. The city wanted to take it over to build offices and an art museum. For Urs, the first in his family to leave the family farm, the rebellion, modest as it was by international standards, showed that the individual can fight the system. And win.

"More fish?" Urs asked after the photography lesson. Hallmark shook his head and Urs smiled. "I remember my first meals with the Penan," he said. "Never thought I'd get to like these little fish."

"You like them now?"

"You have perhaps a few extra Mars bars brought with you?"

The two men, both in their early thirties, talked about their lives, their careers, their families. Urs explained about the simple communal life he had chosen. Robert explained what it meant to be a hungry reporter in a world of pizzas, good wine and hot tubs. Besides the cultural differences, the major distinction was that, when Robert Hallmark spoke, Urs listened; when Urs Gerhard spoke, Hallmark took notes.

"I'm a shepherd, I guess," Urs said, answering one of the American's insatiable questions. He could just as easily have claimed to be an artist, a linguist or a moderately skilled carpenter – a calling which had earned him a berth three years earlier on the Swiss-Danish-American expedition that had explored the great caves of Mount Malu.

Like many great careers, Urs' had been based on nepotism. His sister was married to the expedition's leader, a swashbuckling Zurichois named Bruno Malakoff. Bruno had offered Urs the chance to go to Manusia to supervise construction of the base camp and coordinate supplies.

Urs told Hallmark that he had never heard of the Penan before he had arrived in Manusia, but after listening to expedition campfire tales about pale, shy nomads who caught their own fish, hunted their own game and refused to move to government-sponsored settlements, Urs became intrigued. They sounded not unlike the generation of Urs' parents – shy, isolated, proud mountain people with a distinctive language that was incomprehensible a valley away. After spending some time with the Penan, Urs had a better understanding of his own father, who had such an insular life that he had rarely left his home village of Hungsdorf to descend to the town of Brig in the Swiss canton of Wallis.

Mount Malu was named after a limestone summit that, at 8,350 feet, is the second highest in Borneo. It was surrounded by virgin rainforest and had an ecosystem that some scientists claimed was eighty million years old. It also held an extensive and virtually unexplored network of caves. The entrance led to the world's biggest under-ground cathedral, a natural amphitheater large enough to accommodate three football fields and high enough to host a 12-storey building. To get to the caves, the expedition had to first undertake a four-day boat trip from the town of Bohong and then a three-day trek passing through Penan territory.

During that pioneering adventure, the predominantly expatriate scientists saw no Penan – simply because the Penan did not wish to be seen. But, as Urs learned, the Penan had watched the operation quietly, just feet away, as porters lugged metal cases of food, cameras, geological equipment, plant presses and insect mounting boards.

While the scientists had trekked daily from base camp to the caves to measure the depth of bat guano and collect blind albino spiders, Urs had walked off in a different direction, about two hours from camp. After checking for fire ants, he would lay down his waterproof poncho and sit against a tree. Within minutes, if he was quiet, life around Urs returned to normal. The leeches were immediate visitors, attaching themselves to all parts of his body. He forced himself to sit still, watching the vampire worms engorge themselves to three times their weight until they were so bloated they dropped to the ground where they risked being gobbled by scavenger beetles and wild jungle fowl. By then the thousands and thousands of insects, many probably unknown to science, had screeched into life. If he had been especially lucky, he saw a rhinoceros hornbill, a black and white turkey-sized bird with a horn-like casque that resembled an upturned banana. It flew with a steam engine-like whoosh of wings that could be heard a mile away. On one occasion, Urs had been visited by a chihuahua-sized Malaysian mouse deer, which was featured in local children's tales as the cleverest animal in the jungle.

After a week of trying to be part of the forest, Urs was approached by the Penan. Urs remembered the moment vividly. One moment there had been just rainforest, then two Penan had stood in front of him. Urs offered them water from his canteen. On the second day they had accepted.

In a similar manner to the patient way he had calmed and ultimately tamed deer in the Swiss forests, Urs slowly made friends with the pale natives, first offering them food, then fish hooks, finally sarongs and tobacco. In retrospect, Urs realized that he probably overplayed the scene to suit his own vision of what these people were really like – he could have moved faster, since they are neither fearsome nor all that afraid of Europeans. But *langsam, langsam*, he thought. Never mind. He did it his way. The Penan saw his patience as a sign of respect, something they had in abundance for others in their small bands but a quality they found unaccountably lacking in the 'outsiders' they were occasionally forced to deal with. The Penan invited Urs to travel with them, beginning to teach him their style of communal living and their simple language that was punctuated by so many bird songs and monkey cries that Urs felt like Dr. Doolittle whenever he asked what the weather was going to be tomorrow.

Urs learned much about honesty during those two months. He also learned, from discussions with Russell Alfred, the young American who participated in the expedition to help the Manusians write a management plan for the proposed Mount Malu National Park, that much of that chunk of Manusia had been given as timber concessions to various politicians. It was only a matter of time before the bulldozers moved in.

The expedition had completed its studies. Urs visited the Penan camp a final time.

"You must go," Laki, the Penan elder, had said – as much a statement as a question.

"Yes."

"You will take this." Laki gave Urs his blowpipe and a quiver of poison-tipped darts. "You will need to hunt in your country."

Urs took the gift, hugged the man and walked away. He wanted to promise to return, wanted to say that more than anything he had ever felt, but he could not break a trust. He might never return. It was not that simple.

Urs had kept his unspoken promise to the Penan. He returned to Manusia a year later on a tourist visa, laden with a set of pastel pencils, notebooks, ballpoint pens and a supply of medicines for his new family. He disappeared into the forest faster than you could name one of the Sultan's polo ponies and stayed for more than two years, eluding the authorities who publicly branded him "a dangerous alien, living illegally with the isolated upriver people whom the government is working so hard to bring into the twentieth century."

"What's your next move?" Hallmark asked, startling Urs from his reverie.

"I hope the government will talk. We don't want to hurt anyone. We just want our land."

The journalist smiled. He liked this strange, naive man. "Do you really know what you're getting into?"

"Yes. I think so. For the forest we are fighting."

Hallmark burped. "Urs, did you ever hear of something called the 'Monkey Wrench Gang'?"

Urs shook his head and listened to the story of Edward Abbey and his eco-guerrillas. Fascinated. So, he was not alone.

"OK, so, what's the next step?" Hallmark asked.

"I'm not sure. I must discuss with my friends." He waved his hand to indicate the sober, cautious Penan that sat nearby.

"No other blockades planned?"

"Perhaps."

"Surely you must have *something* planned," Hallmark insisted.

"Why are you curious so much?"

"Look, don't get defensive. I'm a journalist. It's my job to poke into other people's business."

Urs had little experience with journalists. Hallmark was just the second who had taken the trouble to visit Urs in the forest, having got interested after reading a story Associated Press picked up from the *Singapore Straits Times*. Hallmark had first gone to Anjing, asked around and discovered that Urs Gerhard was nobody's friend, especially no-one in the government. The police threatened to arrest Hallmark if he was caught in the Mount Malu area without a pass, which they weren't about to give him. He then tried the back door, entering through Brunei, thumbing rides on timber trucks to get to the common rainforest shared by the two Sultanates. From there, he hitched rides on boats until he reached Long Residan, a Kelabit longhouse at the northern end of the Mount Malu National Park. Hallmark installed himself in the longhouse and let it be known that he was a friend of Urs and would pay generously if someone could set up a rendezvous.

"Hey, I ran into a guy who was real curious about you."

"Yes?" Urs asked.

"Big Korean guy. Named Jong something. He's after your ass."

"I never have hear of him," Urs said, truthfully.

"Well, he sure has heard of you. He runs the timber company that operates the trucks you sabotage. Ran into the guy at a whorehouse in Anjing while I was checking out the story. He was pissed as a skunk. Said that if he ever got hold of you, he'd feed you to the orangutans."

"Then, I would be safe. Orangutans are vegetarians."

"Maybe. But I got the feeling the Koreans can train anything, even orangutans, to do whatever they want them to do."

Camp Trinil

Like any five-and-a-half-year-old, Queenie loved to cuddle. She even had a sign for it, a molding of her thumb and forefinger into an O which she revolved around her ear, which Gerry Schwartz always identified in his notes as 'ballpoint'. It was a little joke between them, although probably lost on Queenie since the orangutan was unable to differentiate irony from a frying pan. She had signs for neither.

"Good girl," Gerry said, slipping his ape student a reward for her last response. Unfortunately, her response was wrong, so she earned only one peanut. If she had been on the money she would have received two and a hug.

It was hell in the tropics, thought Gerry. Stuck in the middle of the jungle, trying to teach sign language to orangutans, with the nearest female days away. Of course, there were women in the camp, but they were off limits. Gilda had her own liaison with Bujang and, even if she was available, one can't very well go screwing around with the head of the project. Further, the native female staff of the camp were out of bounds – although, heaven knows, he'd thought about it. Inter-racial relationships lead to all sorts of complications.

OK, back to work. "Queenie, you little tease, if you get this one right, I'll give you a peanut. Now, *apa ini*?" Gerry asked, waving a frisbee in front of her. What is this?

Queenie climbed onto her teacher's lap and began chewing on Gerry's scraggly red beard. Affectionately, she slapped him twice on the head.

"Was that a sign or are you just pleased to see me?" Gerry joked. "Good girl. You got that one right," Gerry decided arbitrarily, as he rewarded Queenie with two peanuts and rewarded himself with another data entry in his notebook. If she continues at this rate, I'll get a professorship by Christmas, he thought.

"Now, Queenie, let's get serious. We're working on a major breakthrough in communications here," he said, as if encouraging a softball team composed of brain-dead politicians. "You've got thirty-five signs, more than Koko had after studying even longer than you have. Let's go for it. Show me the sign for book," he said, waving a dog-eared copy of *The Lord of the Flies* in front of her face.

Gerry Schwartz was the latest in a moderately long line of linguistic explorers. A student of the famous B.F. Pong at the University of North Carolina, Gerry was the first person to try to teach American Sign Language, or Ameslan, to apes in a semi-wild situation. Previous researchers had worked with captive chimpanzees and gorillas, but in environments that were suited more to the researcher than to the student. Gerry's Ph.D. project was to work with orangutans, which some people considered the most intelligent of the three great apes, in a situation in which they were free to come to class or not, free to play in the trees or learn signs, free to respect their teacher or explore the wonders of the elastic waistband that held up his shorts.

Young orangutans are affectionate, tactile creatures and Queenie craved contact with another intelligent primate.

But while Queenie loved a tickle, she was equally content to wander around the room, nibbling on Gerry's meager and rarely-used wardrobe, crawling into his backpack and licking his moldy running shoes.

Queenie chewed thoughtfully on Gerry's hairbrush. "Damnit, let's have some discipline in class," Gerry said. "Queenie. *Datang sini.*" She shuffled over and sat at his feet, looking up at him with eyes that resembled those of the waifs immortalized in black velvet paintings. She hugged him around his right calf and paid no attention whatsoever to Gerry's admonition that she give him the sign for book. "Come on, Queenie. PLEASE. Just learn these fucking signs and make me famous. I'll make it up to you." Queenie took these warmly spoken entreaties as a sign of reconciliation and she clambered back into Gerry's lap, her orange hair mingling with his reddish chest hair.

Gerry reached around the ape and, as he had done in the past when teaching was slow, wrote in his notebook every once in a while, gently pushing the youngster out of the way so he could see what he was doing. Using the time-honored principle of extrapolation, he speculated that if Queenie had correctly used ten signs the day before, it would not be unreasonable to note that today she had correctly repeated those signs while learning an additional two. "Well done, girl. That brings you up to ... let's see ...

Before Gerry could finish his arithmetic he heard shuffling outside, followed by Gilda's high-pitched voice.

"Gerry, we need to talk," she said, starting the conversation while still ten yards from Gerry's front door.

"Not now, Gilda," he whined. "Queenie is about to make a breakthrough."

Gerry grabbed the toddler-sized animal and tried to put her on the floor. She resisted and only released her grip with a screech when Gerry yanked out a clump of her orange hair.

"Morning, Queenie," Gilda said, without enthusiasm, as she clomped into the one-room house. Then to Gerry: "We've got visitors coming."

Queenie lazily touched her right, then left ear – her way of mumbling a desultory "morning" as she moodily picked up the frisbee and shuffled into the tiny, adjoining kitchen.

"Now, Gilda, calm down. What's happening?" Gerry asked, trying to calm his impetuous employer.

"I just told you," she said, irritated. "Visitors are coming."

It would be nice to have some company, he thought. Hey, I'm a social animal.

"It's a crew from Washington. They're after us," Gilda continued.

"Hold on. Slow down. Who's coming from Washington?"

"I'm not sure. The radio was full of static. Baby … or something."

"And why do you think this Baby or something is after you?"

"Just a hunch."

"Gilda, you haven't been studying chicken entrails again with your boyfriend?"

"Let's leave my personal life out of this," Gilda blushed. "You know, the Federation's been writing those accusatory-sounding letters for months now. Maybe they want to stop our funding. Cut us off."

"Gilda, calm down. They're just asking for the semi-annual reports you're supposed to send them. There's nothing sinister about that. They give you money and in return you promise to tell them how you spend it. That seems reasonable enough, doesn't it?"

"I don't know. I have more important things to do than write reports."

"If you like, I'll do the reports for you again. Anyway, I think I know who it might be," he ventured.

"Who?"

" International Nature Federation's new executive vice president for communications and fundraising. Name's Beatrix Beverly Derek. Calls herself B.B.. Graduate of Stanford, if I remember correctly."

"How do you know that?" Gilda asked, suspiciously.

"Her appointment was announced in the last edition of *Nature's World*. You should read it sometime. We both get it."

"I have enough to do keeping up with the scientific literature."

"Maybe this B.B. person wants to make us famous," he speculated.

"I'm already famous," Gilda said quietly in her barely-discernible eastern European accent. Her small mouth formed A and O shapes that resembled an Edsel's front grille.

"One can never be too thin or too famous," Gerry said, reassuringly. "Oh shit."

"What?"

"Queenie!" Gerry shouted, running into the next room. He returned dragging a frightened bundle of red animal. Queenie squealed as she was spanked.

From outside, Ringo, carrying two ripe durians he had collected for Gilda, watched Gerry's affectionate discipline of Queenie. Had this taken place in Gilda's house, perhaps Ringo would have investigated more closely. But he kept his distance when Gerry and Queenie were together.

"That's an unusual scientific method," Gilda observed.

"If she wants to be treated as a person she had damn well better learn to respect other people's property. That marshmallow cream was mine."

"Maybe if you put your name on it."

"Come on, Gilda. It's enough that I've taught these apes to sign and obey commands. You expect me to teach them to read, too?"

"How is it going?"

"Terrific. Queenie's up to simple sentences, Ringo has maybe 75 signs, Amos and Andy about 30 each and the rest are just goofing-off."

"Can you talk to the orangutans?"

"Sure. Well, sort of. Just the other day I asked Queenie if she wanted to go for a walk along the river to watch the other orangutans and eat watermelon. She understood the whole thing."

"What did she say?"

"Yes."

"That's remarkable," Gilda said.

"Isn't it? I reckon she has an IQ of about eighty. Maybe ninety. She could get a job."

"You better have something serious to show this B.B. woman. She won't want to spend all her time tromping through the forest."

"Sure. I'll get the students to really put on a show."

Queenie climbed onto the window screen, pushed open the loose, wire mosquito mesh and swung down to the dirt path. She followed Ringo to the feeding platform by the river. It was almost noon. Lunch.

"I wonder what she really wants?" Gilda said, again.

"You *really* think it's trouble?"

"I don't know. The last time I was in the INF office, they were having all sorts of discussions about whether nature conservation should be for animals or for people. I said animals. Maybe the people-people won."

"Gilda, there's nothing you can do about it until she comes. Relax."

"Oh, I forgot to tell you. I'm going downriver tomorrow. I have an appointment with the Minister. I'll be gone a couple of days."

Gerry wanted to ask her to pick up some tinned tuna fish and Ovaltine while she was in town, but sensed that she wouldn't be in a mood to run errands.

"Well, I'll look after things while you're gone."

Gilda gathered up her courage, paused ten seconds and blurted: "We'll hold the ceremony tonight."

"Come on, Gilda. Do we have to?"

"Yes, we have to. It's the only way to keep discipline."

"I won't do it. It's demeaning."

Gilda had decided to bluff. "OK. Then, I'll hold the ceremony with Bujang. Put him in charge."

"OK. On second thought I'll do it," Gerry said, with a sulk. "But, I won't kneel down in front of you."

Chapter 4

23 July. 21:00.

Camp Trinil

Bujang lit the joss sticks – large batons of purple incense that cost two cents each and which were used to fumigate Chinese funerals into an atmosphere of smoky piety. Within minutes, Gilda's living room, a large open space cluttered with maps, books, magazines and humble, insect-infested rattan furniture, was filled with the staff of Camp Trinil. There was Hassan, the head of the orangutan feeding platform, Wanita, the cook, Perempuan, the laundry girl and a dozen laborers, assistants and other people who Gilda remembered hiring – but couldn't remember for what purpose. Her ceremonies were the only activities for which the help was on time.

Bujang sat quietly in the corner, strumming his three-stringed *sapeh*. The Kayan guitar gave off a plaintive, not unattractive sound. He was accompanied by Bunyi, an older, but still-active uncle of Bujang, who played the family heirlooms – three brass gongs of varying size which had allegedly belonged to the native orchestra of James Brooke, the first White Rajah of neighboring Sarawak.

Kayans take their time going into trances and their transfer to the world of hornbill spirits and clouded leopard demons is greatly enhanced by the right atmosphere. They found Gilda's house to be quite suitable. Two of the camp laborers were half-way gone and Gilda, too, was doing her best to go into a trance. She sat in a modified lotus position, the best she could do since her legs "didn't bend all funny like those Indian yogis." She closed her eyes. She hyperventilated. She imagined sitting on the seashore. She squeezed her stomach into her kidneys. She visualized herself as Snow White in a deep, deep sleep, with seven tiny people waiting for her to wake up and explain the meaning of life. She felt she was just getting into it, when some idiot gonged the huge brass gong and jarred her from her way-station on the road to infinity. She retreated to the bedroom where she could change.

Several minutes later, amidst the candles, the chanting and the drumbeats, Gilda appeared wearing a diaphanous white blouse and a wraparound orange batik skirt. Gilda wore no underwear for these ceremonies, having heard once that Druid princesses performed their rituals naked. The male members of the staff stared at Gilda and smirked at Bujang, who smirked back.

Gerry, the other key player in this drama, sat cross-legged in the corner. His red, white and blue Chicago Cubs T-shirt – the best piece of clothing he had – was wet with sweat, as were the white cotton pants he had picked up on Kuta Beach in Bali.

"Selamat malam mes enfants," Gilda said. Good evening my children. *"Ich will allez jalan jalan besok matin."* Continuing in the mixture of Malay, French and German, which she thought added a certain mystery and dignity to the proceedings, she continued to explain that she had been called away by the powers that be from far across the water, on business that could affect the future of all the orangutans, the future of all the world's rainforests and, most important, the future paychecks of the assembled gathering. Gilda was going to meet the Minister of the Environment, said by some to be the second most important man in Manusia. But, she did not like to leave the camp without letting the staff know that she was still in charge, although she might not be physically present.

Her voice rising ever so slightly, she undid the rope belt holding her *parang* and held it in front of her. Then came the part Gerry detested. "Gerry, I beg thee to come forth and receive the sword of dominion," Gilda intoned. She took the sword out of its scabbard and, like in the films she had seen of Queen Elizabeth knighting Sir Laurence Olivier, her favorite Shakespearean actor, tapped Gerry on each shoulder. She put the sword back in its holder and passed it to him, speaking clearly and firmly *"Saya kaseh tout le pouvoir parang ini nach du, Gerry. Tu est saya punya wakil until saya return."* Gerry was the boss in her absence and everybody had better respect him. But there was no doubt that this was Gilda's *parang* and when she came back the power reverted to her, as it should, since the sword had been blessed by a local *dukun*, a medicine man skilled in the arcane science of giving spiritual power to inanimate objects. Old Pak Ajaib had demurred at first, since parangs are strong, masculine things and women just don't know how to use the power and responsibility that comes with them. However, when Gilda offered to triple his usual fee and pay the school expenses for his 12 children, he rationalized that, after all, she *was* the chief of the camp. Further, she was a white woman and had appeared on Manusian national television – so maybe she *could* handle it.

Gilda smiled, stretched to her full five foot eleven, raised her hands above her head, took a deep breath and sang the opening bars of 'Casta Diva' in a husky mezzo that she thought could have been a reasonable performing voice – had she had the proper encouragement as a child. "*Tempra Dio, tempra tu de' cori ardenti,*" she sang, quitting the aria in mid-stream after asking the gods to moderate burning hearts. The room was quiet. Gilda spoke quietly in Malay, telling Bujang to turn on the lights. This was the signal for him to put away his *sapeh* and break out the beer. There was always a great party on the night before Gilda left camp.

At times like this, Gilda felt she and Bujang should be discreet about their intimacy. When Gilda wanted to send Bujang a message in a public gathering, she used a private code, stolen from Carol Burnett who used to tug at her ear at the end of her television shows to say hello to her mother. During the beer fest, Gilda caught his eye and yanked on her right ear.

Sometimes, Bujang obeyed her command, other times not. That night, he entered her house at midnight, through the kitchen.

* * * * *

Bujang had mixed feelings about Gilda. He had had contact with other white women, but Gilda was the first *orang putih* he had slept with. The other white women in his life, he thought as he got out his clouded leopard's teeth and strung them through his ears, as Gilda liked, were a far different lot. There had been that fat missionary who lived in the longhouse for two years when he was ten; he remembered how she liked him to sit on her lap during Bible lessons and he had tried to run away because her breath smelled of garlic. There was the Peace Corps woman who used to visit the longhouse school – she had been fun – she would encourage the primary school children to carry their wooden desks to the river in front of the longhouse and, riding the desks as if they were boats, they relived the great naval battles of the Pacific war. Bujang had been too old by that time to play with the younger children, but he and his friends used to hang around and gape at the light brown pubic hairs that escaped from her bathing suit. They had thought how wonderful and how bizarre that a woman would actually let herself be seen in public like that. During his high school days in Anjing, a time in his life he had never told Gilda about, Bujang had seen many white women, usually looking harried, heavy and uncomfortable. Generally, they were amply proportioned. He remembered his English teacher, another big-breasted woman from the American Peace Corps, who always seemed to be laughing too loudly. He and his friends thought that women with big tits were the sexiest things imaginable. And boy, was she a great teacher. She had really taken a liking to young Bujang, lending him *Catcher in the Rye*, *Catch-22* and detective novels. English was Bujang's key to the outside world, making it possible for him to read *Time* and watch CNN. He learned about politics outside Manusia, sports and travel. The language helped set the clever teenage boys apart from their country cousins back home. Bujang remembered the Swedish porno magazine that one of his school friends surreptitiously passed around. Thank God we studied English. The stories accompanying the photos in books like *Teenage Sluts of Scandinavia* significantly helped the boys' vocabularies when they chatted-up the imperious Chinese whores in the Anjing massage parlors.

Bujang had never imagined, never ever in his wildest fantasies, that he would actually sleep with a white woman. What chance did he have? His family had few high-level contacts who could have helped get the young man a job and, after graduating, he had no option but to return to the longhouse and help his father in the rice fields.

Then he got lucky. Mount Malu National Park was created. His teacher and friend in Anjing, George Wee, had explained how social politics worked in Manusia. In order to obtain funding from a consortium comprising the International Nature Federation, the World Bank and the United States Agency for International

Development, the Manusian Government had been firmly instruct-ed to provide one hundred jobs for people living around the Park's borders. The conservationists and development aid officials called this policy "local participation in natural resource management to ensure long-term sustainability of the protected area and its biological diversity." Bujang was simply fulfilling the conditions of a contract between major powers. Even better, he was being paid the equivalent of US$40 a month to do some light labor and screw Gilda every once in a while. He thought it was a pretty good deal.

"I think we should get married," Gilda told him that night, when they were lying together, hot and sweaty, after making love. Bujang had wondered why she insisted on him sleeping with her after fucking. The local girls didn't want that. He didn't want that. These European women are strange.

"What do you mean, Madame Doctor Gilda?" he had asked suspiciously in Malay.

"Marriage," she had yelled at him in English. She calmed down and continued in their lingua franca of fractured Malay. "*Jangan bodoh, lah,*" she said. Don't be an idiot. You, me, babies.

"You have a husband, Madame Doctor Gilda. Mister Mark."

"Mister Mark left me. He ran off with another woman. He took my son. That's desertion. I'm filing for a divorce. You do know what a divorce is, don't you Bujang?"

"Of course. If you're Muslim you can divorce your wife by throwing pebbles at her and saying 'I divorce you' three times. But only men can say it to women."

Gilda had examined Bujang's anatomy enough to be pretty certain he was neither Muslim nor Jewish. She dipped her head along his hard stomach just to be certain.

"No. I'm serious, Bujang. You and I could be a good team," she said as she worked her way south. Her hands roamed over his chest and along his tight neck. She had admired the blue-black neck tattoos of another lad, an Iban, who worked in the camp. Neck tattoos were given only to Iban headhunters a few generations ago, she knew, because only glorious warriors could bear the pain. She wondered what her Iban employee had done to deserve his. Too bad Bujang is Kayan and doesn't have tattoos, she had thought. Oh well, one can't have everything.

Bujang had mixed feelings at being this woman's toy. He was

flattered and honored by her attention and he frankly enjoyed the extra status it gave him in Rumah Sehat, his longhouse. But this sex business, well, he just wasn't too sure about it. Regular sex was okay, although he was sometimes afraid that Madame Doctor Gilda had been stung by a krait the way she carried on, screaming, sweating, writhing and digging her fingernails into his shoulders. It scared him – but it was good, clean, fun. But this, well, it took some time to get used to Gilda's red hair on his thighs, her fingers tracing a line up from his knees, her tongue about to make butterfly motions on a part of his body where neither tongues nor butterflies had previously alighted.

"Mmmm, Bujang, *enak untuk kamu?*" she had asked between slurps. Is it good for you? "Oh God, it's so good, so good," she had replied to her own rhetorical question before she engulfed him again.

Gilda kept her grip on Bujang's pelvis and tried to shift herself into a 69 position. Bujang had tried this once, with Gilda, and didn't think much of it. He thought it was better to continue the conversation which, up to that point, had been very much one-sided.

"Madame Doctor Gilda," he said breathlessly, trying to extricate his head from her haunches. "*Kenapa mau kahwin sama saya?*" Why do you want to marry me? I'm just a small person, a farmer. I have no money. I have no future.

Gilda wriggled her hips, rather larger than the slim hips of the girls in the longhouse, Bujang noted ruefully. She licked the inside of his thighs. "With me you'll have a huge future, Bujang. I'll look after you. You've got something. I'm not sure what, but it's definitely there." What you really have, she had thought, is a body that Madonna would kill for. Further, my dear Bujang, you happen to have Manusian citizenship and, since the wives of Manusians also get the right to take Manusian citizenship …

Gilda's thoughts were disrupted by heavy artillery coming from Bujang's *zakar*. Logic could wait. She didn't want to miss the fireworks. "*Adoo, adoo*" they both happily cried out, more or less together.

CHAPTER 5

24 July. 06:00.

Camp Trinil

Gilda never missed breakfast; a bit of relict behavior she had inherited from her no-nonsense mother. She had become used to sharing the Camp Trinil dining room with an uncertain number of slothful animals, most of whom were not shy about begging for some of her toast and three-minute eggs.

There seemed to be fewer than usual that morning. Perhaps it was too early. Orangutans like to stay in bed if they can, she thought. So do I.

Gilda was finishing her second cup of tea, when Ringo walked into the open-air dining room carrying two ripe mangos he had stolen from the kitchen.

"Little late, don't you think, Ringo?" Gilda said bitchily. However, inside she was pleased, thinking the animal had remembered his task of the day before. Gilda was constantly amused by her ability to ask Ringo to run simple errands. It satisfied her that someone, even if he was an ape, actually paid attention to her. She would enjoy the fruit on the six-hour longboat journey downriver. Ringo contentedly placed his head on her lap while she scratched the back of his neck.

Gilda had never bothered to learn American Sign Language. She spoke to the apes in English and the apes – a few of them at least – replied by signing. They got by.

Ringo was the star linguist at Camp Trinil. He had a fair understanding of spoken English, having been raised since infancy by the Nasibs – a well-to-do, rather pompous Manusian family which had spent twenty years in New York, London and Singapore when the father was with the Manusian foreign service. Ever since Ringo had first been carried into the house as a birthday present for the Nasib's youngest daughter, Fatmi, the family had insisted on speaking English to the affectionate ape.

Like hundreds, perhaps thousands of other orangutan pets, Ringo's mother had been shotgunned out of a tree. Ringo, cushioned by Mom on the fall, survived. He was a bit battered, receiving a nasty star-shaped wound on his forehead that left a permanent scar. He was as frightened as he had a right to be, but he was tough. He survived.

When the Kayan hunter tried to separate Ringo from his inert mother, the little orange ape scratched and bit, before giving up and crying. He was ignominiously stuffed into a rough, brown burlap sack. The Kayan, a striking man with gold teeth, had put his son through Anjing University by trading in wildlife. Capturing Ringo was all in a day's work and later that evening the man gently fed the ape infant milk from a bottle and hugged him until he fell asleep.

The haggling over Ringo went on for days.

"You're asking too much. I've got to be able to re-sell him quickly. You know the government is cracking down. I can't sell orangutans easily anymore," the Chinese trader had argued. "They'll confiscate this little fellow and I'll get fined."

"Okay, never mind" the Kayan hunter had replied in Malay, the lingua franca of the Manusian marketplace. "I'll keep the little fellow. Do you want some hornbill ivory instead?"

The Kayan knew he would make a sale, sooner or later. Both the Kayan and the Chinaman knew orangutans were scarce. Timber felling activity in the forest chased away many of the animals and the ones who remained were fair game for bored Caterpillar drivers who camped out in the forest. If that wasn't bad enough, the 'big people' in Anjing had implemented laws which made it a crime to kill the 'man of the forest'. No, thought the Kayan, this little fellow might be the last one for a while. I'll get my price.

The deal came a month later and the Kayan did well – a portable radiocassette player with omni-directional speakers and the equivalent of twenty US dollars.

Ringo, in turn, was sold to the Nasib family for a hundred and fifty dollars. He was treated like a member of the family – given baths with the Nasib children, fed at the table, encouraged to wear diapers and, when the time came, taught how to, "Go potty, darling Ringo."

Just before Ringo was ready to celebrate his first birthday, he was rudely taken by a policeman, who sanctimoniously announced to the Nasibs that it was illegal to keep orangutan pets since they were a threatened species and the national treasure of not only Manusia, but of the entire world. A few dollars in the palm encouraged the policeman to stop short of arresting Mr. Nasib, but was not sufficient incentive to interfere with the course of justice.

In this case, justice involved sending Ringo to reform school. Not that the animal had done anything wrong. He had simply learned the wrong things. Instead of learning how to follow hornbills to find fruiting trees, he had learned to brush the hair of the Nasib children. He had learned to brush his teeth. Sometimes he even used different brushes for the two actions. He had learned to eat Rice Krispies out of a bowl with a spoon and he had mastered the ability to play the harmonica – admittedly music of a kind best appreciated by other orangutans.

Many conservation officials considered this behavior unsuitable for an ape who belonged in the jungle. Ringo, and dozens of apes just like him, became the focus of a debate that raged in conservation circles about what to do about these problem toddlers.

"Give them a chance to start a new life by re-learning ancient skills," Sam 'Hanuman' Rama, a sensitive poet turned biologist had urged in a widely distributed speech he had given at the general assembly of the International Nature Foundation.

"Make stew out of them and put them in cans," scientist Noelle Hufschmidt had suggested with half her considerable tongue in her equally commodious cheek. "You'll never get them to live back in the wild. A canning factory that processes hundreds of confiscated cute little apes will generate the best publicity you could hope for. Governments and the donating public will have to stop the trade, because if they don't the little darlings will wind up on the table."

Hufschmidt's idea had much appeal, coming as it did from one of the world's leading scientists, a woman who had received International Nature Foundation funding for five years while she headed INF's first (and last) profit-making subsidiary – the ill-fated attempt to establish a breeding colony of gibbons to supply animals for medical research to several of the largest pharmaceutical companies.

The INF had debated the orangutan issue for months. Walter Posthleswaite, the INF's Director of Communications at the time, argued "You can't rehabilitate these animals. Why not make a big public awareness spectacle? We live for big ideas. Kill them on prime time TV and make enough ape curry to feed the starving millions in Ethiopia. The famine-sympathetic audience is 'ginormous' and we've ignored it up to now."

The debate was ended by a rare act of decisiveness by Rod Lawrence, the INF's president. "No, we'll have to find some other way to reach the Ethiopian-softies. We simply can't kill those animals and I'll tell you why," he said sternly. "It's the Shirley Temple factor. Those little fellows are cute."

Someone asked what relevance that had to science.

"It means that our philosophy of carefully-argued scientifically-based conservation action that is essential for sustainable development goes on permanent hold when we have the chance to show a TV clip of an adorable red bundle of fur being nursed by a caring woman. That's what fund raising is all about."

Thus was developed the concept that confiscated orangutans, who, after all, had committed no crime, should be taught how to live in the jungle. After a few months of instruction, conservationists thought, the apes would gladly scamper off into the forest to live happily thereafter, doing whatever it was that wild orangutans do.

However, the apes were not dumb. They quickly realized that by hanging around Camp Trinil they could enjoy life without having to face the rigors of the jungle. Twice a day, Hassan, the head rehabilitation cook/handyman/boat driver/mechanic, would steer a wheelbarrow full of fruit and milk to the feeding platform near the simple wooden dock. He would ring a bell hanging from a tree and some three dozen orangutans would climb out of the woodwork for a free meal and some companionship. Some apes would take a slice of papaya and climb off to enjoy it by themselves; others would try to steal from their friends. One or two of the infants showed remarkable disdain for the laws of gravity by drinking milk out of aluminum cups while hanging upside down. On those rare occasions when Hassan was late, some of the more boisterous adolescent males would good-naturedly pound him on the head, as they had been taught to do while living with humans.

All the rehabilitant orangutans were lucky, but Ringo was the luckiest of the lot. Gilda decided the infant was too young to mingle with the other apes and she brought him into her home. She raised Ringo as a second son. A very spoiled, very undisciplined, very cute son who played freely with Ding-Ding, Gilda's biological son. Ringo's genes were orangutan genes, but his nurture was human – living as he had, in a world of cooked rice, candies, shampoo, language and occasional discipline.

"Time to hit the river," Gilda said, draining her tea. "Will you animals be able to survive without me for a couple of days?"

Gilda now spent almost no time on orangutan rehabilitation. At first she had considered it to be a noble experiment. Gilda was the leader and founder of Camp Trinil. She was pleased to think that people entrusted her with such an important pioneering task. However, she was profoundly unhappy about the whole business. Like a bored English teacher who really wants to write novels, Gilda really wanted to study the red apes' mating patterns, food preferences and territorial ranges. Instead, she was forced to fit spurts of research in between teaching orangutans to stay in the trees and not to slouch along the ground. She was a victim of the marketplace. INF was willing to pay her to run a rehabilitation camp. They were willing to pay her an awful lot less to dissect orangutan droppings.

God, why isn't life simple, she thought, as she grabbed her overnight case and walked to the dock. There she found Hassan filling up the gas tanks, Queenie mimicking Wanita as she did the laundry and Ringo, who saluted as Gilda gingerly sat down in the narrow boat and headed downriver to negotiate her future.

Chapter 6

24 July. Noon.

Hotut River

Gilda tried to make the most of the boat trip from Camp Trinil. Powered by a 30-horsepower Evinrude, it took six hours downriver, ten up. Like a Wagner opera, any fifteen minutes of it was fascinating, but strings of those quarter hours became monotonous in the extreme.

She sat in the cigar-shaped 20-foot longboat, her hips jammed against the sides, her back aching. To pass the time she read back copies of *Scientific American* and *Nature*, when that flagged she looked at proboscis monkeys in the trees that overhung the river. She thought that with their over-developed noses these 'Dutch monkeys', as the Indonesians called them, resembled Jimmy Durante.

She tried to work on the paper she was supposed to give at the University of Arizona in Phoenix, where she was a visiting professor – but she was distracted by the huge logs floating lazily down the wide river. Each time she went to Bohong she saw more and more logs floating towards the sea. Hassan slalomed the boat around these behemoths and Gilda's mind returned to the question of what to tell her dean in Phoenix. She returned to the States every year and they expected new scholarship. She had tried to explain that her project was a longitudinal study of orangutan maternal behavior and therefore they should not expect headline news. However, they needed something, the dean had implored. So while the longboat puttered downstream, Gilda sifted through her notes for tidbits of domestic activity that would appease Sun Belt anthropologists. She thought she had just the thing – possible evidence of communal nursing of an orangutan infant named Norman. That would have to do.

Gilda had written of the orangutans' ability to "be honest in their relationships." "When they want sex, they have sex. When they have babies they just have babies. Uncomplicated. Basic. Beautiful," she had remarked in a cover story in INF's *Nature's World*. Gilda had worked hard on that passage and felt it combined the cutting edge of scientific thought with a touch of poetry that must, she thought, originate from her Hungarian genes.

The International Nature Federation had treated her well, but she was irked because they always seemed to mention her as part of a three-woman series – Maria-Angeles Guzman, Margaret Josephs and Gilda Korda.

Like the late Maria-Angeles Guzman, the sturdy Mexican-American woman who studied gorillas in Cameroon, generally dubbed the "Apes's Angel" in the media, Gilda had helped rid her study area of poachers. Like Margaret Josephs, who studied chimpanzees in Sierra Leone, Gilda had tried to raise a son while studying the behavior of wild primates. Like both, Gilda had devoted the best years of her life to man's wild relatives.

Gilda often thought of the few occasions when the three women had been together. These encounters usually took place at primatology conferences. Beneath the casual banter, Gilda generally felt vulnerable and weak, simply because she had published the least. Yet, unlike the other ape ladies, Gilda actually had academic credentials for the work she did. "After all," she had explained once to a reporter, "Angeles Guzman was a nurse and Maggie Josephs was an English teacher. Isn't there any respect any more for a Ph.D.?"

This is my world, she thought, as she shifted into a marginally more comfortable position. Almost immediately, however, she jerked upright as she watched a fiberglass speedboat zooming upriver. It approached the longboat at a tremendous clip and, at first, Gilda was annoyed by the noise and pollution it spewed. This was *her* river, *her* proboscis monkeys and *her* freshwater crocodiles. The speedboat didn't belong there.

The speedboat passed fifty yards to Gilda's port. She saw a driver and three passengers, one of whom wore a wide-brimmed straw hat. By the time she focused her binoculars all she could make out was a name painted on the speedboat's stern: Hong Neiyi Sdn. Bhd.

Hong Neiyi. Whose name was that? Gilda had heard it before, but couldn't place it. Within seconds, the speedboat was far upriver – it would have been impossible to overtake them and find out what business they had in the National Park.

Gilda's first trip up this river had been ten years earlier. She remembered the early days, when it all seemed like a Disneyland ride – exotic and beautiful and anonymous. No regrets, Gilda, she said to herself. You've made your nest ...

Gilda had not always planned to study orangutan behavior. While at the University of California at Berkeley, Gilda Korda realized, with some dismay, that her future as a marine biologist would be hindered by her constant sea-sickness while on the water and her inability to clear her ears while scuba diving. Rationalizing that one field of biology was about the same as any other, she switched to mammalian zoology and wrote her Ph.D. dissertation on the incidence of common cold symptoms among domestic pigs and cows. She became an expert in the field, partly because her limited social life gave her ample opportunity to visit farms throughout northern California.

Some of her classmates and the few women who had been her flat mates thought that her quiet demeanor and serious attitude was due to an inability to communicate in English, which after all, was not her first language. Actually, Gilda understood and spoke English perfectly. She had virtually forgotten Hungarian and, when invited to the April 4 Liberation Day celebrations by the Hungarian consulate in Los Angeles, she steadfastly refused to speak her native tongue. She had explained to the diplomats that this was because she had left the country when she was a baby. They graciously accepted this excuse and were too polite to mention that her file showed that she and her parents had emigrated to the States when Gilda was 14.

No, Gilda's problem was not language. It was communication. She was the only child of parents who had, between them, a total of 16 siblings. Her father, disappointed because his wife was forced to have a hysterectomy after bearing Gilda, took out his frustration on his daughter. He did this by ignoring her, just as he would have if she had been born in the middle of a brood. Gilda's mother, on the other hand, a modern-thinking woman who had taught herself English and who had slogged away for seven years to get a college degree in economics, spent so much time telling Gilda about her illustrious, wise, brave, brilliant, aristocratic ancestors with paprika in their veins that the young child grew up thinking that the other girls who had nothing better to do than play with dolls – or, later in life, play with football players – were nonentities, not worth talking to, because it was unlikely they would have anything substantial to say.

"I am a child of my times. I seek the golden bough. The sun mirrors my gut-felt desire to touch Monet, the wind echoes my nerve-endings vibrating with Mozart. I live to pick daisies," was how she described her 17-year-old feelings in an autobio-graphical essay that was, perhaps, not too closely read by the university's admissions committee.

Mark Breckenridge was Gilda's first love. She remembered how they had met – in an advanced statistics course. She needed stat because it was required for her masters' degree, he chose it as an elective for his Bachelor's in electrical engineering.

Her first words to him had been: "You're absolutely amazing." He had been drinking a Coke by himself in Quigley's drugstore and was reading the *Los Angeles Times*. The Lakers were hot.

The shy young man wasn't used to compliments, so he answered honestly. "Do you really think so?"

"My God yes. How do you do it?"

Mark wasn't sure what was going on. "Do I know you?" he had finally asked.

By this time, Gilda's unconscious defense mechanisms had taken over and she stood by his side, silently.

"Er, excuse me. I do know you, don't I?" he stammered. "I mean, you know, er, you seem to know me, what I mean is..."

"Spindopholous."

"Oh yes, of course," Mark laughed nervously. He took two sips of his Coke. "Yes, old Ari, well ..."

"Who?"

"Aristotle Spindopholous. The statistics professor?"

Gilda stood by quietly. One corner of her mouth headed north towards her ear, the other started a mild slide south. "Yes," she answered.

"Well, what a coincidence meeting someone else who's interested in statistics."

"Will you buy me a milkshake?" she had asked, without guile.

In time, Gilda told Mark what she had found most attractive about him. Most men, regardless of what they say, want to be admired for their biceps, or their asses, or their eyes or even their hands.

To Mark's dismay, Gilda was fascinated by his mind. Mark, she noticed, was one of those remarkable creatures who sat in the gray classroom and actually appeared to understand what Professor Spindopholus was saying about bell curves. She was so struck by Mark's intelligence that she neglected to notice that they had little else in common except visceral reactions (his was Buddha-like acceptance, hers was abject dread) to standard deviations and Gaussian curves. They lived together for three years.

They had a relationship uncomplicated by vacations or cooking or use of the car or other perils to domestic happiness. Mark left college after receiving his first degree and quickly got a job designing wiring systems for a firm that developed image resonance scanning machines. Gilda stayed in school, attending classes during the day and giving German lessons at night at the Goethe Institute. The couple had discovered the secret to marital harmony by meeting once a week – generally on Saturday mornings – when they would go to the supermarket together and have lunch in an ethnic restaurant – generally Ethiopian or Greek. If it was raining they would go to the movies, preferably to watch a Bergman film. If it was a sunny day, they'd simply walk through the park and feed the squirrels.

Gilda's German students dragged her into the fringes of the women's liberation movement. The idea that a woman should seek adventure and self-fulfilment, doing so with a clear conscience, appealed to her independent nature. It was not surprising that she wrote to Horace Chatwin for a job.

Horace Chatwin was the world's foremost paleontologist. He made his living by scratching around the East African dust until he found the bones of human ancestors. He would then dust them off and announce that each new chunk of fossilized calcium added another piece to the jigsaw of human evolution.

Perhaps because Chatwin studied early man, a distinctly ape-like creature, the raspy scientist was fascinated by the great apes. He often regretted that he had not been trained in biology. Vicariously, perhaps, he funded young women to go off to remote places and study man's closest living relatives.

It was well-known that Chatwin had insisted that his 'angels' endure Abraham-like tests of commitment. He had challenged Maria-Angeles Guzman's resolve by asking if she would have her appendix out before leaving for Africa. He had argued that she would be far from medical care if an emergency should arise so it made sense to avoid messy complications. Guzman did as he asked, never realizing until twenty years later that he had only been kidding.

Gilda decided to have her appendix taken out *before* Chatwin asked. She had elective surgery in Beth Moses Hospital in San Francisco, and, with her letter of application, enclosed a Polaroid of her scar. She received no reply though, since Chatwin was stricken by a near-fatal heart attack two days after getting her letter.

Not one to be easily dissuaded, Gilda innocently turned to Chatwin's scratch-each-other's-eyeballs-out enemy, Jaap Van der Kamp, thereby inadvertently taking sides in a cosmic controversy. For decades, Van der Kamp and Chatwin had been writing nasty letters to each other via the correspondence columns of *Man: The American Journal of Physical Anthropology* and, when the issue was really hot, in *Nature*. Conference organizers salivated at the thought of the two of them sharing a panel, but the two assiduously bobbed and weaved without ever getting close enough to smell each other's breath.

Chatwin had made his reputation in Africa. Van der Kamp had devoted his life to studying early man in Asia, particularly at a site in Central Java not too far from the sugar plantation where he had been born during the Dutch colonial period in Indonesia. Both men had the same overall objective.

The holy grail to paleontologists, at least as far as the public is concerned, is the so-called 'missing link'. This elusive creature is postulated to be the man-ape which marks the transition between humanity's ape-like ancestors and human beings. Actually, the idea of a 'missing link' is based on a misinterpretation of Darwin. The (incorrect) argument is that if men were descended from apes, then there should have been an animal that stood halfway between the two, a transitional creature, that might perhaps resemble a union of man and orangutan.

Actually, Darwin speculated that while man and ape were likely to have had a common ancestor, each most likely evolved along its own lines with considerable evolutionary dead-ends along the way. Nevertheless, the public enjoyed speculating on finding a single man-ape ancestor.

There was no question that Horace Chatwin was the superstar of crumbling bones. Without undue modesty, he and his wife, Lucy, dug up remains of man's ancestors the way young boys collect worms after heavy rain. It would not be an exaggeration to say that he re-wrote the pre-history books.

Jaap Van der Kamp lived in a region which was more modern. He could not compete with Chatwin's discoveries in terms of age, but he had a theory that Southeast Asia, not East Africa, was the place where our ancestors first became human. Van der Kamp, a wild-eyed man who up until the age of 40 resembled a gangly soccer goalkeeper on speed, devoted much of his energy to the neighborhood in which he had grown up – the muddy, not terribly attractive Solo River. It was here in Central Java, at a village called Trinil, that in 1893 Dutchman Eugene Dubois had discovered remarkable skeleton fragments. In time, the scientific community would identify his creature as *Homo erectus*, 'upright man', the first 'modern' man and a direct predecessor to our species, *Homo sapiens*. Having little respect for science, but a great nose for survival, the laborers Dubois employed stole fossils, which they called 'dragon bones', almost as fast as they found them. The 600,000-year-old remains wound up in China where pharmacists, labeling them as 'dragon's teeth', ground them into powder that was sold as medicines and aphrodisiacs.

Some scientists eagerly seek the limelight and, once having achieved a certain recognition outside academic circles, are then loudly denounced as lousy scientists by less fortunate scientists who have yet to be invited to the Tonight show. Van der Kamp sniped away at media-star Chatwin for years, until Van der Kamp's big breakthrough came – the discovery of an entire clan of some thirty people who lived on the cusp of *Homo erectus* and *Homo sapiens* about half a million years ago. The skeletons, found in a limestone cave in Sarawak in Malaysian Borneo, had been found by

Kelabit farmers collecting smelly, nitrogen-rich bat guano for fertilizer. The place was not a cemetery, since these people did not bury their dead. The bones were scattered and many had been chewed. By examining teeth marks and bite patterns, Van der Kamp theorized, in a fictionalized account called Goldilocks in the Pleistocene: Homos Sleeping in My Bed – which he secretly hoped Steven Spielberg would one day make into a film – that a group of late-apes/early-people had taken shelter in the cave from an enemy tribe, only to be surprised by a band of angry bears who did not welcome visitors in what they considered to be their cave.

Jaap Van der Kamp was intrigued by the definitions by which we call one kind of ape an ape, and another kind of ape a human being. He knew it wasn't brain capacity, nor dentition, nor an upright stance, nor group living, that determined human-ness, at least not solely. "What was the unknown quality in human-ness that makes us admire a van Gogh, rather than try to lick the paint off?" he had written in an article published in the INF journal.

Like Horace Chatwyn, Jaap Van der Kamp employed young people to help decipher this enigma, a riddle he considered to be the most sensible question anybody should ever want to ask.

Van der Kamp had spent virtually all of his life in Indonesia, where he had had his choice of girls, boys and, it was rumored, the odd domestic animal.

Van der Kamp's reputation as an aging old goat had a stimulating affect on his female visitors. Gilda, like many before her, made the pilgrimage to Central Java and went into the interview session fully aware that old Jaap liked to seduce the neophytes. Gilda, like many before her, was firm in her resolve that *she* would keep her dress on.

"*Selamat pagi,*" he had said by way of introduction.

Not be be outdone Gilda replied: "*Selamat pagi. Apa khabar Pak Jaap. Saya senang sekali Bapak undangan saya.*"

Van der Kamp smiled, pleased that this woman had taken the trouble to learn Indonesian, even though she spoke it with an execrable accent. She was a bit chunk, and a bit big, her hair was a mousy reddish-brown and she didn't shave her legs, but she had a gleam in her eye. She would do.

"Do you know, my dear – may I call you Gilda? – what – oh, by the way, would you like some tea or coffee? – the tea's more drinkable, really – *Aminah, tolong minta teh untuk kami punya tamu,*" he called out to his servant – "what the single most important transitional factor was that marked the evolution from *erectus* to *sapiens*?"

Gilda had done her homework and thought she had the answer. She glanced around the room and noticed a stuffed rhinoceros hornbill behind Van der Kamp's right shoulder. On its upraised black and white tail was placed an odd elongated conical gourd. "Surely it's communal living and raising children collectively," she replied confidently.

"No, lots of macaque troops do that, not to mention whales, elephants, just lots and lots of creatures," he said in perfect English. His Mephistopheles-like right eyebrow twittered. "Try again."

Gilda went through three other incorrect options – fire, domestication of crops and language – before Van der Kamp changed the subject. He took the gourd off the hornbill's casque and told her about the strange decoration. "It's called a *koteka*. Used by the Dani tribe in the middle of New Guinea. You see, the males …"

Gilda was staring directly into Van der Kamp's deep gray eyes. She felt hypnotized. Perhaps it was the tropical heat, perhaps it was this room overflowing with memorabilia, perhaps it was his Flying Dutchman pipe tobacco, perhaps it was his white-haired presence.

"The males, although they are all quite adequately endowed, feel they have to, well, show-off," he said, rolling the *koteka* through an O he made with his thumb and forefinger. "They take these long gourds and strap them over their penises. Here, I'll show you."

Gilda sat rock still. She heard, for the first time, the overhead fan. Jaap Van der Kamp, 60 years old and a legend, rose from behind his desk and walked towards Gilda. He stood over her. She smelled his Old Spice that couldn't quite conceal the fact that his safari shirt had not been washed recently. Deliberately, he came nearer and reached over her left shoulder to the bookcase. He brushed her hair, as lightly as a breath of wind, as he extended his arm.

"Here's a monograph written by Claeyssans in 1937," he said, handing her a leather-bound volume. "There are some excellent plates showing how the *koteka* is worn."

With that instruction, Van der Kamp excused himself to "take a pee – all this tea, you know. Diuretic."

He returned ten minutes later, during which time Gilda had had ample opportunity to examine photos of negroid men cavorting around wearing nothing but pig fat and long thin *kotekas*.

"I'm afraid I've been having you on, Gilda," he apologized. "You see, my dear, there isn't just one characteristic that separates *erectus* from *sapiens*. There are two things."

Gilda had caught her breath. "And what might those things be?" she asked hesitatingly.

"Well, the first is the deliberate enhancement – but I admit some might call it mutilation – of the male of the species to make himself a better sexual partner."

"Oh really?" Gilda hated herself for not keeping up her end of the conversation, but couldn't think of a better response. She hoped she would remember this discussion to be able to repeat it to Mark – they might have one of their weekly laughs about it.

"Really, no fooling. Did you know that in parts of Borneo men of the Kenyah tribe imitate the anatomy of the male rhino? Did you ever study rhino anatomy?"

Gilda shook her head. Van der Kamp took a step closer. She saw his mane of white hair bounce once, then settle back on his head.

"One reason people think that rhino horn is a sexual stimulant is because the rhino is a great lover. It is not uncommon for a pair to copulate for upwards of an hour, during which the bull ejaculates approximately every three minutes."

"No, I didn't know that," Gilda said, almost in a whisper.

"No, I didn't think you did. Well, the peculiar shape of the rhino's penis supports the perception that the animal is the ultimate mammalian satyr. You see, the penis actually looks a bit like a crucifix – you're not Catholic by any chance – with a crossbar up near the tip. In the rhino it protrudes about five centimeters on each side," he said from about a foot and a half away.

She could see the hairs in his nose. This was the first time she had carefully considered nasal hairs and she gazed at them like a child looking through a kaleidoscope. They were, for the most part, white and gray and black but one orphan hair gleamed red in the sunlight that filtered through the open shutters to her side.

With great effort, Gilda averted her gaze to the diplomas on the wall. They were too far away to read. She instead concentrated on a terrarium and noticed a well-camouflaged lizard yawn as he woke up from a nap.

"As I was saying," he said, lightly touching her wrist, "the Kenyah men, not all of them, of course, and even fewer today because of the bloody missionaries – you can't imagine the mischief they get up to – but that's a different story, but, as I was saying, the men imitate the rhino and have the local medicine man implant a rhino-like *palang* – usually made of bamboo or bone or horn through their penises. They can slide it in and out. I happen to collect odd curios, as you may have noticed," he said, getting her full attention by twisting his black eyebrow with one hand and with the other running his finger in a feather-light caress over her pale knuckles. She was a doe caught in his headlights. "I have one in my own collection." He turned abruptly and went back to his wooden desk. From the top drawer he took out a small jewelry case and a bottle of Dettol disinfectant.

"This is what it looks like," he said, opening the box to reveal a thin, ivory-colored device as thick as a pencil and about two inches long. There were small knobs on the ends through which holes had been drilled. "They say you can even attach ornaments to the ends, just like a Borneo Christmas tree," he said with a festive ho-ho. "Of course, these things have to be well disinfected before they are used.Lots of Kenyah died of septic wounds."

"I'm sure," Gilda said, hearing her breathing, slow, regular and deep.

"Now, can you tell me what the other major transition behavior milestone was?"

"I haven't a clue," Gilda replied, smiling because she looked forward to the answer.

"Ventral-ventral female-supine male-superior prone entry," Van der Kamp said, taking her hand and leading her into his private quarters. "The missionary position."

Three months later, Gilda and Mark were in Manusia, establishing Camp Trinil.

Jaap Van der Kamp had such a significant ego that he would not stoop to allowing things to be named after himself. No, if Horace Chatwin would be pedestrian enough to allow his women to set up Camp Chatwins around the world like so many fast food restaurants, Jaap Van der Kamp would show the world that at least one famous paleontologist had managed to maintain a sense of style.

Van der Kamp would name the camps in Burma, China, Thailand, Vietnam and Indonesia where his women worked after his birthplace, the site of Eugene Dubois' historic discovery, the appellation given to the most famous *Homo erectus*: Trinil. Nor would he stop by naming just research camps after that innocuous little village which had, through no fault of its own, accidentally become famous. To show the world what a modest, unselfish man he was, Jaap Van der Kamp named most of his possessions Trinil. The logotype of the Trinil Foundation was painted on the doors of his Toyota Land Cruiser. The ketch he kept in St Kitts was named *Trinil*, so was his ski chalet in Verbier, as was the line of safari clothing he endorsed, as were two of his sons, not to mention an uncounted number of god-children.

"Are you sure you got the best deal possible out of the old man?" Mark had asked Gilda on several occasions.

"Absolutely. You know I'm, that is, we're getting more money than any of his other researchers."

The great deal Gilda had negotiated was a flat $10,000 a year salary, one way tickets for her and Mark to Manusia and $15,000 to equip, run and develop the research station. Her task: learn as much as possible about the behavior of orangutans so her data and that of other ape scientists could help Van der Kamp come up with a model for what early man's daily grind might have been like.

Managing money was never Gilda's strong suit. Mark easily accepted the task of chief accountant, just as he had taken on the responsibilities of being chief carpenter, chief mechanic, chief personnel officer and, after their son was born, chief dry nurse.

Even with Mark's financial skills, he had trouble making the money last. The budget for operating expenses was supposed to cover the salaries of the local staff and pay for the construction of living quarters, diesel for the generator, binoculars, portable computers and other equipment. He was then expected to have cash left over for semi-annual bribes to the Manusian departments of immigration, environment and research and technology. Mark stayed up nights trying to figure out how to save money. Gilda was happy to leave these mundane tasks to her husband. She had more important business to attend to and was usually in bed by 8 p.m. so as to have the energy to spend all her daylight hours with her orangutans.

Gilda found the orangutans to be fellow-travelers.

"They are loners, spending most of their lives wandering by themselves in search of food and sexual partners," she had written in a popular article. After a while, Gilda trained herself to get out of bed by five each morning, giving her enough time to get herself together. Orangutans are the laziest of the great apes and among the laziest of all forest creatures, sometimes not leaving their nests until 7 a.m., a time when most other forest dwellers have already put in half a day's work. This timetable, though, suited Gilda perfectly. She had time to have a cup of tea and start the day properly.

The Trinil Foundation funded Gilda for the first two years. The continuous shortage of funds put a strain on Gilda's marriage. When the Washington-based International Nature Federation offered to chip in $30,000 a year so that Gilda could supervise their orangutan rehabilitation project, Gilda and Mark thought things were turning in their favor.

Their lives, however, became more chaotic as a result of the INF windfall. By this time, Gilda had given birth to a son whom they named Ding Ding, after the boy's godfather, who was the headman of nearby Rumah Sehat longhouse. The Korda family shared living quarters with half a dozen apes. That situation lasted for five years, during which time Ding Ding learned to speak excellent Gibbon and developed a deep friendship with Ringo, with whom he communicated in their own version of American Sign Language.

Mark, however, thought that it was inappropriate for his son to climb trees before he could ride a bicycle. He felt it was misguided to allow the boy to slurp water from a stagnant pond while never having learned to use a spoon.

Mark also thought that it was somehow unfair that he did all the work around Camp Trinil while Gilda got all the glory.

These were serious problems which bothered Mark intellectually. There was another problem, perhaps equally knotty, which sliced at his emotional wellbeing. Gilda, to be polite, was a big girl and she got bigger, at least around the hips, the older she got and the longer she stayed away from polite company. Mark realized that he liked slim girls.

Ultimately, Mark jumped ship, taking Ding Ding and returning to California with Manis, the Malay cook. It was a serious blow to Gilda. Good help was hard to find.

She hired Bujang a year later.

As the river widened and became the color of *café au lait*, Gilda returned to the problems at hand. What if Bujang doesn't marry me? That means my only hope is Taffy? But what if Taffy doesn't help me with my work permit?

Gilda dozed off in the midday sun.

Penan encampment

Life in the Penan camp had become considerably more interesting since the timber blockades began. The threat of arrest scared some Penan, excited others.

But, life goes on and Urs had much to learn.

"And this one, you say, is for not having babies," Urs said to Maya, his wife.

"Yes. You asked me that earlier."

"Sorry. All these twigs and leaves look alike. How do you use it?"

"The woman holds it between her knees," Maya giggled.

It had taken Urs some time to get used to the earthy ways the Penan viewed sex. It was like all the other bodily functions. Perfectly normal.

Avalon shyly entered the clearing in front of the crude shelter that Urs and Maya called home. "Mail, elder brother." He handed Urs several envelopes that reached the Swiss through convoluted mail drops. They eventually were delivered to friends at Rumah Sehat, one of Urs' safe houses. Urs saw that Maya looked at him with quiet admiration. She had told him that no one else in Penan history, as far as she knew, had ever received any mail.

His 14-year-old wife had been a welcome-back gift from Laki. It was not normal Penan behavior to offer your daughter to a visitor, but Urs' homecoming was a special event. Laki saw it as a ceremonial unification of two nomadic bands. Both groups were acceptably pale, but the representative of one was significantly taller, hairier and had a funny nose. Aesthetically, the newcomer was distressing, but the Penans were pragmatic. They realized the importance of mixing genes.

Urs didn't mind the mixing bit, but he was still bothered by the fishbowl existence. Urs compared his private life to that of the orangutans. You could do pretty much what you wanted, but you always did it under the scrutiny of the others in the band. He realized he might never again be able to slip into a city café for a quiet, private drink. He could not ride his bicycle down a deserted country lane and he and his woman could not make love – like a married couple should.

How could he explain to this simple girl that in a month or so, after he had taught Laki some sabotage techniques, he would leave.

He still wasn't sure whether Maya had a concept of romantic love. Maybe she just hasn't had to think about life in those terms. He smiled as he remembered their first five minutes of lovemaking, when Urs had learned how to kick dogs. His instinct and his European upbringing told him that dogs were your friends. The theory was: treat them right and they'll treat you right – but the first night he had coupled with his Penan wife, the dogs had come sniffing at their soggy genitals. Urs had unleashed a size ten foot that sent the mangy critters flying.

Urs had not had many experiences with women. One of his fonder memories was of an English secretary who worked at the United Nations in Geneva. He had met her while he was trying, unsuccessfully, to round up support for his adopted cause from the international organizations which proliferated on the comfortable Geneva lakeshore. Her name was Jill and he remembered writing a poem comparing the sound of her name with the tinkling of his sheep's bells. Her breasts smelled of talcum powder and made him sneeze. Urs remembered the domesticity of having to move her pantyhose in order to take a shower in her apartment. He remembered sleeping all night in a proper bed and waking up, privately, just the two of them, the not-so-small English girl lying on his forearm, giving him a cramp. It was a good memory. Maybe even it would happen again, he thought.

In the meantime, Urs and Maya coupled every few weeks in the dead of the night, in an open-sided lean-to like shelter that stood ten feet from identical constructions. This was funny, Urs thought. Even though we live in a forest that is so big that it takes months to walk across, everybody sleeps and makes love within farting distance of each other.

Once the band had decided to accept Urs, the Penans patiently put up with his constant questions and frequently bumbling mannerisms.

His discomfort was partly physical, since their world was designed for people who were rarely much taller than five feet three. The bigger problem was that, as far as the Penan were concerned, Urs did not speak a known language.

As his language ability improved, the Penan were able to include him in more of their activities.

"We're going hunting tomorrow morning," Laki had said early during Urs' apprenticeship. "You can come, but do try not to stomp around like a water buffalo."

This was the breakthrough he had waited for. Up to that point, the men had usually slipped away in the early morning hours, leaving Urs alone with the women and children. His first foray into the world of blowpipes and wild boars was predictably hilarious to the Penan, predictably sobering for the Swiss. However, within several months Urs learned to keep the prey upwind, how to identify different monkeys and birds by their calls, how to handle a blowpipe and how to start a fire with a vine, a stick and some tinder.

All the while he kept notes and documented every aspect of Penan life. During the first six months he filled five thick notebooks with a Penan/German dictionary of 350 words, including seven that described different types of rain, the six words for 'us' and eleven for various poisons used in making blowpipe darts. He illustrated medicinal plants and the technique of weaving baskets. He described childbirth and the method of constructing a lean-to shelter out of a few branches and leaves.

Gradually, the Penan realized that Urs had become useful. He could hunt. He could fish. He could skin an animal and climb a tree to collect honey. He became a Penan man.

Almost as soon as he had arrived, Urs heard the chain saws of the timber cutters and saw the bulldozers clearing roads through the forest. The area was a national park, but the legal delineation of the area did not matter to the Penan. It was their home and had been for many generations.

The Penan were inclined to move further into the forest to avoid the noise and chaos. Their hunting had been disturbed already and they had to travel further to find wild boar and deer. They were frightened when they saw the scars made by the timber operators and reacted to the noise of chainsaws as Urs reacted to a dentist's drill. Almost every day now, while walking in the forest they would come to a stream and find that a tractor had defiled it. Bad for fishing, bad for collecting frogs, bad omens for the future. Where the trees had been cleared huge open gaps formed; the Penan avoided these wounds, so hot, so exposed. The Penan would climb a ridge and see red zig-zags through their homeland, many of which defiled sacred sites. No non-Penan could have identified these sites as holy, of course, since they were subtle in the extreme – just a special tree, or an unusual waterfall where the spirits took refuge. More than ever, the Penan realized they were on the bottom of the Manusian social ladder, the yellow-brown dregs in a land ruled by the tawny-brown Malay aristocrats.

The event that rearranged Penan thinking had occurred one drizzly morning. The band had camped for two weeks in a riverside clearing where they extracted starchy, tasteless sago, one of their staple foods. Avalon rushed into the clearing. "Come quick. All of you. But be careful."

The excited band had followed the young man for several miles. They could not have imagined a more horrible end to a morning. A bulldozer from one of the timber companies was constructing a road through a ridge top forest that contained the remains of five generations of Penan. A simply carved burial pole lay crumbled by the side of the road.

"We must stop them," Laki had argued.

Their first inclination was to seek change peacefully. Unlike other tribal groups, the Penan are not aggressive by nature. They have a well-developed timid streak that rarely puts them in conflict with any outsiders.

They sent two of the teenagers who spoke some Malay to the district office, a five-day walk. There, the boys were received by a gruff Malay clerk. He listened to what they had to say, gave them three Manusian dollars each from a petty cash fund allocated for "tribal entertaining" and told them to go to the marketplace, buy a beer and enjoy their time in civilization.

The timber activities intensified. So, too, did the search for Urs. The authorities knew he was somewhere in the Mount Malu area, but had no way of finding him. However, they realized that he was with one of the Penan bands and Urs did not let any of his group go to town again for fear they might be arrested and questioned. He was not afraid for himself, but did not want to put any more pressure than necessary on his adopted family.

Urs realized that his most effective role would be as stage manager and publicist. The result: a series of blockades of timber operations that resulted in an expanding number of news stories that were increasingly embarrassing to the government in Anjing.

All the Penan who had not gone out hunting sat quietly around Urs as he opened the first envelope. Robert Hallmark's note was cryptic in the extreme. "Thought these might interest you, R." He tore off the stamps from America and gave them to one of the children. Urs had once tried to explain world geography to his adopted family, but did not get much further than "many, many days of longboat travel away."

Urs unfolded a story that had appeared in the *Wall Street Journal* five weeks earlier and did his best to translate. 'Manusians Promise Rural Development Program to Penans,' the headline read. 'No Timber Activity in National Park, Minister Claims'. "Scheisse," Urs said under his breath. The second article was from a publication called *Tribal Rights International*, produced in Berlin by a group of civil rights lawyers with anthropological inclinations. It told of the Huonari tribe in Ecuador which had murdered fourteen Ecuadorean and foreign workers who had tried to set up an oil exploration camp in the middle of the Huonari homeland.

Liebchen, feeling left out, climbed onto Urs' shoulder. He absent-mindedly scratched the monkey behind her ears. One of the hunting dog puppies, which would remain cute for another few weeks before growing into skinny, dirty, body-sored adulthood, nibbled on Urs' toe. Urs scratched him as well and a jealous Liebchen scooted down to bite the dog's tail and send him yelping. She then resumed her perch.

The second small package was from the director of the group in Sydney that called itself "Rainforests for the People."

"Dear Urs. As always, I never know whether this letter will reach you. I got a note from our friend No. 2 asking me to stop sending him your mail because he fears the authorities have been opening previous letters and he's frightened for his safety. So, I send this through route No.3 and hope for the best.

"How are you? We received the film you sent and enclose a set of prints for your own files. I particularly love the reaction on the lorry driver's face when your monkey pissed on his head. All the papers ran the story and I enclose some clips for your scrapbook.

"Our mailing list now has 3,000 people worldwide, our website gets hundreds of hits a week and the next newsletter will feature the Penan rainforest story as the lead article. We'll start a postcard campaign to try to put pressure on the Manusian government to stop logging and declare the Mount Malu area a biosphere reserve. I see that the Global Greens in Brussels are trying to get one of their environmentally-sensitive Euro MPs to introduce a bill in the European Parliament to condemn the timber activities and protest against the abuse of civil rights in Manusia. Also, the US activists are trying to put pressure on their congressmen to impose economic sanctions.

"I need news of new actions, both from your side and from the timber operators. Also, it would help if you could send some photos of domestic Penan life – adds a bit of human interest. Please also send some more of your dynamite drawings – they add so much to the articles. I know you don't like to feature yourself too much, but it really does help publicity when we have photos of you. Teach your friends how to use the camera so they can include you in the picture. I enclose some more film, some pastel pencils and a watercolor set. Also, a little treat. How I wish I could come and visit you. Would that be possible? I'm good in the forest and I'm in pretty good shape. I climbed Ayers Rock in just two hours last year. Here's a photo of me at the top. I'm the one with the red hat and the sunburned shoulders.

"I hope to hear from you soon. Until then, keep up the fight. Forests for the people.

"With sincere admiration and affection from your friend in Oz, (signed) "Jennifer"

Urs opened the small bottle of Vegemite. He dipped his index finger in the black glop and tasted the downunder delicacy. Only an Australian could consider that a gift. He passed it around. Most of the Penan did not go back for seconds. Even Liebchen gave it a wide berth.

* * * * *

"This is not a fucking game," Jong Il Kim shouted at his director

71

of security at the morning inspection of the timber camp's security guards, scaring the Rottweiler puppy Manja, who always followed him around. "Do I have to make a list for you?" he asked. "Okay, I will make you a list," he said when the silence became too thick. Punctuating each problem with a calloused finger, he listed the disasters. First, the Penan had toted-up their fifth timber truck hijacking. Second, the mail contained a clipping sent by the Minister of the Environment. It was from the *London Times*; a long article on the earlier hijackings and an impassioned editorial supporting the native cause. Third, the Minister had made it Jong's problem, which meant it was their problem. Surely that was Asian solidarity.

"The Minister has told me to stop those bastards and I'm telling you to stop those bastards," Jong shouted at his Chinese deputy, thereby causing Ramsay Wong to lose as much face as a single human being can lose.

"Yes, I agree," Wong, the equally burly ex-army officer replied. "But it's hard to know where they will attack."

"You call a bunch of skinny, naked men an attack team? Come on. Just get them."

"But we have forty trucks and they drive all over this miserable jungle. They probably cover, I don't know, maybe 300 miles of road. Not easy, *lah*."

"If it was easy I wouldn't have interrupted my coffee break, *lah*," Jong said, mocking the Singaporean's speech. Jong ran the Hong Neiyi Timber Camp as a military exercise. There was no room for weakness in the face of the enemy. He took pride in his work, he thought, as he scratched the puppy behind her ears. He took particular pleasure in ordering around a Chinese, just as he had pleasure imagining dead Penan and, most of all, seeing Urs Gerhard in handcuffs. "Bastards, bastards, bastards," he swore, savoring the word as he might a grilled slice of beef with *kimchi*.

Hotut River

Gilda slept fitfully as the longboat cruised down the river towards Bohong. It was hotter downriver and the river became muddier and wider. Gilda awoke as they approached Bohong. She knew the scenery by heart – the hills and forests of the upper stretches of the river had given way to flatter land where farmers grew small holdings of rubber and vegetables. Every few minutes she was jolted awake when Hassan steered clear of a big log. More dangerous, she knew, were the branches and debris that floated just below the surface.

On the upriver outskirts of the town, she was startled to see a new dock with a small fleet of speedboats, supply boats and, high on shore, large cranes hauling giant logs out of the river. The sign read: Hong Neiyi Timber Company.

CHAPTER 7

24 July. 16:00.

Bohong

Mustafa bin Kayu kept Gilda shivering in the over air-conditioned waiting room of his 'up-country' office in the Hotel Niagara. Good for this western woman to learn a bit of patience, he reasoned.

The Minister of the Environment watched Gilda through a peephole in his inner office. She thumbed through the packet of mail for Camp Trinil that she had picked up at the post office. He knew what was in the bundle. What's the point of being a Federal Minister if you can't give orders to the head of the Central Post Office? Back copies of *Parks* magazine, *Nature's World*, *Ms.*, *Working Woman* and *Vogue*. A letter from Mark, containing the final divorce decree. A packet of papers from the INF. Assorted missives from various friends and professional colleagues. Invitations to speak at conferences in Monte Carlo and Gothenberg. Some mail for Gerry, which Mustafa bin Kayu hadn't bothered to examine.

Gilda glanced at her watch. She glanced at her blurred reflection in the mirror on the wall. "Bad hair day," she mumbled. "Do you ever notice my hair, Taffy?" she said quietly, flicking a wayward strand behind her ear. "You're such a big shot. Big, big, big shot Taffy."

Mustafa bin Kayu smiled, pleased to be a complicated character. He was a world star in the rapidly growing firmament of ecological super-novas. He was an environmental lion, a rare creature: an articulate third-worlder who spoke out about environmental destruction. As a result he had won virtually every accolade

dreamed up by first-world environmental groups and governments. The Minister spent much of his time attending banquets,
making speeches and massaging the egos of those people who felt
that by awarding honors to a brown man they were helping to save
the world.

The Minister and virtually all his colleagues at senior levels were
Malays, conservative coastal-raised Muslims who claimed that
their birthright as Sons of the Soil made them more equal than
other Manusians.

The Manusians, like nationals of most countries, jealously
regarded their prerogative to screw-up their own country as they
saw fit, much like parents will generally defend their right to smack
their own child but will damn anyone else who tries it. The senior
level Manusians were well educated and the inner core was dubbed
the "Sorbonne mafia" by the international press in honor of the
university where the all-powerful Sultan, who doubled as Prime
Minister, and five cabinet ministers had done graduate work.

Internationally, however, the Manusian leaders, many of whom
were vaguely related to the royal family, resented that they were
treated like groveling third-worlders. When they attended major
UN conferences they disliked to the point of indigestion having to
be lumped together in developing world caucuses with nouveau-
riche Nigerians, odiferous Yemenese, Indians in shiny grey suits
and Peruvians who ate guinea pigs.

One way the Manusians felt they could set themselves apart
from the crowd was by embracing nature conservation, just like the
big boys – the Americans, the British, the Germans, the Dutch and
the Swedes.

The western nations were so thrilled to have a counterbalance to
the xenophobic environmental cataclysms of Brazil and Malaysia,
that they encouraged Manusia's green politics and gave Manusian
politicians a world platform from which they could show the world
how wonderful they were. There was plenty of development aid
money available, provided the projects claimed to be environmentally-sensitive, a vague term that more often than not meant
that some European or American expert in sustainable development had a lovely holiday spending six weeks in the country
writing an environmental impact assessment which was then
widely circulated and promptly ignored.

One cold February morning, in the cavernous UNESCO auditorium in Paris, Mustafa bin Kayu had addressed the annual general meeting of the World Heritage Convention. Dressed in a charcoal gray suit tailored by Justmen's Shop in Singapore, wearing highly polished Bally-tasseled shoes and sporting a burgundy Italian silk tie emblazoned with the koala insignia of the INF, the Minister, whose remit included national parks and nature conservation, had stood on his tiptoes to peer over the lectern and made an impassioned plea that the Mount Malu National Park should be given World Heritage Status, a distinction several hundred other natural places had been given by virtue of their being, quite simply, the world's best places.

That year, the committee, which acted on behalf of the hundred nations which were signatories to the World Heritage convention of UNESCO, had rejected requests for World Heritage status at sites in Bulgaria, Colombia, the United States, Fiji and China. They accepted Manusia's proposal, however, noting in their report that "the proposed site contains some of the world's largest and barely explored limestone cave formations thought to provide evidence of human development. Perhaps of equal, if not greater, importance is the area's large stand of relatively undisturbed lowland and montane rainforest containing a biological diversity of exceptional abundance, including Borneo's largest population of orangutans and other threatened species. The intact rainforest also forms the watershed for the major rivers which irrigate farmland in Manusia and neighboring Brunei, Indonesian Kalimantan and Malaysian Sabah and Sarawak."

That night, the Minister hosted a private celebratory dinner at Archestrate and his party, which included his charming French assistant Mimi, dined on *langoustines en papillote de poireaux* and *canard apicius*, washed down with a modest Margaux 1948. Mustafa bin Kayu had just secured half a million dollars in funding for Mount Malu. He felt he was justified in taking a small bit of that in advance.

Mount Malu National Park

Some of the best hunting is just before sundown and Urs, Laki, Avalon and his brother, Seridan, were en route to the Hotut

River in the hopes that they might stalk a deer. As they crossed one of the numerous timber roads that snaked through the forest they saw, in the far distance, a timber truck inching forward.

Blockading timber operations had become a sport with some of the Penan. Penan five, Hong Neiyi zero.

"Dinner can wait," Avalon declared. "Let's stop these big people."

Bohong

Gilda thought the Hotel Niagara looked like the architectural mistake of a mad pastry chef. The hotel's five red brick-terraced storeys rose uncertainly above miles and miles of oil palm and rubber plantations. Rooms had fifteen-foot-high ceilings covered with reliefs carved in teak. Brass railings wound along marble stairs, the floor tiles were vintage art nouveau and there was a sinister algae-encrusted swimming pool – all of which reminded Gilda of Pontius Pilate; something about the decadence and decay brought to mind images of ancient Rome. Stained glass windows were etched with the initials of Lim Boon Jing, the Chinese rubber baron who constructed the building as a private residence in 1910. Even though the hot water didn't work, the toilets were without seats, the loudspeaker of the next door mosque was aimed at the guest rooms and guests were charged for soap, it was Bohong's finest hotel.

"But why is it called the Niagara?" Gilda had asked Mustafa many years ago during the first time she had visited him in Bohong.

"Nee-ah-ga-ra," he had corrected. "Well, as you know, my dear, this place used to be a private residence. Designed by a Brazilian architect, they say, although God knows what he was doing in these parts. Can you imagine the parties they had here? Well, after independence and all that drama, the government nationalized old Lim's rubber estate and used the building as a district headquarters. Then, about 15 years ago, when the tiresome Muslim reactionaries got more power than they knew what to do with, oh dear, I really shouldn't be saying these things, those towel heads said this place 'wasn't representing the Islamic nature of the country.' Can you imagine that?"

Never too quick off the mark, even when she knew something about the subject, Gilda had curled up the tip of her nose and prepared a comment. She missed the one-second pause in the conversation though and had to wait until the Minister's next deep breath.

"So, the dim-witted government sods sold the building at auction and it was purchased by another Chinese. God, those Chinks are all over the place, aren't they? You can't turn around without their taking over something else. So this guy turned it into a hotel in this Godforsaken corner of paradise."

Gilda saw her chance and pounced. "But why the name?"

"Good question. Bloody good question. I have no idea. Could it be that the owner had spent his honeymoon in upper New York State and wanted to recreate the magic of those first nights?" he said, pouring her a glass of Bollinger.

Ordinarily, Gilda drank very little. Not out of prudishness but because it made her fall asleep. Drinking in the middle of the day made her especially tired, a lesson she had learned during their first meeting. It had been noon. The air conditioner in the room rumbled and sputtered but produced precious little in the way of cool air. She had opened her backpack and took out some worn papers.

"Mister Minister," she had said. "You invited me to Bohong to talk about the Park. I know how busy you must be and I prepared a list of points that I would appreciate your looking into."

"Park? Plenty of time for those national parks. They've been around for millions of years and we've got all day, haven't we?" he had joked, admiring his non-sequitur. "You're not in any hurry, are you?"

"No. No hurry, not at all. I just thought ..."

"First, a little lunch."

Mustafa bin Kayu was a man of not-quite medium height and medium build with a great shock of black hair that he waved back with the aid of liberal doses of Brylcream. He wore stylish tortoise-shell eyeglasses of a similar shade to his rust-colored Lacoste tennis shirt. There was little that was exceptional about him except his energy and his ability to find ways in which to rid himself of tension. He had long ago learned that man's most important duty in life was to collect cosmic karma points and, through personal experience and a series of mystic encounters which he would someday write about so others could share his philosophy, he had learned that he could earn a maximum number of points by giving other people the opportunity to make him happy. 'It is truly a win-win situation,' he had explained once to Gilda. 'I give you the chance to make me happy, which earns you future credits in whatever afterlife you might wind up in. Have some paté, my dear."

The Minister had learned that the hotel's kitchen did not match its architectural achievements. Instead, he carried a modest picnic when he flew from the capital Anjing to the backwater town of Bohong.

Gilda, who had been living on rice, vegetables, tinned corned beef and wild boar, timidly, but gratefully, accepted the liver-topped cracker.

"Don't be shy. That's a good girl. Now, smoked salmon or caviar or smoked oysters?"

"Mister Minister, I hope you will be able to visit the Park headquarters sometime soon. There are problems and opportunities. You must really see for yourself."

"How far is it from Bohong?" he asked, guardedly.

"Going upriver, about four hours in a speedboat, about ten in a fast longboat and maybe twelve in a Chinese launch."

"And the accommodation once I get there?"

"Simple, I'm afraid. But it's very peaceful. You'll find it quite relaxing."

"I'm sure."

"So you'll come?" she had asked, excitedly.

"I would love to visit you. But I am so busy these days. Cabinet meetings in the capital Anjing, then over to Washington to see the World Bank, then to Geneva to see that Union of Nature thing, then Stockholm to see Swedish Aid, then Nairobi to see those tedious UNEP bureaucrats, then to Bogor to see the CIFOR folks, then over to Yokohoma for that blasted tropical timber nonsense, then ... you have no idea how thankful you should be to stay in that peaceful little corner of yours."

"I don't understand. You're the Minister in charge of national parks. This is Manusia's newest Park and the one getting the international attention. I'm confused. Maybe it's the wine."

"You have no idea how much I admire you."

"Uh. You do?"

"I do. You're almost unique. How many other women would give up the comforts of California and go live in a place like Camp Trinil?"

"Oh, I don't know if it's that extraordinary."

"It is, dear Gilda," he said quietly. "You are a most extraordinary woman. With the most magical eyes. They remind me of the blue sky of Mallorca."

The Minister had explained several things to Gilda that first afternoon without really saying them. He would be her patron and ensure that her work permit was renewed annually. He would make sure that she got whatever supplies were in his power to provide. He would allow her to study orangutans to her heart's content provided she did not meddle in local politics.

Gilda had known the Minister for ten years. Each time they met she would urge him to visit Camp Trinil, each time he would plead that he had to return to Anjing the next morning to open a scientific seminar or escort a visiting delegation from UNESCO to view the 14th century Madjapahit Empire temples or accompany the Manusian national polo team, of which he was captain emeritus, on a tour to Pakistan. It became a bad joke between them. Gilda sensed he was afraid to travel the 100 miles up river from Bohong to Camp Trinil, but she couldn't figure out why.

The reason was quite simple. Mustafa bin Kayu liked his creature comforts. The small town of Bohong, which to Gilda was civilized and sophisticated, was to the Minister as pathetic as a Calcutta slum. He could reach Bohong by a scheduled daily flight from Anjing – two hours – not too bad on the discomfort scale. Bohong would be his field visit. "Why should I go all the way up to Mount Malu?" he had rhetorically asked one of his cabinet colleagues. "Such a dreary trip. Anyway, this Gilda person comes down to Bohong whenever I want her. At least there they have clean sheets."

Mount Malu National Park

"Do you think we have enough people?" Seridan asked, hoping that Laki would over-rule his head-strong brother, Avalon, before the truck reached the small group.

"Afraid?" Avalon had prodded, gently. "No need. Nothing has happened yet. They're afraid of us. Brother Urs says the big people are afraid to hurt us. He says they're afraid that the newspapers would write about cruelty to natives."

"Avalon, you still think this is a game for children," Laki finally replied. "Put yourself in their shoes. You are destroying their property. Yes, I know it is evil property, but it is theirs. How would you feel if strangers stopped you on the path and broke your blowpipe and smashed your *parang*? You would be angry."

"That would be vandalism and we would have a right to be angry," Avalon said carefully, realizing he might have overstepped his place. "We're just fighting for our home," he said defensively. However, he had made up his mind. "Anyway, I'm going to stop these foreigners," he said, as he walked calmly into the path of the timber truck.

Reluctantly, Laki and Seridan joined Avalon in the middle of the jungle road.

Urs, as was his custom, remained hidden on the sidelines. He shivered, unsure whether it was the wind that had rapidly picked up, signaling a storm, or the onset of another bout of malaria.

The timber truck stopped, almost on cue. The driver stepped out of the cab and angrily approached the Penan blocking the road. They held him at bay with their spear-tipped blowpipes.

Suddenly, from the other side of the cab, two Hong Neiyi security guards pushed open the door and leapt to the ground. Their dramatic entrance was marred by the fact that, on hitting the ground, their knees buckled and they tumbled onto the dusty road. It had worked all right in practice, but they had neglected to compensate for being scrunched out of sight in the truck's cab for three dusty hours. They regained face by quickly scrambling to their unsteady feet and pointing shotguns at the bewildered tribesmen.

Bohong

The Minister and Gilda had reached an understanding. She admired his worldliness. He admired her red underwear. The Minister had turned the hotel's bridal suite into his private residence. For good form, he had installed filing cabinets and a desk in the outer room. On the wall he had stapled an educational poster illustrating the importance of tropical rainforests to the welfare of rice-growing peasants in India. Another poster featured the birds of Costa Rica. A third showed the acid rain cycle in Germany. A fourth explained, in laborious prose, the intentions of something called The World Conservation Strategy – a vitally important document which no one had ever read and which the Minister took great pains to praise at every public gathering that had the pleasure of listening to him. He had installed a carpet. He had paid, out of his private Ministerial Administration Fund, to have soundproof double-glazed windows mounted and three Carrier air conditioners installed. When he was present, the suite was kept at a constant 60 degrees, chilly enough to ensure that Gilda left every meeting with him with a chest cold. Yet it was not cold enough to properly chill the South African Chardonnay, which reposed in an ice bucket awaiting Gilda's entry into the inner sanctum.

"Gilda, my dear, how wonderful to see you," he greeted her. He smoked a meerschaum pipe. Vivaldi tinkled.

"And it's good to see you, too, sir." Despite their often intimate relationship, when they had their clothes on Gilda always ad-dressed Mustafa bin Kayu with respect. She had been brought up to be polite to those in positions of authority.

During the years, the Minister had put on a few pounds. Gilda saw his stomach beginning to bulge beneath his green batik shirt. Curiously, it was a similar pattern to the one she had chosen to liven up her dress – the sacred Hindu eagle Garuda.

"Minister, I can't really stay very long this time. I'm expecting visitors."

"I know."

"You do?"

"Of course. That woman from the INF."

"I'm flabbergasted. I mean, do you know about every visitor to Camp Trinil?"

"Just the important ones. You forget. People need visas. Especially foreigners who want to visit the Mount Malu area. Because of that Urs fellow, things are much stricter. But there's no need to get worried – unless, of course, you're hiding Urs in your orangutan school," he joked. "So, how is it going up there in jungle land?"

Gilda wanted to pour out her soul to the older man, now beginning to lose his hair. He was still good looking, but he had slowed down noticeably in recent years. The one thing that hadn't slowed considerably was his sexual appetite. She had asked him for his secret, about a year earlier.

"Secret?" he had laughed. "You make it sound like one housewife admiring her neighbor's laundry and asking which detergent she uses. There's no secret. Just *jamu*."

Gilda had begun a self-taught course in the Indonesian herbal medicine, widely used in Manusia, and found, to her delight, that it works just as well for women as for men. *Jamu* made men big and copious. A different formula made women tight and dry. If she owed the Minister nothing else, she owed him for his suggestion to drink a packet of herbs – which taste like broiled cardboard mixed with cigarette stubs – with some honey every morning.

She could still taste her morning's *jamu*. She touched her face and was pleased that it still felt soft – another benefit of the herbs. The tropics can play havoc with a white woman's skin, she realized. She knew she wasn't beautiful, but, to some men, at least, she was attractive.

"Minister," she ventured. "I'm getting a lot of pressure from Washington to speak out on the timber issue. Don't you read the papers? Every school kid in Italy knows that loss of rainforests affects agriculture, cuts down on rainfall and …"

"We've got quite enough as it is, my dear," he said gently.

"Uh, quite enough of what, Minister?"

"Rain, of course. Just last Saturday I had to cancel my golf game *for the third time this month* because of the blasted rain. If only we could export moisture, then maybe we'd solve some of our horrendous financial problems. You have no idea what a crunch we're in."

"Darn it, the *Park* is in a crunch," she exclaimed in frustration. "Something has to be done."

Quietly, Mustafa bin Kayu took a sip of his wine while holding Gilda's eyes in his gaze. He stared at her for fifteen seconds. The tendons in his neck twitched.

"Young lady. You are not in an American shopping mall where you can shout at will. You are my guest. A female guest, I might add. In my country. Don't ever raise your voice again like that."

"Sorry."

"You say something has to be done," he lectured. "Well, you're right. Something has to be done about our country's budget. You foreigners go on about tribal rights and development. Do you know that in the last five years we've built three hundred new schools, constructed seventy five new markets and several hundred medical clinics, started a flying doctor service, tripled the number of telephones and introduced television into the most remote backwaters of this country? Do you know that Manusia's literacy rate has gone up from twenty percent to sixty percent in the last decade? That the average life expectancy has increased by fifteen years? That the per capita income has nearly doubled? Don't lecture me about 'something has to be done.' Something is being done. And it's being paid for by exports of tin, rubber, palm oil, spices and rice. And timber."

"Yes, I know that, I'm not a fool. I know about the economy. But the Park is important for itself."

"The Park is important for its watershed function. The rest is icing on the cake. You say you know about the economy. Do you know that oil prices have dropped 30% in the past three years? Tin is down, so is everything else. If the country doesn't make money from timber then we'll all be eating orangutans instead of taking pictures of them and your cute little ass will be on the first plane back to the land of the lotus eaters because this little Sultanate won't be able to afford the luxury of Gilda Korda Breckenridge sitting in the forest pulling leeches off her neck."

Gilda thought that with age the Minister might have acquired understanding. She knew the arguments against his tirade. She had even taken the government's side sometimes during press interviews. She had discussed them in Malay on Radio Manusia. However, she was cowed by this dapper, middle-aged Asian aristocrat. The words didn't come. Only the regrets that they couldn't communicate. She wanted to tell him how angry she was about the continued presence of the timber operators, who were now cutting trees inside Park boundaries. She wanted to tell him that she wanted to marry Bujang and become a Manusian, just like the Minister. However, she was frightened. No, now is not the time, she thought. She instead accepted a glass of white wine and ran her hands through the Minister's slick black hair as he bent forward to unbutton her dress and nuzzle her neck.

"Taffy, can I ask you something?" Gilda said after their love-making.

"That depends."

"I've never asked about your personal life – and it's none of my business, but I know you have a wife. Do you tell her about us?" she asked, as she traced a series of circles on his chest.

"Just what are you getting at, Gilda?"

"Well, maybe I could go with you on one of your European tours. It would be good for you to have someone along who is actually working in the rainforest."

"You couldn't have suggested that at a worse time."

"What do you mean?"

"Gilda. What I'm going to tell you now must never – and I mean never – go any further than this room. Swear?"

"Of course I swear. What's this all about?"

"At the cabinet meeting last week, the Sultan said he wanted to throw out all foreigners working in the field."

"But he already threw out the missionaries once," Gilda said guilelessly. "They came back."

"He's not just talking about missionaries. He means all foreigners."

"You mean people like Gerry?"

"He means people like you, Gilda."

Gilda had not wanted to consider that was what he meant.

"But why? I don't understand."

"It's because of Urs Gerhard. The Sultan is furious that he's still running free, making fools of our secret service. If we could get Urs out, then things might settle down. Until then, well, the Sultan has given us a month to find him before we clear everybody out."

"But Urs is just one man. Most of the foreigners here are scientists, teachers and businessmen. What good would it do to get rid of them?"

"Think, Gilda. Urs must have some foreign contacts working for him – to bring him supplies, collect his mail. Cut off the connections and you isolate Urs. He'll have to come up for air sometime."

"My god, you don't think that I ..."

"I don't know what to think. The Sultan has told us to check everyone. He specifically mentioned you by name. I'll protect you as best I can, of course. But this has become serious. The Sultan doesn't like to read on the front page of the *New York Times* that his peaceful little country is 'engaging in cultural and environ-mental genocide.' One month. From the big guy himself.'

Damn that Urs, Gilda thought. "I was going to ask your help to renew my work permit. It comes due in September."

"Not a snowball's chance in hell with that Swiss around."

Gilda thought about her options. It took her exactly four seconds to decide.

"Taffy, I'll tell you what I know. One of the camp's laborers ran into some Kayans on the other side of the park. They bragged to him that they had had dinner with Urs two nights earlier. That's all I know. He's around somewhere."

"Keep your eyes open, Gilda," the Minister instructed. He lay flat on his back, stretched out to his full five feet four. "Eyes open."

Mount Malu National Park

"They won't shoot us," Avalon said, with more bravado than conviction. "I think they want to arrest us."

"Never," Laki said softly, the fear of an enclosed prison in his voice.

"Okay, punks," the taller guard said in English, pretending he was Dirty Harry. "Put down your weapons."

"*Jatohlah kamu punya sumpit*," the darker-complexioned guard repeated in Malay. Throw down your blowpipes.

The Penan had never rehearsed a contingency for being arrested. They stood motionless, impassive, as a heavy, hot rain began.

Without drama, Urs walked out of his hiding place and faced the Hong Neiyi employees. He threw his hand-carved blowpipe at the guards' feet. "I am the one you want," he said in English. "Let them go."

"Ah, we were hoping you might join the party. Yes, we certainly do want you, *Tuan* Urs. But we want your friends as well."

Urs' body convulsed. *Ja*, malaria, he told himself, but it's okay if they think I'm frightened of them. Without taking his eyes off the guards he instructed his friends in Penan: "Listen to me. Laki and Avalon slowly back off towards the forest to the right. Seridan, be prepared to run to the left. Wait for my signal."

"Here I am," the European said in English, walking towards the guns. He held Liebchen in his hands in front of him, almost as a peace offering. When he was within two feet of the Malays, he threw the monkey to the younger security guard and grabbed the barrel of the taller guard's weapon and wrenched it out of his hands. "Run, run!" he shouted at his friends. Urs twisted and dived over the embankment into the brush. Liebchen, who had been thrown to the ground during the turmoil, scampered after him. The security guard in whose face Urs had thrown the monkey, regained his composure and fired at the quickly disappearing figures of Laki and Avalon.

Seridan, who had not dropped his blowpipe, quickly loaded a poison dart once he had reached the security of the forest. He aimed at the Malay guard and hit him in the thigh. The man grunted when he felt the dart's prick, then screamed when he saw what it was and realized that he might die, painfully, from the poison.

Urs crawled down the hill for thirty yards, then moved parallel to the road to a blind curve a hundred yards behind the truck. There, hidden from view, he crossed the road and quickly ran through the forest on the uphill pitch. When he reached the others, who had stopped after scrambling no more than a hundred yards, Urs gasped with sympathetic pain.

Avalon was helping his father, Laki, whose kneecap had been shattered by the blast. Urs grabbed his father-in-law and tossed him over his shoulder like a dead wild boar. "We go," he said in Penan to the others. "*Schnell*, for the love of Christ."

PART III

VISITORS

CHAPTER 8

25 July. 16:00.

Camp Trinil

It was a hot ride back upriver and when Gilda stepped off the longboat the last thing she looked forward to was a welcome-back reception line that had formed on Camp Trinil's rickety dock.

"Madame Doctor Gilda. Buttercup *mati*," Bujang offered. Buttercup was dead.

"Hello, you must be Gilda Breckenridge," a white woman standing next to Bujang said pleasantly, offering her hand.

"Hi, Gilda," Gerry called. "How are tricks with the Minister?"

What the hell is going on here? Gilda asked herself, unconsciously returning Ringo's salute. She decided to order her priorities.

"You must be Ms. Derek," she said, as politely as she could. My visitor is already waiting for me, the host, in *my* home. Loss of face. I lose points for this one.

"That's right. The office couldn't get you on the radio and I thought I'd take a chance and come on up – I hope you don't mind. I was lucky – I hitched a lift on a speedboat that was heading up here. We must have just missed each other."

"Well, I hope you've been well looked after."

"Oh, Gerry and I have been having some fascinating discussions about orangutan intelligence and your workers have been super-kind," she said, patting Bujang on his shoulder.

"Great. I don't know about you, but I'd like something to drink," Gilda said, marching along the dock. Ringo climbed on her back.

When they reached her living quarters, Gilda went to the

kerosene-powered refrigerator used for storing drinks and a small selection of medicines and took out a couple of beers – one for her, one for B.B.. Gerry then got one for himself. "I'll leave you two alone," he said, slamming the door behind him.

"Sit down, relax," Gilda said, trying to be gracious. "So, how long do you plan to stay?"

Gilda knew she had said the wrong thing as soon as the words had left her mouth.

"Oh, just a few days. Have to get back. Lots of work in the office. You know how it is."

Gilda wanted to reply that she had never worked in an office a day of her life. "Certainly."

"Oh, by the way, I bring regards from Ambassador Fangar. I think he's a Californian, like you. He wanted to come up with me, but couldn't get away."

"Oh, that would have been nice," Gilda offered. "Well, Ms. Derek, anything special you want to do while you're here?"

"I don't want to impose, but I thought we might go into the forest, look at some wild orangutans, have a chat, get to know each other," B.B. said hopefully, swatting at a forty-decibel mosquito.

"Sure. We'll work out a program at dinner."

Gilda smiled at B.B.. B.B. smiled at Gilda.

"You're all settled in the guest house? Everything okay?"

B.B. nodded. "It's a little hot, isn't it?"

"Listen, you just relax. You must have jet lag and all that. Grab a beer and take it easy. I'll get you later, after I freshen up."

After Gilda visited the latrine, she *sotto voced,* "*Bujang, datang sini. Lekas.*" Get your ass over here. Now, what's this about Buttercup?

* * * * *

B.B. had assumed the American ambassador was going to come along, but she was glad that he had declined. She preferred to operate on her own. As she reviewed her notes, she realized how valuable his briefing on Mount Malu and Manusia had been.

The interests of the United States in Southeast Asia, he had explained, were jeopardized by the uncertain political climate in Manusia. The Malay minority – only thirty percent of the population – exerted its power by hereditary rule, not by a democratic process. Yet, while the Malays and their Sultan held the political strings, they had little real influence over the Chinese and Indians, a powerful minority of twenty percent of the population – the Chinese controlled the economy and the Indians controlled the civil service and the education system. To further complicate matters, native peoples – including the Iban, Bidayuh, Kayan, Kenyah, Kelabit and Penan tribes – accounted for 40% of the Manusian population and they were not happy.

B.B. had been somewhat surprised by the ambassador's candor. It sure helps to have a letter of introduction from the president of a major nature group, she thought. That's the way the world works. Of course, it was useful that Rod Lawrence, her boss, had gone to Princeton with the ambassador.

B.B. knew little about foreign affairs, but sensed that Richard Fangar's job was to put out political brushfires before they devoured everything in sight. One particular geopolitical bombshell that Fangar had his eyes on was the island of Natuna, just 250 miles northwest of the Borneo coast, which was under Indonesian jurisdiction. It was also claimed by Malaysia, China, Vietnam and Manusia. The Americans hoped to build a naval base on the island. Above all, the Americans believed that the strategic island must not, at any cost, fall into communist control – since it could then be used as a stepping-stone for the newly-rejuvenated domino theory that paranoiacally predicted a Marxist infiltration throughout the region. The Indonesians were 'on side', but the Manusians were 'playing their own ball game', which meant, in State Department parlance, that they were liable to screw things up by selfishly acting in their own best interests.

Manusia, until recently, had been stable, reasonably prosperous and reasonably easy to deal with, albeit quirky, inbred and corrupt – as many other developing countries. However, Sultan Ibrahim bin Akbar Harrods was getting old and the line of succession was unclear. The country had overspent its income and was falling into debt with the international lending agencies. Further, they were playing both sides of the environmental card – a small, but annoying point.

Unluckily for Manusia's self-appointed Prime Minister, his rule was not seen as being in the United States' best medium-term interests.

It wasn't that Sultan Ibrahim was uncultured. Just the opposite – he had attended Dartmouth and the Sorbonne, had the finest wine cellar south of Hong Kong and painted 'very modest *aquarelles*' – as he once described them to a *Wall Street Journal* reporter. However, he had four wives, three more than most Americans, and countless mistresses – including, it was rumored, the wife of a senator from Colorado who was touted as a potential presidential candidate. As Sultan and chief law-dispenser, he sat in judgement on people accused of crimes both major and minor – and was not averse to subjecting a guilty party to the "*buaya* test", in which the man (and on four occasions a woman) was tossed into a crocodile pit. If the accused climbed out after two minutes he was considered innocent. If necessary, he was fitted immediately for prosthetic devices, which were provided free of charge under the generous British-style socialized health services scheme the Sultan had instituted. When criticized by skeptical observers from Amnesty International and the International Society of Jurists, Sultan Ibrahim had impatiently explained that the judgement-by-reptile was an ancient custom whose Semitic roots dated back to King Solomon. "Criticize me and you criticize Israel," he taunted. However, when the visitors failed to agree that the punishment was eminently suitable for the twentieth century, the Sultan threw out most foreign missionaries (who filtered back in when the uproar subsided), temporarily withdrew his ambassadors from Washington, London, Bonn and Canberra (the French, having gone through and tacitly supported a similar situation with Emperor Jean Bokassa in the Central African Empire – who preferred lions as the jury of choice – kept a quiet neutrality) and arrested New Zealander Clovis James, the effervescent *Far Eastern Economic Review* correspondent who had broken the story.

* * * * *

Gerry retreated to his quarters and looked at the mail Gilda had brought. Two letters for him, three letters and a thin packet for Urs, addressed to 'Jerry'. Boy, I wish I knew what they contained, he thought. Gerry's own friends had been sending him newspaper clips about the strange man living in the vicinity. "Is this guy anywhere near you?" they had asked. "Have you met him?" "Are you helping him?" Up to now, Gerry had remained quiet about his involvement with Urs Gerhard, but he had begun taking notes and planning his retelling of the story. His version would be quite exciting. Flashman stuff. Maybe he could get a book out of it. At least a piece in the *Washington Post*.

In the meantime, he realized he had better run these up to Nirvana. Urs had instructed Gerry that when mail came, he should wrap it in a plastic bag, tie it underneath the lean-to platform and alert Urs by tying an old T-shirt to one of the support posts. This mail drop marked Gerry's first delivery and he didn't want to screw it up.

On his way out of camp, he noticed Gilda and Bujang, deep in conversation. He didn't think they noticed him as he moved stealthily into the hills, bird book in hand. Queenie considered following, but stayed with the other orangutans.

* * * * *

"Oh, you're a cute fellow," B.B. said to Ringo as he sniffed her groin. "Wherever did you learn that?" she asked lightly, in the same voice with which she spoke to her Irish setter whenever he made similar vaguely cute, vaguely obscene advances. She tried to push Ringo away and found that he wouldn't budge. "Now, you get out of there," B.B. said again, more sharply, trying to be polite, but sincerely wishing the ape would get lost. Ringo held on to B.B.'s right calf with one elongated arm and looked up into her eyes with a funny-sad gaze that she found strangely moving. "I don't care if you are, maybe, man's closest relative," she said. "Piss off."

Ultimately, B.B. remembered her baby-sitting training. She reached across the table and extracted an energy snack from her daypack. She ripped it open and, as she had hoped, Ringo turned his attention to the treat. B.B. lost no time in walking quickly to the door. She wasn't sure, but she thought that Ringo looked hurt.

* * * * *

"*Saya tidak tengoh, Madame Doctor Gilda, tapi Hassan tengoh semuanya.*" Bujang explained that he hadn't seen the murder, but Hassan had.

Gilda shuddered as she heard the story. Hassan had been

feeding the orangutans a normal breakfast of bananas, milk and bulgur wheat donated by the the people of the United States to provide nourishment for starving Manusians. Buttercup, a young sub-adult male of about six, had mischievously grabbed Ringo's stockpile of fruit and raced off to enjoy the bounty. Ringo let out a screech and chased Buttercup to the edge of the river. Buttercup had long since dropped the bananas, but Ringo, apparently, was out to use Buttercup to teach the other orangutans a lesson. He grabbed the smaller animal by the neck and shoved his face into the shallow, dark water. Then, just before Buttercup drowned, Ringo relaxed his grip momentarily, grabbed a rock that was within arm's reach and, as the younger male gasped for air, smashed in his skull.

"Oh God, I don't believe this. Bujang, are you sure?"

Bujang looked at her like a puppy that had been scolded for no reason. "Why do you think I lie to you?"

"Of course I don't think you lie. I just find this so … incredible. Ringo is like a son to me."

Their conversation was interrupted by B.B.'s urgent exit from the house.

"Oh, hi. I just needed some air," B.B. said breathlessly. Gilda and Bujang, standing on the walkway that led to the latrines, continued to stare.

"I think I'll just take a little walk for a while. See you at dinner?" B.B. finally added.

Ringo left the house shortly after, chewing on a blue and yellow paper wrapper that read "Champion Bar".

* * * * *

Following the bungled attempt at capturing Urs the day before, Jong Il Kim ordered all workers and security guards at the timber camp to turn-out on the rock-hard soccer field behind the motor pool.

"Mr. Ramsay Wong has told you of the increased security procedures," Jong bellowed. "Our illustrious security chief," he said, sarcastically, "had put patrols on a timber truck. These two men," he shouted, pointing at the humiliated security guards, "were stopped by a band of natives. They had the leader, the Swiss Urs Gerhard, within their grasp and let him escape."

Jong then slapped the two men responsible for the failed operation. The fact that one of them, "that useless Susah fellow", was doubled-over in pain from an infected poison dart wound, did not endear Jong to the other twenty members of the timber camp's security forces. However, Jong was a manager of a timber camp which was threatened by savages, not a camp counselor. If these guys were not tough enough, they could go work in an office somewhere.

Susah was taken to the camp infirmary, where he spent a miserable day, vomiting, hallucinating about flying monkeys and in his few lucid moments, wishing he was back on the coast helping his father grow coconuts.

* * * * *

That evening, Jong reluctantly made two radiophone calls. The first was to the Deputy Minister of Internal Affairs, who was directly in charge of the police effort to catch Urs.

His second call was to Mustafa bin Kayu, the man the Sultan had assigned to orchestrate the public spin on how the Penan were being treated and the destructive role Urs was playing in national development.

"The Minister is out of the country," his assistant, Tusau Padan, had replied. "Tell me what happened."

"The Minister said that I should only speak to him," Jong answered.

"Mr. Jong, I know you're a powerful and important person up there in that timber camp of yours. However, I assure you the Minister has left instructions that if anything happened that he should know about he wanted to be alerted to the fact earlier rather than later."

"I have to inform you of bad news," Jong said, reluctant to apologize to someone younger than himself. "Our security forces had Urs within their shotgun range and let him escape," he continued, fumigating the mouthpiece with garlic. "I have punished the men responsible.

Jong told the Minister's assistant the story as he had been told it by his staff. The number of Penan attackers had increased to twenty-five during the retelling. The security guards and the driver had valiantly fought, not only for their own survival, but also for the pride of the Hong Neiyi company itself, long may it extract timber from the otherwise useless forest. He explained that one of the guards was seriously ill from the blowpipe dart. Tusau Padan asked several questions and finally said, simply: "Listen carefully. Call me back on this frequency in one hour. Do not talk to anyone in the meantime. One hour."

* * * * *

Tusau Padan had no idea where his boss was. He hoped the Minister hadn't shut his mobile phone off while servicing one of those white women he seemed to like so much. Just what we need, a Sukarno wannabe with a taste for fine wine and loud women, Padan thought.

* * * * *

Mustafa bin Kayu answered his mobile with a non-commital, "Yes."

"Sorry to bother you, sir," Padan said, "but there is some news you should know about."

"Go on."

"By the way, where are you?"

"Never mind." The Minister had made a quick and quiet trip to Singapore to check up on some Chinese businessmen his wife thought she might do business with. The Chinese had proven to be surprisingly agreeable to a renegotiation of the timber contracts his wife silently owned, especially when they learned that the allowed out-take was going to be trebled very soon.

Luckily, the Minister had finished early. He was pleased to learn that his friend, Monique, who ran La Brasserie at the Singapore Westin, was free. They had been enjoying a light, room-service meal at the Raffles when the phone rang.

"I'll get right to the point." Tusau Padan explained the situation. Mustafa bin Kayu listened while he stuffed a last bite of *salade de crevettes* into his mouth.

"You have a recommendation, I'm sure," Mustafa bin Kaya said.

"Well, actually I do."

Mustafa bin Kayu sipped the Alsace Riesling, chewed slowly and noisily, then was silent for several moments before grunting assent to his assistant's suggestion.

CHAPTER 9

25 July. 22:00.

Rumah Sehat longhouse

Urs liked visiting Rumah Sehat, but he often felt like a once-welcome guest who had contracted a contagious disease. In the Kayan longhouse there would be food, conversation, civilization. In the longhouse there would also be the possibility of entrapment and the fear of involving innocent people in his illegal actions. It was, to Urs, a classic example of yin and yang at work. There are two sides to every coin.

Before Urs entered any settlement, he or his friends sat outside the immediate vicinity for hours, quietly, seen by no one, just watching for suspicious activity – such as a government longboat moored by the river. Urs and four Penans arrived at Rumah Sehat late in the evening; after the recce team had pronounced the long, ramshackle building clean of enemies.

Bujang came out to give the final all-clear. His reassuring call, the mellow 'pwok-kwo-oo' of the collared scops owl, brought Urs from the shadows.

"Nothing strange?" Urs asked in English. The two men stood behind the elevated kitchens. Neither man seemed to notice that they were standing amidst organic rubbish. Small pigs rooted nearby.

"No visitors now. But last night, yes," Bujang replied. His English was a bit rusty, but retained the slightly British accent that most educated Manusians had when they spoke the language of the BBC World Service.

"Gerry slept in the longhouse last night," Bujang told Urs. "They said he was acting strange. He was asking everyone in Rumah Sehat how they felt about Gilda and whether they thought she was doing a good job."

Urs listened carefully. "Your sister told you this?"

Bujang nodded. He knew Urs had a crush on Mimes but kept out of their business.

"What did Gerry ask else?" Urs asked. One of the Kayan women threw a bucket of dirty dishwashing water out into the darkness and the soapy water splashed on Urs' calves.

Bujang told the tall Swiss man what he had heard. Gerry had asked about the timber blockades, obliquely, by enquiring whether the Kayan's hunting and fishing had been disturbed by increasing timber activities in the region. He had asked if he might buy a ceremonial *parang*, as a souvenir. He wanted one with a handle and scabbard embellished with hornbill ivory and deer antler, one which had been hand-forged and, most curiously, one which had been endowed with magic power by the head dukun of the upper stretches of the Hotut River. Gerry had left at dawn.

"What does this mean?" Urs asked.

"Let's go upstairs and eat," Bujang said.

Urs Gerhard and his friends slipped into Ding Ajang's kitchen area through a trap door which had been cut to enable Urs to escape if the authorities stormed the front entrance.

They sat in one room of a large, well-constructed longhouse that ran parallel for the Hotut River for seventy yards – long enough to have 25 'doors', behind each of which a family ate, slept and went about its business.

Urs knew that outside, on the communal porch, men cleaned their shotguns, or mended monofilament fishing nets, or carved wooden statues to sell to traders – who, in turn, sold them in the hotels in Anjing. He knew that on the porch, the women, many of whom were nursing babies, wove mats or baskets. They repaired clothing. They laughed. They drank. Some small children smoked hand-rolled cheroots. All this domesticity was forbidden to Urs. Although he knew that his presence was not, could not, be a secret in the community, he nevertheless felt it was safer not to wander among the others, not to jeopardize his own security or, any more than necessary, that of the people of Rumah Sehat. He was a prisoner, locked away on the outside of life. I wanted to quit after one or two hijackings, Urs thought. Then Laki got hurt. How much longer will I have to live like a stranger?

Ding Ajang's wife served a plate of little pastries which tasted much as Urs had expected tiny green, purple and pink things to taste. She placed a ceramic teapot on the eating mat on the floor. The pot camouflaged freshly-made *tuak* rice wine, which tasted like fermented lemonade, only thicker and milkier. The teapot was a modest attempt at religious harmony. The animists in the longhouse, including Ding Ajang, did not like to deliberately antagonize the other half of the longhouse's population, which was composed of fundamentalist Christians. The animists, who believed that spirits lived in wind, water, stones and trees, had no qualms about drinking alcohol. The sober people, who drank wine that represented the blood of Christ, refused to drink for pleasure.

Urs noticed the Penan looking around at the strange surroundings. Ding Ajang's quarters had running tap water and electricity produced by a noisy generator. They sat on gaudy linoleum floors. Posters of Italian film star Ornella Muti and Brazilian soccer hero Ronaldo were tacked to the walls. From the next-door family's quarters, children giggled as they watched television – probably avoiding homework as children back in Switzerland did.

"Delicious," Urs said to Ding Ajang. "Your wife is a wonderful cook."

"Eat all you want, Tuan Urs. My wife always says you look too thin."

Ding Ajang's daughter rocked sleepily on her father's lap. Her right foot was heavily bandaged. "What happened to you, little Bunga? Did you fall playing games?" Urs said in Malay to the seven-year-old girl.

The little girl was too shy to answer in the presence of the white and yellow foreigners.

"She cut her foot in the river," Ding Ajang said angrily, explaining that there was so much debris in the river due to timber operations that simply taking a bath had become a hazardous occupation.

"Serious?" Urs asked.

"One of the women in the longhouse had government training. She has a medical kit. She gave Bunga an injection and sewed the cut."

"You should take her to Bohong for proper treatment," Urs recommended.

"Yes, perhaps."

"Laki has also been injured," Urs said. "He was shot in the leg by the security men of the timber *kampeni*."

The Kayans waited, as was the custom, for Urs to continue. He gratefully accepted a heaped bowl of red rice – a little soggy, but still a great treat. He reached into the jumble of dishes that cluttered the floor and scooped out a portion of ferns boiled with onions and garlic.

"Laki sends his regards," he said, nibbling on a chicken wing.

"I hope he will continue to have good hunting," Ding Ajang said as a roundabout way of asking whether the Penan would ever walk again.

"This is delicious venison," Urs said. The Penan with whom he lived had many virtues, Urs thought as he tucked into his meal that night, but cooking was not one of them.

"Have some more Guinness, *Tuan* Urs," Bujang offered. He sang the beer's well-known advertising jingle: "Guinness Stout. It's good for you."

"*Bapak* Laki, my father, may live, if the spirits agree," Urs said, perhaps too melodramatically he realized. "But he will stay in the camp with the others," he added, indicating that Laki would be relegated to the sedentary life of infants and the elderly.

The conversation to this point had been between Urs and the Kayans from Rumah Sehat. If this exclusion bothered the Penan they did not show it.

Urs knew the good citizens of Rumah Sehat had trouble meeting the Penan on equal terms. If Urs had not been there it would have been unthinkable for the Kayans to have invited the shy, virtually unclothed visitors into their living rooms. The Kayans considered themselves aristocrats with well-defined social hierarchies. They were the establishment – at least in the forest. The Kayans lived in sturdily constructed settlements in which they cultivated an eclectic lifestyle that encouraged them to take the best modern society offered, provided it helped them retain their independence. In contrast, they viewed the Penan as rural, somewhat untrustworthy innocents, who had mastered arcane acts of metaphysics which enabled them to survive in the dark of the forest.

Urs ate quickly – a bad habit, he knew – but the food was so welcome. As he stuffed rice and tinned sardines into his mouth, he mused on the twists of fate which had made Kayans, Kayans and Penans, Penans. Both groups were descendants of people who came overland from northwest India or Burma some 20,000 years ago, walking to Borneo at a time when sea levels were considerably lower than they are today and the island was connected by land bridges to mainland Southeast Asia. These pioneers domesticated plants and had been the dominant racial group throughout the region. They were the true sons of the soil, Urs observed. Now, one group was higher up the totem pole than the other.

Urs dredged up memories of the anthropology texts he had read. The Kayan and Penan ancestors were followed by relative newcomers, represented in modern times by coastal Malays and Indonesians, who were the predecessors of Sultan Ibrahim. These coastal folk originated in southern China, a people with distinctly Mongoloid features who used their knowledge of rice cultivation, pottery and improved stone tools to take control of the fertile coastal and lowland valleys, thereby pushing the earlier immigrants into the hills. This was part of a domino effect and the Penans were subsequently shoved into the back corners of the island – the wrong side of the anthropological tracks, and became isolated in the deep forest equivalent of Appalachia. The Penan had little opportunity to exchange women with other tribes and retained facial characteristics they must have had millennia ago; their bland, long, wide-eyed faces bear a striking similarity to the faces of isolated Amazon Indian tribes half a world away with whom the Penan may have shared ancestors.

In the hierarchy of society in Manusia, the further one goes from the coastal, urban civilizations the more tribal and uneducated you are considered. Because the Kayans wore western clothes – simple though they were – and because they brushed their teeth, sent their children to school, understood Malay and had been to Bohong, or even the capital Anjing, they considered themselves superior to the Penan. There was no guilt about the conclusion. In Malay, the term *ulu* defines the upper reaches of a river. However, it refers to far more than geography. To many people, including those of Rumah Sehat, it describes a way of life that gets more primitive, alien and unattractive the farther inland you go.

Nevertheless, that night the Kayans had to ignore the 'we' vs 'them' dichotomy because both Kayans and Penans were in the same boat. The Penan were losing their homeland, but so were the Kayans. Ten politically-minded Kayans of Rumah Sehat joined the feast. They brought Urs and his friends antiseptic for wounds, film for his camera, pencils and notepads. Ace bandages and chocolate bars. *Parangs* and plastic water bottles, worm medicine and advice. Mimes shyly handed Urs several thick envelopes that had arrived via one of the convoluted mail circuits.

"The head of the province's internal security force was up here last week nosing around," Ding Ajang told him in an odd combination of Kayan, Malay and English, which Urs translated, as best he could, into Penan for the benefit of his friends. "Be careful. They seem to know you're around here."

"What did you tell them?" Urs asked the group.

"We just behaved like upriver innocents," Robin Nawan Bala, the local schoolteacher, said.

"And they believed you?"

"Certainly not," Ding Ajang declared. "But what could they do? Arrest the whole longhouse? If they tried something like that, all the Kayans and Kenyahs in the river valley would march into Anjing and parade for the newspaper reporters."

Urs opened his mail. He unfolded several of the clippings of articles that supporters had placed in newspapers in Switzerland, UK and the United States. Everyone huddled around the strange Swiss man. The world, well at least small parts of the world, were paying attention to their home and their problems. "It is working," Urs said quietly. "They've got to give in sooner or later."

The group discussed tactics. There was a rumor that the government would try to bribe its way out of it.

"*Ja*, they offer money. In my country, too." He turned to his Penan friends. "Would you take the money?"

They shrugged like Paris waiters. Nobody had ever offered them any money for anything.

"Would you?" he asked the more sophisticated Kayans.

"Who knows?" Ding Ajang replied. "I wouldn't, but I don't speak for all. How could I take money after what happened to Bunga?"

"Excuse me, *Tuan* Urs, we are not getting what we want," Bujang argued. "True, you get newspapers to write about our problem. And what do the 'big people' do? They shoot *Bapak* Laki. They injure Bunga. They cut the trees that protect our crops. They ignore us like a fly on the back of a water buffalo. This is a war. We should do something dramatic."

"Such as what?" Ding Ajang asked.

"I don't know," Bujang stammered, looking to his friend Robin for support. None was forthcoming.

"You, brother Avalon. You have been quiet," Urs said to the young Penan. "Now that your belly is full, your mind can think. What should we do?"

The Penan was emboldened by the rice wine and surprised himself by speaking out. "You have told us that the foreigners will press the government to stop the timber. I don't know about the foreigners and I don't know much about the government. But we must be strong. But I do not like violence. It is not our way."

Urs thought the discussion that night resembled the deliberations that must have taken place during the early days of the civil rights movement, or the Vietnam War period. He had read about those heady times, moments in history that convinced him that rebellion was okay if the cause was just.

"I have it," Bujang blurted. He exhaled a cloud of Marlboro smoke. "We should kidnap a minister, or maybe blow up the district office in Bohong."

"Is there good hunting now?" Urs asked obliquely, hoping to redirect the debate, just as one might distract a child.

"Not so good. The tractors scare away the animals," Ding Ajang answered. "We have to walk further and further into the national park."

"Are you allowed to hunt in the park?" Urs asked with mock innocence.

"Of course not," Bujang answered. "But what choice do the people have?"

"But you're breaking the law," Urs taunted.

"The *kampeni* is breaking our laws," Ding said angrily.

"Didn't you ever hear of Gandhi?" Urs asked sarcastically.

Robin, who had recently graduated from teacher training college in Anjing, nodded his head.

"And what did Gandhi teach?" Urs asked the black-haired

teenager.

"You get what you want by non-violence."

"*Ja*. Exactly."

"But *Tuan* Urs," the young man asked, confused. "Gandhi broke lots of laws to get what he wanted."

Debate was not Urs' strong point. He was tired. He was weak, having had four bouts of malaria in the last two years. He had sores on his body. He had worms. He had a minor case of beri-beri. He needed to see a dentist. He had eaten too much roast pork and had gas. "What do you suggest we do?" he asked Robin wearily.

The Manusian school system did not prepare young men for decision making, nor did it provide a fertile ground in lateral thinking. But Robin Nawan Bala, who was the younger of two primary school teachers at Rumah Sehat's four-class school, gave it his best shot.

"What we're doing is good. We continue the blockades. But we need something more dramatic," Robin said.

"Remember the story about *Singalang Burong*?" Mimes asked.

The group turned to her. It was not forbidden for women to speak during a gathering such as this, but, up to now, Mimes had kept her peace.

The Kayans nodded in acknowledgement. The Penan listened quietly, unknowingly. Urs asked, "What is this *singalang burung*?"

"*Singalang Burong*, the ancient God of war," the young girl explained. "People in the longhouse today saw it – it's like an eagle. It flew over the longhouse for an hour."

The Kayans began to murmur amongst themselves.

"*Und?*" Urs asked.

"He's the God of war, of good fortune and of peace," Mimes explained. "The Ibans downriver claim he is theirs, we claim he is ours, the Kelabits probably say the same. I don't know."

"We all saw it today," another man said quietly, rolling a cheroot. Next door, a baby cried.

"Maybe it is a sign," Bujang suggested, somewhat pompously. "A messenger of the gods telling us to be bold."

A middle-aged man named Joseph Tama Weng, who up until now had been quiet, angrily spoke to Bujang. "You, my nephew are a Christian. You were baptized John – I held you in the river and you cried like a stuck pig. What is all this talk about omens? You are blaspheming. And you, Ding Ajang. Your sister and your brother are Christians. I am a Christian. Half of this longhouse is Christian." He continued in English: "You, *Tuan* Urs, *you* even have Christ's white skin and you talk about spirits." Joseph reached for Bujang's glass of *tuak* and threw it across the room. It landed near the cassette player and sent the Skeeter Davis tapes flying. "This bird, this eagle you talk about, is just a bird, not a God. There is one God."

"And what did your God do for us Kayans?" Ding Ajang asked bitterly. "What is he doing for the Penan? Will your Jesus make the timber *kampeni* leave?"

Urs translated as fast as he could, not too accurately he regretted, but quickly enough to get the sense of the conversation to his Penan friends.

Ding Ajang's wife, who had been quietly listening to the conversation, moved to clean up the mess. She then went into the kitchen to get some prawn crackers. Outside, on the communal porch, a fighting cock woke and crowed. Several other roosters answered his challenge. The men looked at each other, embarrassed to have been arguing.

"This newspaper from Singapore says that Manusia's income from oil is going down because of the decline of world oil prices," Urs said, once again trying to mediate. He spoke each phrase in Malay, then in Penan, a laborious process since his Malay was sloppy and the Penan language had few words to describe macro-economic practices. "That means that they will have to cut more and more trees to pay the bills. I do not think they will stop cutting timber."

Robin Nawan Bala spoke. "We must do more. And we cannot just let our Penan friends take all of the responsibility."

Ding Ajang looked sternly at the younger man. "And what do you suggest?"

"Bujang," Robin said to his friend. "You remember when we were together in Anjing and we went to the cinema and saw *The Godfather*?"

CHAPTER 10

26 July. 07:00.

Camp Trinil

Gerry rushed through breakfast. He felt like a 12-year-old who couldn't escape to his baseball game until he had finished his dinner. When Gilda and B.B. had finally decided they had drunk enough tea and should go for a walk, Gerry nonchalantly headed the other way. "Okay, see you guys later," he said, cheerily. "Have fun in the jungle."

Gerry raced to his hideaway. He knew it was unrealistic, but he hoped he would run into Urs.

Instead, he ran into Queenie, who wanted to come along. She climbed on his shoulders for twenty yards. Ringo trailed behind, finally catching Queenie's eye. She climbed down and the two apes went off to play by themselves.

He arrived at Nirvana in an anticipatory sweat. He found the mail packet was gone and his T-shirt had been neatly folded and placed on his lounge chair. He had a few minutes to kill. He took a bath in the waterfall, rolled a monster joint and settled down with an old Isaac Asimov article in *Penthouse* about the medical breakthroughs mankind could expect if the US was to establish laboratories on Mars. He awoke three hours later.

"Shit." Late for work again.

* * * * *

It was 8 a.m. and it was sweltering. Before she had gone twenty paces behind the collection of ramshackle buildings that was grandly called Camp Trinil, B.B. knew that she had once again proven her ability to dress properly for the wrong occasion.

The first stream convinced her that the expensive leather hiking boots, which had served her so well in the Austrian alps, were not jungle caliber. She dragged her feet after that, squelching with each miserable step.

Damn you Mister Levi Strauss, you Jewish bastard, she cursed as the sweat began to build on her legs. Can't you make denim that breathes? She felt her inner thighs become a sweaty breeding place for all sorts of bacteria that she dared not even contemplate.

At least she had the sense to wear a sensible shirt – a lightweight, short-sleeve Washington Redskin's jersey. Bujang was pleased too, since he could time his stride to the flopflop of B.B.'s ample breasts. It was as close as he ever got to a military mindset. Flop-one-two, flop ...

Gilda tried to make conversation, which was as awkward as two sumo wrestlers trying to dance Swan Lake. Their worlds were too far apart to talk about grown-up things and they both internalized anything that was even remotely emotional, so there was little sisterly bonding.

Nevertheless, Gilda had finally taught Ringo not to use her toothbrush, so she had some skill as a communicator.

Gilda found it was easy to get B.B. to talk about herself.

"This is my first big fundraising campaign," B.B. had explained. "Back in the office, we like to think we're creating a new frontier in conservation fundraising."

"How so?"

"It's the first campaign which features the ecological services of the rainforest." B.B. explained the logic. The campaign was called 'Jungles for Judith', Judith being a fictional 'everywoman' who was the beneficiary of the rainforest's ability to regulate climate and provide medicines. On a higher plane, by supporting rainforest conservation, 'Judith' would receive substantial personal gratification in the knowledge that the people who lived in the forest, dramatically less fortunate than she, slept better that night because their hot and sticky homes were intact. All this was possible by donating a minimum of ten thousand dollars to join the 'Judith Fund'. Entry was limited to 6,000 individuals, that being the number of native groups whose lives, the INF had calculated, were directly threatened by rainforest destruction.

"I think I've just about convinced Peter Weir to produce a short film for us on this campaign," B.B. had explained proudly. "And, well, I hate to count my chickens, but it looks like Sean Connery will do the voice-over."

"And Judith?"

"She doesn't exist of course, but I was thinking of Mia Farrow for the film. Independent. But vulnerable."

Gilda was afraid to ask, but did anyway. "Where does Camp Trinil fit in all of this?"

"That's what you have to tell me," B.B. said. "Convince me that your project helps people. That's the bottom line in fundraising today. Development aid. Rural bootstraps. Nature for people."

"It used to be nature for nature."

"*Passé.*"

Gilda didn't like the direction this conversation was heading, but couldn't think of a way to change it. She squinted her eyes and pursed her lips. Usually the forest could restore her psychic balance. Not this time.

"I thought we might just walk through the forest and you could show me the world you live in," B.B. said, as they squelched through the fourth stream of the morning. "Human interest stuff. Then we can get on to development issues."

"The only development issues worth talking about involve timber," Gilda said.

"Aren't you worried that talking about timber could get you into a lot of trouble?" B.B. asked provocatively. "Remember David Ferdiaz, our researcher in Sabah? He gave an interview to CNN about illegal logging in the Mount Kinabalu National Park and got his cute little butt thrown out of the country for being an anti-Malaysian subversive."

Gilda was preparing a reply stating that sometimes principles are more important than political correctness, but was interrupted by Bujang.

"*Tengok*, Madame Doctor Gilda. *Ada banyak orkid*," Bujang said, pointing out bright flowers high in the trees. He climbed to fetch several for the women.

"He's quite handy around the camp, I suppose," B.B. said to Gilda, as they watched him encircle the tree trunk and shimmy up.

"Yes."

"Has he been with you long?"

Gilda wasn't sure what that meant. "About two years."

"Bright lad," B.B. said. "Does he help you with your research?"

"Increasingly. I'm teaching him about orangutans."

"How wonderful. The INF likes to involve local people."

"I might make him my assistant one of these days," Gilda said, trying to earn a few points.

"I suppose he knows most of what's going on."

"What *is* going on B.B.? Why all these questions about Bujang?"

"No reason. Sorry, didn't mean to upset you," B.B. apologized. Gilda remained silent. "Let's continue walking and you can tell me about orangutans. Maybe we can figure out a human angle."

Gilda was too reticent to be a natural story-teller. In fact she was often annoyingly slow and careful in her comments. However, Gilda did know a few things about orangutans. After all, she had logged hours upon hours of field observations, the record for any individual studying primates – and was more relaxed explaining orangutan behavior than she was talking about herself. She told B.B. that the male orangutan is territorial. That the gestation period is eight months. Gilda speculated on the orangutan's relationship to man. "We share 99% of our DNA with the three great apes," she said, "and at least one scientist, Jeffrey Schwartz at the University of Pittsburgh, thinks that the orangutan is our closest relative, although that view is not generally accepted."

"What's that, Gilda?" B.B. asked, looking up, as they entered a clearing.

"Oh, a kite. Or maybe an eagle. I get them confused."

"A kite, I think," B.B. said.

"How can you tell?"

"Forked tail. At least that's the difference in North America."

"Could be. Ornithology isn't my thing. It's all very well for you amateur bird watchers who have time to study books. Mother-infant behavior. That's what I've spent most of my time on. It's really incredible how they act, well, just like mothers and children."

"And that?" B.B. asked, referring to a sound more appropriate to an asylum for the insane than a rainforest.

I know this one, Gilda thought proudly, like a little girl in class. It was the call of the rhinoceros hornbill, one of the most startling and dramatic in the jungle. It starts as a series of mellow hoots uttered at rather long intervals, gradually rises in pitch and frequency until the climax is reached, an unbroken series of shrill, demented chuckles which, in turn, fade away into a mocking laugh.

"One of the hornbills. It's got a big casque on its nose. The natives think it's sacred."

"Sounds incredible."

"Yes. It's a real important bird. The orangutans follow it to find fruit trees."

B.B. and Gilda followed a few yards behind Bujang. Gilda had briefed him on his role and every five minutes or so he came up with another curiosity for the visitor.

"*Tengok*, Madame Doctor Gilda. *Jika perempuan minum daun ini, dia tidak menjadi hamil.*"

Gilda muttered to herself. "How interesting. So that's what it looks like."

"What did he say?" B.B. asked.

"Bujang says this plant can be used for birth control."

"Does it work?"

"Well, I, er some of the women in the camp take some concoction made from plants. The cook brews it up for them. Might be from this plant."

"And it works?"

"That's what they say."

B.B. giggled. "Anything you're hiding from me, Gilda?"

Gilda was angry at the invasion of privacy. Although everything she did was unwittingly public knowledge, she had lived a decade in a society that knew everything, but did not probe.

B.B. changed the subject. "Can I get a photo of you ... and your helper ... with the plant?"

Gilda and Bujang posed for the pictures. Gilda then threw away the branch.

"Oh no," B.B. admonished, as she picked it up. "I want to take it back with me. Ethnobotany is hot right now. What's the scientific name?"

"I'm not sure."

"Could we look it up back at camp? I saw a sign on one of the buildings that said herbarium."

God help me if she gets a look at that miserable, old closet filled

112

with rotting sticks and leaves. "Listen. It doesn't pay to be too hung up on academic things out here," Gilda said. "Anyway, that's a job for the taxonomists."

"But, surely this could be important. This is news. A natural birth control substance found in a threatened Borneo jungle. You *must* know the name."

Gilda looked to Bujang for help. *"Apa nama pohon ini?"*

"Daun hijau besar."

Gilda tried not to giggle as she repeated the Malay words phonetically to B.B., who wrote them in her notebook. Bujang had identified the plant as "big green leaf".

"Gilda, *this* is what conservation is all about," B.B. admonished, waving the branch. "Benefits. End users. Reality. Show me more of these things."

Triple-pause time. "I can show you 21 varieties of wild figs that orangutans eat."

"Look, I know your orangutans are important to you," B.B. said sympathetically. "But they're old hat. That's old-style fundraising and now every mom-and-pop nature conservation organization in the western world is flashing pictures of cuddly orangutans." B.B. wiped the sweat from her forehead with the bottom of her T-shirt. "The INF publicity machine has evolved with the times. People want to give money – and I'm talking about big money, not your ten dollars here, thirty dollars there – to projects which benefit people."

Gilda went quiet. Her future depended on good publicity, she knew that. Some three-fourths of the annual budget of Camp Trinil, which had skyrocketed to about $75,000 per year since the shoestring days when Gilda had first arrived, came from the INF – which, in turn, came from millions of supporters worldwide. However, that income had always been generated by appeals to save orangutans. Had the world gone mad?

B.B. explained the change in direction at INF. "Wait until you see the next issue of *Nature's World*. It's got articles about water catchment forests in Venezuela and how the beer you drink is improved by wild barley from Ethiopia and how the happy, poor people in Zimbabwe kill *kudu* that wander out of the national park."

Gilda knew the power of *Nature's World*. The monthly magazine, with a circulation of some ten million, was INF's showpiece. Gilda had been featured in it three times. INF fundraisers timed their direct mail appeals to coincide with the arrival of the magazine. The mailings were produced by the same bunch of creative geniuses who also wrote the mailings for the Republican National Committee, the National Rifle Association and the Eldridge Cleaver Memorial Scholarship Fund, among other clients. The last mailing in aid of Camp Trinil, some three years ago, featured Gilda holding an infant orangutan, with the headline: 'Why Gilda's Adventure in Borneo Affects Little Queenie's Future'.

"You know, I wasn't too happy with that last mailing piece you guys sent out," Gilda complained, as she re-tied her bootlaces.

"What do you mean?"

"This isn't an adventure. It's my life."

"Well, first of all, it happened before I joined," B.B. explained. "But anyway, it didn't pull as well as INF had expected. I read the file – I think you pulled a two percent response on the American Express list and a three percent response on the previous over-fifty-dollars donors list. Which is okay, but it was an expensive piece to produce, so our average contribution, if I'm not mistaken was, oh, maybe fourteen dollars. Not great."

"Those are just figures. What about the message?"

"We've found that the greater the donation, the greater the message comprehension. Anyway, those were the old days – and I refuse to take responsibility for what my predecessors did. We've got a new team in place now. Very exciting times," B.B. said enthusiastically. "In any case, fundraising is a highly technical discipline and I wouldn't expect you to be familiar with all the ins and outs. I think you're being a touch too sensitive. We don't meddle in your work, surely we should be allowed to get on with fundraising as we see best."

"But what I don't understand is if that approach worked so well why do you want to change it?"

B.B. looked at Gilda as if she had ordered a Pepsi at a Coca-Cola bottlers' convention. "Haven't you been paying attention? It worked so-so. Not great. Not terrible. But the response to your project has been declining over the past six years. It's crunch-time. If you can't find a way to show, at least a teeny-weeny bit, that this project is relevant to the local people, then INF can't fund you anymore."

114

Gilda paused. She smoothed her short hair back over her ears. The filtered sunlight that came through the trees highlighted red streaks in her hair, a minor bit of inadvertent cosmetic improvement that resulted from the henna-like plant sap that Gilda rubbed into her hair three times a week to keep it thick and healthy.

"What do you suggest?" she asked.

B.B. made some notes in her steno pad before replying. "Well, if I can suggest a basic change in ..."

She was interrupted by Bujang, who touched B.B. on the shoulder and pointed upward.

Just thirty feet above them, a female orangutan and child had swung over to have a look at Gilda and Bujang, familiar figures, and B.B., a novelty. B.B. got out her Nikon, attached a 200-mm telephoto lens and began snapping. After a minute of 'being stared at', the mother ape became angry at the perceived aggressive behavior of the strange, terrestrial, female ape and took retaliatory action. While hanging on to the wild mango tree with one hand and one foot, she grabbed a dead branch on a nearby tree. Rocking back and forth between the two she managed to break off the branch and fling it towards the humans. Bujang saw it coming and pushed both women out of its path.

"Wow," B.B. said, catching her breath. "*Toreemi kaysee*," she said to Bujang, squeezing his shoulder. Thanks. She added to Gilda, "Did I say it correctly?"

"Close enough."

"You know, I really admire the way you've been able to survive out here in the forest. Not too many women, hell, not too many men, could do what you've done."

"Well, you get used to it," Gilda admitted, with a hint of pride. "There's a certain order to things, in a way."

"Don't you get lonely?"

Quiet.

"I mean, don't you miss not having other white people around."

"There's Gerry."

"Yes, I forgot about him." B.B. was getting nowhere.

"Gilda, you've been out here for, what, ten years now?"

"Eleven in a couple of months."

"Right, eleven years. Could you summarize what you've accomplished?" B.B. asked, formally, holding out her tape recorder.

"Well, me and my team have accumulated seven thousand hours of observations of wild orangutans. That's more than any other researcher, far more."

"Yes, it certainly is a lot. But what has it proved?"

Gilda scrunched up her left eye and took a while to reply. "We've accumulated samples of sixty plants that orangutans eat. We've named about fifty wild orangutans in the national park and kept records of how old they are. We've captured ten and put radio collars on them so we can track their movements. We've compiled over a thousand pages of notes on mother-infant relationships."

"Now we're cooking. Tell me about the radio collars."

"Well, it really didn't work too well. The radio transmitters either broke or the orangutans managed to rip them off. We did track one orangutan, though, for three months. Jelly Roll we called him – because of his fat, little stomach."

"And what did the data show?"

"Basically, that he kept pretty close to his mother."

"And the mother-child relationships?"

"Well, as you know, the father abandons the female after impregnating her – it's a very macho life. Say, that's an idea."

"What is, Gilda?"

"Well, you're the direct mail specialist, but maybe you could do a mailing to subscribers of *Ms* magazine, the women's libbers, and tell the story of how the male orangutan just buggers off after screwing the female and how the female successfully raises the infant, without any paternal help."

"Let's think about that one a little."

"Well, you're the expert."

"Anything else of significance?"

"Oh, lots of things. It's all in the paper I'm writing."

B.B. knew that Gilda's scholarly output was limited to quite unscholarly writings – a few articles in *Nature's World* and regular , though generally tardy, reports from the field. The scientific world was curious as to whether Gilda would ever produce a scientific paper.

B.B. suggested that it was high time for her to write a paper with Latin names and footnotes.

"Oh, but that's not the point," Gilda said. "My being here is the story, of course," she said. "Me and the orangutans in the camp have become a symbol for nature conservation all over the world. And the timber people don't dare come too close because they know that I would chase them out."

"And the park is threatened because of outside pressures on the forest?" B.B. asked.

Gilda was not going to be drawn into a political discussion. The Minister had told her to keep her powder dry. She had already said too much.

"That's what some people say."

"Some people?" Then louder, in exasperation, "*Some people*? What do *you* say?"

"I'd rather not talk about it."

"Whoa. Hold on. You're standing here telling me that you've spent ten years playing around with these orangutans, that you've devoted the best years of your life to this forest and you don't want to talk about the fact that it might all be destroyed in a few months?"

Gilda disliked being between a rock and a hard place. In this case, her principles swayed like bamboo, leaning in the direction of the most recent wind.

"I'll tell you a story, if that's what you want."

"That's what I want. That's what the INF wants."

"Did you hear what those bastards did on the north side of the national park?"

B.B. got it all on tape. The Manusian Government had granted a timber concession to a Philippine company which was operating just outside the boundary of the Mount Malu National Park. The Filipinos, however, perhaps by appealing to ASEAN solidarity, somehow convinced the Manusian Forestry Department that the only way they could get the logs out would be by building a road *through* the reserve. Of course, roads are expensive – so to pay construction costs, the concessionaire negotiated a special permit that allowed him to cut 'just a few' hardwood trees that grew within a half mile of the road.

"Well, I flew over the area with one of the missionary pilots," Gilda continued, "and do you know that the logging road they built looked like it was made of spaghetti! It curved and curled back around on itself for miles to form huge U-shapes. You couldn't imagine a less efficient road."

"I don't get it. So they built an inefficient road."

Gilda looked at B.B. like she was a Martian. "Don't you see? The guys who had the timber concession, before they surveyed the route for the road, first surveyed the location of the most valuable trees in the reserve. Then, all they had to do was build the road so that it gyrated within a half mile of each precious tree. They made a killing. "

"That's a great story, Gilda."

The scientist glared at her.

"I mean it's a fascinating story. Those bastards are all over, aren't they?" she said, rewinding her Sony Professional Walkman a few feet and testing to confirm that she had it all on tape.

"You were recording that?"

"Of course."

"You can't use that."

"Why not? You spoke eloquently, forcefully. It came from the heart."

"You would get me thrown out of the country if you used that," Gilda argued, barely noticing that Bujang was sitting nearby, trimming his toenails with his *parang*.

"Is the government that sensitive to criticism?"

"Of course it is. I'm a visitor here. They can do anything they want with me. I told you that for background. For color. Don't use it. Please."

"How about if I attribute it to 'an informed source'?"

"Please."

"Okay."

Gilda wanted to ask B.B. to swear on her mother's grave, but thought it would be carrying things a bit too far.

"But *someone* has to stand up to these people. The INF can do it, if you cooperate," B.B. said.

"No, I told you that would just create more problems."

"Well, how about someone like Urs? Can he make a difference?"

"What do you know about Urs?" Gilda asked guardedly.

"The whole world knows about Urs Gerhard. His articles, his drawings, appear everywhere. Non-governmental organizations throughout Europe raise funds for the Penan blockades. Have you met him?"

"No."

"He must be right around here, no?"

"I said forget it. We're here to do conservation, not to incite riots. Keep your nose clean."

"*I'd* sure like to meet him and write a story about him. I think you're wrong. What Urs is doing is just as much nature conservation as saving cute red apes. Fighting for the people."

Gilda remained silent. She looked at her visitor, at her brass-hooped earrings, at her curly blondish-reddish hair, at her pale, freckled face.

"Sure you don't know how I can reach him?" B.B. pushed. "Wave a flag from a treetop? Pound the tom-toms? Surely someone around here knows him. He must get supplies from somewhere."

Gilda spoke as clearly as she had for months. "Do not even think about getting near Urs. He's trouble. He's bad news. The government wants his ass and if they know that you're even thinking about contacting him we'll both be on the next boat out of here."

B.B. was clearly disappointed. "Not the response I expected."

Gilda spoke immediately, something she rarely did. "What response am I expected to give you? Fine, go ahead and see Urs and ruin everything I've been trying to build for the better part of my life?"

"Now, settle down. I didn't mean that."

Gilda hated herself for becoming hysterical, the female characteristic she tried most to avoid. This woman might decide my future, Gilda thought. Finally, the scientist changed the subject. "I think Gerry is waiting for us." In her ragged Malay, she told Bujang to clear a path through a thicket.

* * * * *

Tusau Padan's role model was Henry Kissinger. Fast as a speedboat. Incisive. Convincing.

Even Mustafa bin Kayu liked the idea. It was really quite elegant, Padan thought. Announce that Taib bin Susah, the unlucky security guard wounded by a Penan blowpipe dart, had died and been buried in the forest. Martyrs were useful.

"Only a handful of people know where he really is," Tusau Padan had told his boss. "He's playing dominoes in a secure military hospital outside the capital." Padan was pleased with himself. The Minister was so impressed by the opportunities for disinformation offered by the elegant deception that he neglected to consider that Padan was too clever by half. Besides being one of the few Kayans ever to make it to an overseas university, the bright-eyed young man was a student of contemporary American history. Remembering the golden days of Watergate, Padan had deftly implicated the Minister in the cover-up through a series of memos he had placed in the confidential file, indicating that he had concocted Taib's fabricated death on his superior's explicit orders. Padan lit a cigarette, called the Ministry's senior accountant to his office and ordered him to prepare a substantial check for Taib's family to ease their bereavement.

* * * * *

Gerry laughed to himself. Here he was, stuck in a jungle where people can't tell you if it's Tuesday or November and he was worried about arriving late to teach a bunch of primates whose natural response to a watch is to stick it in their mouths. Still, a teacher had to keep discipline in the class, a lesson he had learned during his first semester as a teaching assistant to Professor B.F. Pong, a brilliant researcher who had absolutely no interest in teaching Psychology 101, the university's way of humbling even the most luminous academic stars. Gerry had been one of a half dozen graduate students entrusted with holding forth to 175 bubblegum-popping teenagers who had signed-up for Psych 101 in order to be introduced to the wonders of learning, perception and stimulus-response mechanisms.

The first term, he had treated the predominantly freshman audience as friends. He paid dearly for that lapse. Class attendance fell dramatically in subsequent weeks, papers were late – if they arrived at all – and no students, particularly no cute female students, came to his miniscule office cubicle to seek scholarly inspiration and career guidance.

The second term, Gerry decided to get tough. He insisted that he be called Mr. Schwartz and let it be known that he was just a few semesters away from the cherished Ph.D.. He wore a suit to class, gave surprise quizzes each period and graded them with the mercy of Attila. Gerry was surprised by how well it worked. Students feared him – and a few even respected him. He was sought after. He was in graduate students' heaven.

Gerry was privileged to be one of the handful of students B.F. Pong selected each year as Ph.D. candidates. Professor Pong was generally acknowledged as the world's leading expert on ape intelligence – although, Dr. Rheinhold Bertlesman, of the University of Heidelberg, had his own vocal following. Both men would have been close to Nobel prizes, had there been a category for cross-species communication.

Pong had emigrated to America from Shanghai in 1947, together with Dr. An Wang, the genius who went on to found Wang Computers. While Wang went to MIT to invent new memory systems which were to revolutionize the technology of data processing, Pong went across town to Harvard Medical School, specializing in brain physiology. His goal: identify the chemical changes that occur when somebody 'learns' something. Dr. Pong soon learned that there are some enigmas man is unlikely to ever comprehend and he turned his attention to comparative learning. He did a second residency, this time in psychiatry, and worked with brain-damaged patients to analyze how they perceive their world. It was a simple step to move from injured human beings to healthy gorillas and, shortly thereafter, Pong convinced the University of North Carolina to establish a major center for the study of primate intelligence.

Pong's laboratory was filled with expensive, endangered primates – lesser apes, including three varieties of gibbons, and the three great apes – chimpanzees, gorillas and orangutans. Through a combination of skill, hard work and luck, Pong's human students managed to teach several of the great apes to speak using sign language and taught others to communicate with a logical series of grunts that meant yes, no and maybe. Some of the apes – most notably the orangutans – appeared not to communicate at all, yet showed remarkable skill in solving tactical puzzles. All in all, they were a bright lot; Professor Pong liked to boast that his ape students had a higher median IQ than the average inner-city high school class.

Professor Pong had become the most recent star in a long series of ape educators who were proving that their hairy charges could learn an astounding variety of bits of information.

Koko the gorilla, studying at UCLA with Francine (Penny) Paterson, learned several hundred signs in Ameslan. Koko even invented imaginative new phrases such as 'finger bracelet' for ring, 'white tiger' for zebra and 'eye hat' for mask.

Washoe, a chimpanzee, lived with Allen and Beatrice Gardner for over six years and mastered 132 words, but the Gardners estimated she passively understood perhaps three times that number. Washoe learned rudimentary grammar and occasionally invented new signs. She learned the sign 'dirty' to refer to feces and then used the sign to invent insults such as 'dirty monkey' for a macaque who angered her and called researcher Roger Fouts 'dirty Roger' when he refused to give her sweets. She invented the phrase 'water bird' when she first saw a duck.

A chimpanzee named Lana even learned "a primitive form of counting", according to Duane Rumbaugh at the Georgia State University and Yerkes Regional Primate Research Center. He claimed this was the first time counting behavior had been demonstrated in any animal other than man.

Not all researchers were as sanguine about the intelligence of the great apes. Several critics felt there is generally a 'clever Hans' syndrome at work in which the ape responds to a variety of facial, body and vocal cues issued by the trainer/tester. Dr. Herbert Terrace of Columbia University believed that the success he had in teaching sign language to a chimpanzee named Nim Chimpsky (named in recognition of the linguist Noam Chomsky, who had written that apes would never really speak in the sense humans understand the term) can be explained as "merely prompting on the part of the experimenters and mistakes in reporting the data, since much of the ape's behavior is pure drill."

The careers of many professors are judged by the success of their students. Pong's ape students were brilliant, but he was still dissatisfied. There was one lingering and fundamental problem that needed to be resolved. Pong's work and the studies of his compatriots were all done with apes bred and raised in captivity. The apes were already familiar with human contact and human communication. What is the wild ape thinking? Pong wondered. How intelligent are apes in their natural settings? What would they learn if they didn't *have* to learn?

Pong was getting old and he realized that he would not be able to carry out the next stage of his life's work – the study of apes in an ape-environment as opposed to a people-environment. For this task, he selected a small number of graduate students who had, he felt, the right temperament and the determination to see a project through. Pong made his choices based on intuition. Gerry was one of his first protegés.

Gerry proudly felt that his selection marked a milestone in his lifetime quest for social success. As a teenager, he had suffered from acne and he was relieved when he entered college and could grow a beard to cover his pocked face. Realizing that he would never be more than a mediocre athlete, he abandoned the idea of playing football or running track and instead tried competitive frisbee. When he missed making the Chicago under-21 team that was going to La Jolla for the national championships, he tried amateur theater. After failing to get the role of a tap-dancing Macbeth at a suburban dinner theater, he gave square dancing a shot. It was not until he hit on behavioral psychology, that he saw an opening for his life's ambitions.

As Gerry became immersed in the rigors of academia and the dog-eat-dog environment of searching for grants, he quickly gave up trying to have a good time and instead developed a healthy and finely tuned cynicism that confirmed what he had always suspected but could never prove – he ought to look after his own skin first.

This philosophic tidal wave had two effects on his life. It made him a more attentive student and, since success in graduate school is based as much on willingness to support a particular professor's pet projects as it is on success at exams, Gerry's academic career soared. In the process, he discovered that his reluctance to engage in any activity which was not self-serving was an aphrodisiac to dozens of women who thought it was terribly refreshing to sleep with a man who had a purpose in life – even if that purpose was furthering his own career.

Gerry's quest for a Ph.D., Gilda's need for outside funding and the presence of several dozen infant orangutans in Camp Trinil who needed babysitting, came together like the fortuitous configurations of planets that astrologers claim will cause earthquakes and enable people to fall in love.

Gilda had gone to Chapel Hill to interview Gerry, although she really had no alternative but to accept him. With Gerry came the funding from the University, the US National Institutes of Health and the American Psychological Society. Gilda was not the best judge of people and her interview procedure consisted primarily of watching his table manners as they had lunch. She saw that he had clean fingernails, that he did not wipe his nose on his forearm, that he rarely dribbled his iced tea, that he did not chew on her ankle. He was more sophisticated than the apes she had spent several years with and would be a good role model.

Gilda later told Gerry that she had an ulterior motive for wanting the sign language project to go ahead. Ultimately, Gilda hoped Ringo would become fluent in Ameslan and return to the forest. He could then act as her jungle agent and come back with regular reports on what life was like out there – his opinion of logging, people, other animals, how he finds fruit and females, whether he dreams. Ape life. Gilda and Ringo would go on the David Letterman show together.

Gerry was working with six orangutan students at Camp Trinil. Queenie, his personal favorite, was not the smartest. That honor went to Ringo, the aggressive adolescent who had been raised from infancy by Gilda's human family and who Gerry optimistically estimated had an IQ of around 80-90. Ringo had been brought to the rehabilitation station when he was four years old – old enough to have spent many of his formative years living as a child, yet young enough, the researchers thought, to get used to a jungle existence if shown how to return to the wild. Gerry, too, had visions of grandeur very similar to Gilda's. Ringo's story was the complement of Tarzan's. It would make a perfect movie, he thought. Gerry would play himself.

"Sorry I'm late," Gerry grunted to his students in the trees as he climbed up to the feeding platform, an open bamboo structure built on stilts and about ten feet off the ground. He rang the bell that usually signified lunch. Several curious orange bundles, led by Ringo, crept out of the woodwork.

"Now, let's get started."

Gerry offered Ringo a banana bribe. The ape shuffled over to the end of the platform. Being quadridexterous, the ape somehow managed to simultaneously unpeel the fruit, pick his nose and slowly manoeuver a Rubic's Cube, one of the signing props. He couldn't solve the cube, of course, but he seemed to enjoy watching the colors change sides. Gerry placed a metal cup on the wooden 'teacher's stand', a simple, small table.

"Ringo. Pay attention. *Apa ini?*" What's this?

Ringo curled his index finger and made a half turn on the horizontal axis. He chewed the last bit of banana and tossed the peel over his shoulder, a trait he had learned from watching his teacher.

"Good, Ringo. Cup," Gerry said, rewarding the ape with two peanuts.

He replaced the cup with a tuning fork.

"*Apa ini?*"

Ringo replied by flicking his two index fingers together and got two peanuts. Gerry noted the correct response in his notebook, which contained the data that would later be analyzed by a program called Advanced Primate Elucidation. Gerry was certain the ultimate printout would contain impressive graphs showing learning curves so that Gerry's students could be compared with the ape students of other Pong protégés.

"Very good, Ringo. We're really cooking today. Now, how about this one?" Gerry asked, placing a well-chewed, plastic flip-flop slipper on the table.

Ringo thought a moment and crawled a yard away to lick the place where the warden had spilled milk during the morning feeding.

"Ringo, pay attention." He held out one peanut to encourage the ape to return to class. Gerry waved the flip-flop and smacked it down on the platform in front of the orangutan. "*Apa ini?*" he said harshly.

Ringo continued to ignore Gerry, which forced Gerry to take a nearby stick and give the orangutan a gentle whack on his thighs. Ringo put his wrist to his mouth and sputtered a Borneo version of a Bronx cheer. Gerry whacked him harder. The ape shuffled over, took a look at the slipper and made the correct sign.

B.B. and Gilda approached, not too quietly.

"Looks like class is already in session," Gilda whispered.

"Would it disturb them if I took some pictures?" B.B. asked.

"No, I don't think so. They know you're here anyway. Just don't get too close. They have a limited attention span."

"Okay, Ringo, enough revision," Gerry said, for the audience.

He placed a spoon, an empty jar and a banana skin on the table. "Ringo, pick up the spoon," Gerry said in Malay and signed in Ameslan – clearly making the spoon sign, a revolving fist.

Ringo picked up the spoon and sucked on it. He then used it to scratch his chest, then offered to place it in Gerry's mouth.

"Good, Ringo," Gerry smiled, giving the animal two peanuts. "Now make the spoon sign. Good," he praised, passing over another couple of peanuts. "Now let's try …"

Class was interrupted by Queenie. "Hello, what are you doing here?" Gerry said happily, as the young ape clambered up to the platform and jumped into his arms. "Queenie, you know you shouldn't be over here," Gerry admonished, nuzzling her. "Now, you scoot." Queenie stayed right where she was and reached into Gerry's shorts with her left foot.

"Now, where were we, Ringo? How about counting? Let's see the number three. Show me three fingers."

Queenie tried to enter the conversation by forming an O with her thumb and forefinger and revolved it lazily around her ear.

"Gilda, can you take Queenie?" Gerry called down.

"Come here, Queenie." The small ape went to the queen of the apes, who passed her to B.B. for a cuddle.

During this brief interlude, Ringo got tired of school. He swept the props off the table and retrieved the banana skin.

"Ringo, sit down," Gerry instructed.

The ape ignored Gerry, slid down the platform's support pole and gave the banana skin to Queenie, who held B.B. around the neck. Ringo pushed Queenie's little rump aside and stuck his flat nose against B.B.'s sweat riddled T-shirt. B.B. didn't know what to do. She tried patting him on the head with her free hand. Ringo kept his face on her breasts, breathing deeply, making gurgling noises. Finally, Queenie climbed onto Ringo's back and they tumbled to the ground. The two apes then climbed into the neighboring trees and sat on a branch some 15 feet directly above Gerry.

"Ringo, come back down here. You know we're not finished yet."

Ringo ignored Gerry.

"Ringo. I mean it."

The ape replied by pissing down through the leaves.

"I guess class is over," Gilda said morosely. "Come on, B.B. It's almost lunch time."

Anjing

The Cabinet Ministers had never seen Sultan Ibrahim bin Akbar Harrods so angry. During the emergency meeting, he had screamed: "You mean they had that bugger Urs covered with shotguns and he escaped? What is this? Disneyland? No, I take it back. In Disneyland things function properly. We can't even catch a single Swiss man? This is just Mickey Mouse."

The bottom line to Mustafa bin Kayu: take charge of the spin and hit the road to "spread the truth about that subversive Swiss."

CHAPTER 11

26 July. 23:00.

Camp Trinil

Where the hell is Bujang? Gilda thought. If he knew how serious things are, he wouldn't be off drinking *tuak* with his buddies. "I need you, Bujang," she said to herself. If people is what B.B. wants, then she'll get people. Rumah Sehat. Full of people. People who rely on the forest. Local, brown people. People who fish in the forest, who hunt there. People who collect rattan and fruit and even die in that dark wilderness. We'll fill her pompous head so full of rice wine and human aspirations that she'll write a direct mail piece on the spot. And if that doesn't work, well ... She finally allowed herself to add – And I miss you, you naked savage. Where are you, Bujang?

* * * * *

It was black hole time for Gerry. How perceptive is that B.B. woman?, he wondered. After that performance today, he'd be lucky if she ... oh, never mind. I'm not responsible to the INF. I don't need their money. Just let me get those three letters after my name. Ph.D. He turned up the volume. The Stones always soothed him.

A scratching on the door. Queenie. She leapt into his embrace. "Queenie. You're awfully sweet. But why aren't you a little bit smarter? Can't you learn just a little bit faster? At this rate you'll never make the ape hall of fame."

Even with the loose scientific method Gerry employed, he estimated that he needed another six months before he could collect enough data to write his dissertation. Six months of apes signing with such strong accents that their 'speech' was incomprehensible to all except Gerry.

He saw now that the ape was frightened. Queenie made a sequence of signs Gerry had never seen. "What is it, girl?" She repeated her signs. Gerry picked up Ringo's name, two fingers on each hand crossed on the diagonal. He recognized, too, the second sign, a molding of her thumb and forefinger around the thumb of her opposite hand, a cuddle, but couldn't place it in context. He had never seen Queenie so upset. He made a generous gesture and offered her a Mars bar from his private stock.

She settled down and was soon dozing in his lap. Gerry, too, drifted off to sleep, without noticing Ringo peering through the window.

Penan encampment

Orange sparks from the forge flew into the dark sky, attracting hopeful, male fireflies. Laki pumped the bellows tirelessly. He sat on the ground, his left foot folded under his useless right leg, which was wrapped with aromatic plants.

The Penan made spears and *parangs* from scrap iron and, in recent years, from old automobile springs. While they increasingly traded for many of their needs – cooking pots, cloth, fishing line, needles and thread – the jungle nomads felt almost ritual satisfaction in making their own tools and weapons. Although three monkeys or a hornbill casque would earn them a *parang*, the handmade version could be imbued with power that was lacking in store-bought versions.

This night, Seridan and Avalon pounded the metal into a different kind of weapon – eight-inch long, metal spikes. The Penan had learned to hammer them into mature hardwood trees, a tactic first recommended by Robert Hallmark and then independently suggested by one of Urs' Greenpeace pen-pals in America. When a chainsaw comes in contact with the difficult-to-see spikes, the chain will break. At the very least, the result will be a broken saw. In some cases, the severed chain will snap back into the face of the laborer, sometimes with fatal results. Many workers in the United States national forests, where the technique had first been used, understandably refused to work if they knew the trees had been 'spiked'.

Urs watched the procedure with detachment. A group of Penan making weapons of war did not fit his vision of nomadic life. The fire was a place for tales of wind spirits and giant boars, for stories of mouse deer outsmarting the crocodile. It was not a place for hammering metal against metal to injure someone. He moved away from the fire towards his shelter, where Maya waited. Liebchen jumped down and danced in front of the embers.

Camp Trinil

Defecating in strange places was always a drama for B.B.. At least in Camp Trinil she didn't have to worry about dirty seats. There were no seats. Just a hole in a wooden floor in an enclosed platform some 50 yards behind the 'guest cottage' where she slept. She half expected to find an old Sears Roebuck catalogue and was delighted to find, instead,Tiger Lily toilet paper, made in Shanghai.

She visited the latrine several times that night. She couldn't decide whether her nervous stomach stemmed from something she ate, jet lag or her run-in with Gilda. B.B. hadn't wanted to confront Gilda so directly, but the woman had as much subtlety as an ironing board.

It was that blasted durian, B.B. decided, as she squatted for the fourth time that evening. Gilda had insisted she try the spiky fruit after lunch. The whitish, sticky pulp tasted like strawberries and cream mixed with onion custard, with the aroma of a poorly kept public toilet. Which was where she was at the moment.

"I hope that's it for the night," B.B. said, as she closed the latrine door behind her. She shone her Eddie Bauer miniature torchlight on the raised wooden path, let out a loud burp and headed to bed.

"Madame Baby." A whisper.

B.B. shined her light around. Nothing.

"Madame Baby." The voice was louder. From the shadows a dark figure emerged and came closer. B.B. focused the flashlight.

"Bujang. You scared me."

He smiled and came closer. B.B. wasn't sure what he wanted, what to do. He remained hidden in the half shadows under the walkway.

"I sleep go," B.B. said in baby English, indicating that she was going back to her cabin. God, that's probably the wrong thing to say, she thought. Now he'll want to climb into bed with me.

Instead, Bujang leapt onto the raised, wooden walkway. He stood before her, wearing just a pair of faded basketball shorts. The moonlight glanced off his shoulders. He reached into his back pocket and extracted a crumpled note, which he handed to B.B.. She focused her flashlight on the paper.

"Dear Fraulein Bee-Bee,
I understand you would like to meet me. Please follow Mr. Bujang at 05.00 this next morning and we can talk. Please do not anyone tell."

It was signed: "Urs Gerhard."

PART IV

DIPLOMACY

CHAPTER 12

27 July. 06:00.

Penan encampment

Even without having to carry two cameras, two photo flash units, six lenses, a tape recorder, notebook, film, tapes and assorted gifts, B.B. would have found the early morning trek to the Penan encampment difficult.

Bujang gestured that he would carry her pack. She stumbled after him in the grey mist, her heart pounding too hard for her to be able to appreciate the dawn chorus of birds, monkeys and insects that signaled a new day in the rainforest.

It had been Urs' idea to invite B.B. to his encampment. Bujang had been frightened, suggesting that Urs instead meet the woman in the middle of the forest. "No, we meet here," Urs had decided when the two men discussed the rendezvous the previous day. "She doesn't know the forest. She can't find her way here again. And this place adds location color."

Even so, Bujang didn't want to give away the location of the Penan encampment and he walked her in many circles so that the trip, which normally would have taken half an hour's stroll, took an hour and a half. B.B. arrived in a clammy sweat, totally disoriented because of the lack of horizon in the vast, green maze. The early morning air had turned from fresh to musky, with the heavy scent of rotting fruit rising from the jungle floor. The Penan day was in full swing by the time Bujang and B.B. arrived.

Urs' initial greeting, "Have you eaten?" took her by surprise.

"Uh, no. Hello. You must be Urs," she said to the pale man.

"That is the way the Penan greet each other. Food is important

135

in our culture. Sit," he said, as he unrolled a hand-woven mat near the small fire.

Maya came to the group with breakfast wrapped in leaves.

"Please," Urs said to B.B., offering her a packet. His hand shook slightly due to the weak malaria fever he was fighting. B.B. did not notice.

She unwrapped the leaves and was faced with a glutinous ball studded with pieces of what might have been meat. Bujang lost no time in digging into his portion. B.B. was afraid of upsetting cultural traditions, particularly since all twelve people of Urs' Penan band stood around watching, waiting for her reaction to Penan cuisine.

She gingerly inserted her fingers into the white mass and pulled off a piece in a similar manner to the way she used to pull taffy with her grandmother. She dropped it into her mouth. It tasted of many things and of nothing. Like a combination of library paste, plain oatmeal and raw potatoes. The Penan were content. The white woman had shared food.

"It takes some getting used to," Urs said sympathetically. "It's sago. Not very nutritious, but it's filling."

"And this?" she asked, daintily nibbling on a grey chunk of meat.

"Squirrel."

B.B. looked more carefully and saw the remnants of rodent hairs that had not been completely seared. Liebchen scampered over to investigate as well, and snatched the meat from her hand. B.B. was grateful.

B.B. and Urs talked for an hour. About life with the Penan. The incursions of the timber operators. How they just wanted to be left alone. Several of the Penan joined in, shy at first, with Urs asking their opinions and translating for the American. They showed her their medicine chest, a faded red sarong folded around a witch's brew of leaves and sticks.

"She asks if you are a doctor," Urs translated, as an old woman mumbled something incomprehensible.

"Why? Is she ill?"

"She is getting glaucoma. It is difficult for her to see."

"All I have are these drops I use for my contact lenses. They won't cure her, though. Come here," she said to the woman. B.B.

got the old woman to lie down with her head on B.B.'s lap. B.B. held open her eyelids and squirted in a few drops.

Others approached. They showed her sores on their bodies and asked for medicine. One woman pushed her three-year-old daughter forward. The naked child was thin, but with a distended belly. "Why do the children look so fat? You don't have much to eat here," B.B. observed.

"It's not fat. It's worms. Everybody has them. That is not the problem with this child. She has tuberculosis, I think."

B.B. had no response. Instead, she escaped into a series of photographs of Penan life, asking questions to prove her assumption that the people of the rainforest led rich, productive lives.

"Urs, could you ask this man why it is important to keep the rainforest healthy and to stop cutting it?" she asked, motioning to Laki.

When told the question, the newly-crippled, old man smiled wanly. "I am just a poor Penan, but I have been to Bohong and I have seen your stores. You have a store that sells only medicines, wonderful medicines from all over the world, many days' walk away. If I was sick in Bohong and I needed medicine, what would happen if I went to the store and broke the glass to take what I wanted? It would be illegal and you would put me in your jail. But that is what the big people from Anjing do now. They send in their foreigners and break the glass of our drugstore. They cut our trees. The spirits are not pleased. This is our home. Leave us our home."

"What happens now?" she asked. With a glance, she included Bujang in her question. He remained impassive.

"We need your help," Urs replied. "Our modest road blockades are not working. We are too few. We have no voice. *You* have the voice. We ask you to help."

"Yes, but how? I can write about you in *Nature's World*, oh, I almost forgot, I brought some extra copies – thought you might like to read about what is happening in the rest of the world."

"No, we need more than nice pictures. The only thing that will stop the government is strong outside pressure. Inside, they are too strong. Can you make our story a big issue? Talk to your parliament and get them a resolution to pass stopping trade with Manusia. Get your President to telephone Manusia's Sultan and ask him to stop. Convince the European Community countries they should stop buying timber from Manusia. Make the World Bank stop giving development money to the country. Big things. The people ruining our forests are big people. They only understand big things. Please. Before it is too late."

It was time to leave. B.B. sensed she would never see this man again and thought how odd it was to cross paths with someone so ... alive ... and then for each of them to continue on separate journeys, seeking different ends of the rainbow.

"Bujang will take you back," Urs said cordially.

Something didn't quite click. "How did you know I wanted to see you?" B.B. asked.

"I just took a chance. An educational guess, I think you say. I'm a tourist attraction around here. You wouldn't go to Orlando without seeing Disneyworld. Most visitors to Mount Malu want to see Urs and the Penans."

CHAPTER 13

27 July. 10:00.

Camp Trinil

"Squawrk". The short-wave sputtered into life for the morning review of gossip, news and useless airwave rubbish that was accessible to anyone on the open frequency.

After the open broadcast session, individual messages were passed on specific frequencies. "Personal. Personal awrk for Gilda," the familiar voice screeched. "Seventy seven point four." That was the frequency that Gilda was to tune into in order to receive any personal messages and other listeners on the general frequency were supposed to stay put. In practice, many usually tuned into the new frequency.

"Urgent communication just received from the honorable Mustafa bin roawrkk, Minister of screech. Gerry Schwartz terrank to scrork Manusia within one kwark due to awrk activities. Letter to screerch shortly." That sounded like bad news.

"Repeat. Message indelible," Gilda said into the radio. "Repeat."

"Thweerk." Then static as the urgent communications ran into a rain cloud.

Gilda was stunned. She felt like she imagined a sailor aboard the USS Arizona would have felt watching the first Japanese planes fly over the Pearl Harbor horizon.

Gilda turned off the radio and started it up again. She punched in the emergency frequency of Taffy's office in Anjing. She heard a gagging pterodactyl, a wounded water buffalo and a recently castrated cat, but no voice that was even vaguely human. She gave up in disgust. Better not tell Gerry anything. Could have been anything. Don't upset him.

She had to get out of the house and see her charges. It was claustrophobic in that little, wooden room.

The last person she expected to see, in fact the last person she wanted to see, was B.B. However, it was unavoidable. The INF executive was walking towards camp, on the same path Gilda was taking to commune with the orangutans.

"Early morning stroll?" Gilda asked politely.

"Uh, yes. It's so refreshing out here in the morning," B.B. bubbled. God, she looks post-orgasmic, Gilda thought. Damn these bubbly Americans.

"Where are you off to?" B.B. asked politely. She appeared eager to end the conversation before it began.

"Oh, just for a walk. I mean, actually, I wanted to check up on one of the females who is going to give birth in the next few weeks."

"Sounds interesting."

Gilda wanted to be alone. "Could be. But she's pretty nervous. I think a stranger might spook her."

"No, you go along and have a good time." B.B. sounded like a space cadet, Gilda thought, as they continued along their previous paths. Ringo saluted as they passed on the path.

As usual, Gilda did her best thinking after she had acted. Shit, I forgot about the longhouse thing. Better make it sound casual. "Oh, B.B." she called after her. "I forgot. Feel like going to see the longhouse this afternoon? Local color and all that. They're expecting us."

CHAPTER 14

27 July. Noon.

Nirvana

Gerry rolled a joint and stripped down to his underwear. He lay in the sun at Nirvana and felt its warmth seep into his tired, tired body.

He leaned back in his cot. He was sweating, but the day was overcast and his discomfort had psychological roots, not physical. He had no desire to unpack his hoard of treasures. He looked at the notepad hanging over the cot, where, at the end of his last visit, he had written the mystery of life he promised himself he would contemplate the next time he came to his sanctuary. It read: "Why do Asians use so much chili in such a hot country?" It seemed to him to be both significant and utterly ludicrous. He unlocked the chest and took out his harmonica. He knocked out snatches of *The 59th Street Bridge Song*, *The Impossible Dream* and *Let it Be*. He would have given up his Ph.D. then for an ice cold beer and a ticket to a Cubs game. Since he was likely to get neither, he lay back, almost comatose, and tried to make sense of the strange events of the last few days.

Gerry was confused about life. He tried to rationalize his existence. He really wasn't a bad guy, but somehow everything kept going wrong. Damn these women. Why can't they be sensible and easy to figure out? Why couldn't they be like Queenie?

Got to stop that, he thought, thinking about Queenie like a person. His hash-battered brain tried to figure out why he was upset about the little ape, with her silly, trusting grin and calm, wide eyes that seemed to see everything yet saw nothing. Was it a latent, fathering impulse that made him feel affectionate towards the little orangutan? Or was she merely triggering memories of his liaisons with human students? Some of the best sex he had ever enjoyed had been with students, particularly when they called him professor. Well, only one had actually called him professor. He had not corrected her.

Gerry took a last puff and popped the roach into his mouth. He sipped on a warm beer.

Let's establish a hypothetical situation, Gerry thought to himself. What if a man fucks an orangutan? What would happen? Could he impregnate her? What would come out? He wasn't thinking of fucking Queenie, of course, that would be against the will of God, or something, and it was somehow immoral even to think about it. But what if he had fucked Queenie? He didn't know much about biology, but could she become pregnant? Wouldn't that be something? Imagine, Gerry Schwartz, the founding father of a new race – half orangutan, half human. They could be called *Pongo sapiens*. Thinking apes. Imagine the gymnastic teams they could produce. What an infantry. Probably would be too short to play very good basketball and they would likely to be too lethargic to be much good at volleyball, but what about swimming, with their incredible arm length and those huge shoulder muscles.

He lit another joint. And Gilda. Shit, what a performance. She was really pissed that he had let Ringo quit the class like that, embarrassing her in front of this Derek woman. Gilda made it sound like it was his fault. Didn't that bitch realize all he had done for her? How he had saved her ass by writing her reports for her, by taking photographs she put her name to, by figuring out strategies to deal with the government and the funding agencies? And what about glory? Gilda had been messing around in that swamp forest for donkey's years with nothing to show. Gerry had been there just two years and was making major breakthroughs that would get him worldwide attention. Stupid bitch. She could be part of that if she had played her cards right. Anyway, why did it …

Gerry sensed a presence. He looked around and saw nothing. He turned to the other side. "Urs?"

"*Ja.*" An invisible voice.

"Er, can I help you?" Gerry asked, turning to the left.

The Swiss appeared to Gerry's right and stood silently until the

American noticed him.

"You surprised me. Want a toke?"

"*Entschuldige?*"

"Want a drag, Urs? Lighten up, man. Things can't be any worse for you than they are for me."

Urs remained standing. Gerry was glad he was wearing his jockey shorts.

"So, Mister Urs of the Penan. How's it going?" Gerry asked.

"*Ça va,*" Urs replied.

"My *Asiaweek* magazine came with eight pages torn out. Was that a story about you?"

"Yes. A good story. Lots of photos. Very embarrassing to the big people in Anjing."

"How do the reporters get in to see you Urs? You're not really what one might call an accessible figure."

"If I want to see them, there are ways. You are curious, Gerry."

"Sure, I'm curious. I'm a scientist. It's my nature."

"I am cautious. That is my nature."

"Hey, whatever works."

"Gerry. You have a film I can borrow?"

"Film? Sure. Kodachrome or Ektachrome?"

"Either one."

"Right. No problem, but it's down at the camp. Do you want me to mail it to you?"

"Would you please leave it here tonight? I will come back."

"Listen, we've got important overseas visitors in camp. I've got to entertain them and later we're going over to Rumah Sehat. Can't we make it tomorrow?"

"It would be a big help to me if you could give me the film tonight."

"Listen, it's a long way down and a long way up. Couldn't I leave it for you closer to the camp? Or maybe give it to someone to give to you?"

Urs stared at the curly-haired man. "What do you mean?"

"You must know other people in the camp. Don't make me do all the work."

"You are curious again."

"My man, Urs. I can't figure you out. Lot's of people would be willing to help you if you just opened up a little. Be a touch more friendly, man. It can't hurt."

"And be caught by the special forces. You know they are for me looking."

"No, but it doesn't surprise me."

"It doesn't?"

"No, after all, the timber blockades are all around here and people know that you are behind them, so, put it together and ..."

"Do you think I am behind them?"

"Yeah, I suppose so."

"And did you tell that to the police?"

"Urs, my man, what are you saying?"

"I say only this. I have been captured once. The next time they get me, they will, how you say, throw away the key. And the police are very close. Very close, Gerry. Someone has been telling them where I was. And I don't like that. I get angry. But if I get angry it is okay. I am European and I can live with it. We are Catholic in the Wallis. But my friends here do not understand other people who are not friends. I cannot control them."

Urs disappeared as quickly as he had come.

Mount Malu National Park

Gilda went into the forest in search of orangutans. Perhaps they could put some sense into the events of the last few days.

Gilda quickly found Diane and Rosebud, mother and daughter, and watched them for an hour. Rosebud relied completely on her mother, even though she was just becoming old enough to wander around in the trees by herself. Diane never let her get more than a few yards away. Gilda wondered whether Diane was a better mother than she had been. Gilda had done her best for Ding-Ding, but it was really no place for a kid. Mark had been so frightened that the infant would be savaged by the apes that he insisted Ding-Ding be kept in a cage for his own protection. That didn't seem to bother the boy. He had toys to play with. But, in truth, Gilda had to admit that the language skills the child learned were, well, somewhat unusual. There isn't much need for a young boy to learn how to speak Gibbon in California, she whined to Mark just before their departure. But Ding-Ding had made a small, but significant, contribution to science. Gilda remembered how extraordinary it was watching him and Ringo talk to each other with made up signs. He was a bright boy. He would do well with Mark. She remembered her son fondly and wasn't too concerned that she couldn't visualize his face. Maybe Mark would send a photo. Diane and Rosebud moved off towards the north. Gilda followed, her binoculars at the ready.

Rumah Sehat longhouse

Two men from the Hong Neiyi Timber Company, a flabby Chinese and a skinny Malay, roared up to the dock of Rumah Sehat in a red and white speedboat and clambered up the rough, log ladders to the longhouse. Instead of waiting politely for permission to enter, they barged onto the communal porch and demanded to be taken to the headman, Ding Ajang.

A frightened, young boy showed the strangers Ding Ajang's rooms. They knocked. Getting no reply, they walked in, frightening Ding Ajang's aged mother, who was lying on cushions on the linoleum floor playing with her infant granddaughter.

Ding Ajang had been in another part of the longhouse when the boy fetched him. He walked slowly to his own quarters and confronted the men.

"Good afternoon," he said in Malay.

"Good afternoon. You are Ding Ajang?" the Chinese visitor replied, his Malay accented and harsh.

"Yes. Who are you?" Ding Ajang asked, looking at their mud-caked shoes soiling his home.

"We are from Hong Neiyi. May we sit down?"

Ding Ajang pointed to the floor. His mother slowly walked upstairs with the child.

After a few minutes of discussion about the weather, the river levels and the fate of the national soccer team, the strangers came to the point.

"We have received the letters you have written complaining about various aspects of the timber operations," the Malay said in his native tongue, using vocabulary that Ding could not totally comprehend. Ding's wife, acting on a stimulus-response reaction ingrained through decades of waiting on visitors, arrived with a pitcher of sweet, milky tea and stale biscuits she had purchased the last time the provision boat had stopped at the longhouse.

Ding Ajang replied: "And it's gotten worse. Bad hunting. No fishing. Dirty water. Noise. It's so dangerous you take your life in your hands just going for a bath."

"We sympathize with you, Ding Ajang, we really do. Which is why we are here today. Our owners, who are powerful people – you would recognize their names if we were empowered to tell you – have asked me to express their regret. They are willing to express that regret in a tangible way and would like to give you a gift of three hundred dollars for your trouble."

"Three hundred! For a poor, illiterate villager like me?"

"That's right."

He turned, without rising, and called out: "Bunga. Come down, please. Now."

The group turned to the stairway that led to Ding's upper quarters. A bright little girl appeared at the head of the stairs and slowly eased her way halfway down, holding the railing and walking with a pronounced limp. "What is it, Papa? I'm playing."

"Nothing, honey. Go back to your toys."

She muttered something about grownups never knowing what they want and eased herself back up.

"That's my daughter," Ding Ajang said proudly.

"Beautiful girl."

"She doesn't walk too well," Ding Ajang added.

The visitors kept quiet.

"She cut her foot on one of the branches in the river. One of your branches. She cut her heel tendon. She will never walk properly again.

"Surely you can't blame us for sticks in the river?"

Ding remained silent.

"Look, we are sorry. We didn't know you had suffered personally, I mean your family. We can certainly increase the gift to five hundred dollars."

"And in return?"

"You sign a receipt. Here it is."

The paper was written in Bahasa Melayu, the official language of Manusia, which in its formal, written form is nearly as unapproachable as literary French. Ding could not understand much of it, but saw enough to force him to put it down. "This is a receipt?"

"Yes."

"Anything else?"

The two strangers looked at each other. "Actually, it is more than a receipt," the Chinese man said, turning on a 'let's be pals' smile that is often found in the repertoire of insurance salesmen. "It makes you a partner in future timber extraction around Rumah Sehat. There could be substantial money resulting for you … and your longhouse, of course."

"I am not an educated man. But I think you are asking me to give you permission to cut trees on traditional, Kayan land."

"Excuse me, Ding Ajang," argued the Malay. "There is no such thing as traditional Kayan land. The forests on the upper Hotut River belong to all the people of Manusia." He switched into his lawyer's patter. "The lands are, therefore, under the jurisdiction of the Government of Manusia. Which has leased the lands to Hong Neiyi. Our generous managers wish to share the income with you and your friends."

"You think my daughter's foot is worth five hundred dollars?"

"No, of course not … but …"

"And you think I will give you permission to rape the trees on our land?"

"But, as I explained, it is not your land. It belongs …"

"We have a saying, among the Kayan. When you go to the river and see a fruit floating on the water, before you grab it you should first make sure that it is not attached to a crocodile."

"Please be reasonable, Mister Ding. This is a good deal. You will earn a lot of money and …"

"And what?" Ding Ajang said, cutting off the Chinese.

"And if you don't accept the offer, you will wind up with nothing. Because, regardless of what you do, we will continue to cut the trees on our land. And how smart will you look then?"

"Get out of my house before I break the law against head-hunting."

"Look, you idiot. You natives think you own this place. You don't. Take what's coming to you. You'll be happier. I promise."

Ding's neighbors had heard this increasingly violent exchange. Several men walked in just as Ding Ajang slugged the Chinese, breaking his nose. Blood dripped on the ginger snaps.

The two men from the timber company pushed their way out of

the rustic apartment. The Kayan group looked for a sign from Ding that they should stop the men from leaving. Instead, Ding indicated that the strangers could go. The Chinese and the Malay from Hong Neiyi scurried to their motorboat, but before pulling away from the dock, the Malay turned back to the throng and shouted: "You jungle bunnies don't know what you're up against. Come see us when you change your mind. We're just up the river." The boat pulled away. "Assholes," he muttered under his breath in English.

CHAPTER 15

27 July. 16:00.

Rumah Sehat longhouse

When she lived in San Francisco, Gilda sometimes took her out-of-town friends to see Alcatraz. The few visitors she had at Camp Trinil were treated to an afternoon at a genuine Kayan longhouse.

The day before, she had sent Bujang back to his home with instructions to set up a small party. A little *tuak* rice wine. Some dancing. Some conversation – there were always a few young Kayans in residence who had completed enough school to speak English reasonably well. In exchange for this hospitality, the longhouse people got the chance to sell a few handicrafts, meet some new people and pay back Gilda for having hired a dozen men from the longhouse to work at Camp Trinil.

However, Bujang had a more complex brief than usual. Gilda had told him that B.B. Derek was after something specific and Bujang's job was to arrange a seemingly-natural parade of residents who would perform in support of Camp Trinil's future.

Gilda, B.B., Gerry and Bujang crowded into the camp's longboat, a twenty-foot long, narrow, wooden dugout whose sides rode four inches above the water level. The boat wobbled and leaked, but it arrived in half an hour, thereby saving the group a two-hour walk

During the trip downriver, Bujang, who was at the helm, deftly avoided snags and debris from the timber operations. Two Hong Neiyi speedboats passed heading upriver, their rooster tails spraying the passengers in the Camp Trinil boat. B.B., unable to make conversation over the 'bebberroom' of the straining outboard

149

engine, tried to take photos of the passing, forested shore, but was frustrated by the boat's motion and the sweat that dripped into the viewfinder, obscuring her vision.

The longhouse stood on a bank that overlooked the Hotut River. The river was low and muddy in the dry season, but even so some women washed their clothes while small, naked children splashed in the shallows. The longhouse dock was sitting lopsided on the mud and about eight feet higher than the edge of the river. However, a huge log was anchored into the river and Bujang leapt out of the boat onto the tree trunk, into which the Kayan residents had cut simple, shallow steps.

He reached down and helped B.B. out of the boat, grabbing her left hand with his right, then tightly holding her upper arm to steady her.

He gestured to enquire whether she wanted help up the ladder.

"It's okay, I can manage," B.B. said to both Bujang and Gilda, with a hint of annoyance.

"*Dia mau jalan sendiri, Bujang,*" Gilda said. She wants to try it alone.

The ladder was actually a series of four tree trunks chained together that led to the longhouse. Minutes before the Camp Trinil expedition had arrived, a giggling band of children had scampered up the log, leaving it slippery from mud. B.B. managed to take two steps before finding herself precariously balancing on one leg, like a tightrope walker, before losing her equilibrium completely and being forced to leap off the log into the mud. By twisting and breaking her fall with her arm and the right side of her body, she was able to barely avoid a savage-looking branch embedded in the gook. B.B. sunk to her knees, two feet into the brown-gray ooze, and became stuck. Her US Army surplus, dark green, bush pants were plastered to her legs.

Gilda, still in the longboat, watched the scene with satisfaction. Now, if only I can make it up without slipping …, Gilda thought.

Bujang resisted the urge to laugh. Instead, he calmly reached down and pulled B.B. back onto the log. Schloorp. One foot was wrenched from the mud, minus a shoe. Schlerp. The second foot, similarly denuded. The mud had eaten her Reeboks. Bujang shouted at one of the young boys who were laughing from the longhouse porch and the lad scampered down the tree trunks to retrieve the shoes from their muddy tomb.

This time, B.B. gratefully held Bujang's hand as he guided the woman to her grand entrance. Gilda thought he held her a little tighter – and a little longer – than he needed to.

"Hello. *Selamote deenger haree,*" B.B. said to the curious assembly, who had the good manners to pretend she was speaking decent Malay.

Gilda arrived next, pleased with her safe passage. "*Selamat tengah hari, teman teman*" she articulated.

They were greeted by an old lady who offered glasses of a pale, milky, fermented brew.

"No, thank you very much, I hardly drink," B.B. said.

"Oh, but you must. It's a big insult if you refuse," Gilda whispered to the American. So B.B. downed a tumbler of *tuak* before being whisked away to the family's rooms by Bujang's sister, Mimes.

"Here, you can wash up," Mimes said in English, taking B.B.'s hand and leading her to a screened-off part of the kitchen which served as an informal bathroom. A huge, green, Chinese, stoneware jar, decorated with dragons, was filled with water. The wooden slats were damp and felt refreshingly cool.

"I think it will be more comfortable if you change from your pants to a sarong. I will give you some of my clothes," Mimes said as she left the American.

Minutes later, B.B. emerged, feeling much better in a red and green flowered, batik sarong and a faded, blue T-shirt which read: "A woman's place is on top."

The unexpected diversion had given Gilda time to choreograph the longhouse residents by placing them strategically along the common porch of the longhouse. However, first Gilda had asked for refreshments and the group, hosted by Bujang, his mother and two sisters, sat down for rice wine and warm Sprite.

"Thank you again for the clothes, Mimes," B.B. said.

"You're welcome."

"You speak such good English. Where did you learn?"

"Oh, no. I make many mistakes. I still am still taking my studies."

"Here in the longhouse?"

"No, we just have a primary school here. I go to the secondary school in Bohong. Now we have school holidays."

B.B. felt comfortable. Maybe too comfortable. A little dizzy, actually. Must be the sun. Surely not the rice wine, which tasted, she thought, a bit like weak lemonade mixed with milk. It wasn't very strong.

B.B. looked around the simple room. "I didn't notice the TV before."

"But you have seen TV, certainly," Mimes said, confused.

"Of course," B.B. answered, looking at the fuzzy black and white picture of a *Baywatch* episode.

"Your clothes fit me well. We're about the same size. Eight?" B.B. guessed.

"Medium," Mimes answered. "The color of your skin is good with the sarong."

"Funny, I was just thinking that I'd kill for skin like *yours*," B.B. said to the younger girl.

"But my skin is dark and ugly. You skin is white and beautiful."

"*Your* skin," B.B. corrected. "Y-O-U-R"

"Your skin. Thank you."

"Odd, isn't it? In America, most of the girls would lie in the sun all day to get a skin color like yours."

"Why would they do that?" Mimes asked.

"It's supposed to make them attractive. When you have a tan you look healthy."

"*You* don't have dark skin."

"Mimes, with red hair you get freckles. Freckles are my curse."

"Freckles, Madame Baby?"

"These things," she said, pointing to her forehead, then her nose, then her arms. "When I go out in the sun they become more and more orange and then my skin burns and I peel and I look like an apple that's been left in the sun too long."

"Then you are like us."

"How so?"

"We don't like the sun, either. Sun makes us ugly. White skin is good. You skin is good."

B.B. and Mimes talked and giggled for ten minutes, until Gilda broke in.

"Mimes, maybe Madame B.B. would like to take a walk and see the rest of the longhouse. Will you come with us?"

B.B. scooped up her cameras, her notebook, her tape recorder and weaved after the group. Gerry followed right behind, so he could position himself to make sure he was in any photos that might appear in *Nature's World*.

They strolled along the solid, hardwood *ruai* – the communal, partially-enclosed porch of Manusian longhouses which is the center of social interaction. The visitors from Camp Trinil attracted the attention of a black hunting dog – scrawny, mangy and with infected ears. He came by to sniff and was kicked out of the way by Bujang. The animal sulked by pissing on the guardrail.

Teenage boys stared at B.B. as she passed. Little children watched, fascinated, from a distance. Gerry went over to a group of urchins and made what he thought was a funny face. Two of the older youngsters laughed nervously at this strange man, but three of the toddlers, who had been brought up on tales in which evil, bearded giants ate naughty children who didn't finish their dinner, took one look at Gerry's curly, red beard and ran screaming to the nearest grown-up. Gerry turned and saw Mimes watching the scene. He smiled at her, turning on his boyish charm. She smiled politely and continued walking.

Bujang had arranged a cultural smorgasbord of traditional life styles. Tony Weng sat crosslegged, smoking a pipe, while he mended his monofilament fishing-net. He offered the visitors some rice wine and spoke, first to Bujang in Kayan, who explained to Gilda in Malay, who finally explained to B.B. in English, how his life depended on fishing, but things were difficult now because of the timber operators. Too much dirt washed into the rivers, killing the fish.

"That's a good shot," B.B. said as she focused. "Nice back light coming through the net. Uh, Gerry, would you mind moving a bit to the side, please? You're in the frame."

"Varoom, screech." A ten-year-old boy laughed as he provided sound effects to accompany a remote-controlled, toy car. The battery-powered Ferrari weaved between B.B. and Gilda and swerved to torment a puppy. Although the nearest race track was three countries away, the lad drove his toy with visions that he was at the wheel of one of the Formula One racers that were pictured in the magazine his father brought back from Singapore. The man was a foreman in the Hong Neiyi timber camp and twice a year flew to

Singapore for a holiday. He had promised to take his family later in the year and the boy was practicing so he could be cool like Singapore kids. His father had told him that there were stores there with dozens of different toy cars and the boy wanted to be able to 'drive' each of them perfectly, first time out.

The visitors stopped and chatted and sipped wine with Akan Ajang, who cleaned his shotgun and spoke about hunting. "No, I never hunt in the national park itself," Gilda ultimately translated, "but just outside." He took them into his family quarters, through the living area and out back into the cooking area, to show them a small deer he said he had found wandering near his vegetable garden, near the longhouse. B.B. got some nice shots of the man holding the fawn. By shifting her angle and zooming, which eliminated the distraction of Gerry peering over the man's shoulder, she was able to get some attractive close-ups.

B.B. was fascinated by old Usun Laing, who carved frightening masks and demon-like figures with huge phalluses. Gilda looked at Bujang. That was his cue to ask the man about the use of the masks. After making sure that B.B.'s glass was topped up, he explained, in Kayan, that he just used his imagination and made them for the tourists in the Hilton in Anjing. By the time the translation got sifted through Bujang and Gilda, B.B. learned fascinating information about how the upcountry Kelabits and, to a lesser extent, the Kayans, rely on omens in the form of migratory birds to determine when to plant the rice and when to seed, weed and harvest. The masks, she heard, were for those occasions when the bird horoscopes didn't quite work and the farmers needed to exert external influence with the fickle, agricultural gods. She bought several.

Once again, the toy Ferrari zipped into the crowd, bounced off a wooden figure whose phallus curved between its legs to become a monkey's tail and varoomed to an abrupt stop, when Bujang swept it off the ground and held it aloft, the toy's wheels still spinning. "Cut it out," he said to the boy in Kayan.

B.B. took photos of women weaving mats from strips of rattan they had collected in the forest. She bought two, without considering how she would get them home.

"That's a pretty bag," she said, pointing to a cylindrical, woven sack that had the walnut-colored patina of age. "Did you make that?" B.B. asked the woman.

It was time for dancing. The music started – a simple, insistent rhythm played on a three-stringed *sapeh* guitar. The women started it off and B.B. was transfixed at the grace and dignity of the women, regardless of their ages, as they crossed their feet as if each performing a *ronde de jambe*; each went into a *pirouetto* that would have been tricky for a professional dancer and weaved their hands through the muggy afternoon like cosmic painters creating wisps of fluff, their fingers arching back to wave the feathered gloves they wore.

"I wish I could dance like that," B.B. whispered to Gerry. For, although B.B. had studied ballet for five years as a schoolgirl, her hips had blossomed more quickly than her passion for Tchaikovsky and she had reluctantly turned to academia and tournament chess.

As soon as Mimes finished dancing, she determinedly approached B.B.. She and several other women pulled B.B., protesting, to her feet, quickly tied on the feathers, placed the rattan cap with the hornbill feathers on her head and stood around her in an admiring circle.

B.B. was too drunk to feel overly self-conscious. She waved her arms and imagined herself floating on a cloud; the insistent music helped her imagine she was a celestial traffic cop directing the wind. She danced for ten minutes, until she glided back to earth, exhausted and happy. She burped her goodbyes while Bujang led her back, in the early, evening dusk, to the longboat.

Hong Neiyi timber camp

The Hong Neiyi timber camp stopped work around four in the afternoon and Jong Il Kim went back to his lonely quarters and poured himself a large shot of Courvoisier cognac. He dozed off for several minutes and awoke when his Rottweiler puppy, Manja, snuggled against his neck. It had been a bitch of a week.

First, those jokers had Urs in their shotgun sights and lost him. Then, the assistant to the Minister had radioed back. "Listen carefully, Jong," Tusau Padan had said, in carefully enunciated American English, as if he was speaking to a child. The Korean had fumed at the Malay's insolence, remembering every word.

"Send this unfortunate Susah fellow downriver in a speedboat tonight," Padan had ordered. "Explain only that you believe he is dying and needs urgent medical treatment. Send him only with a single boat driver. Someone you trust. Instruct the driver that, when he gets to the Hong Neiyi harbor in Bohong, he is to make two wide circles in a clockwise direction and head back upstream for a mile to the first big right bend. Someone will take the patient. Your driver is to return upriver immediately. I mean immediately, Jong. Tell him that if he goes into town and looks for whores, like all your drivers do, we'll feed his balls to the wild pigs."

As he stood under the cold shower, Jong Il Kim meticulously reviewed the new security measures he had created. He was skeptical, however, that these ding-dong Manusians had the skill to implement his plan. It would work, though. He would order that each timber truck be equipped with a specially-designed compartment, camouflaged as a huge tree trunk. Two armed guards would crouch in the hollowed-out log and a third in the cab. They would be ordered to shoot troublemakers on sight.

CHAPTER 16

27 July. 18:00.

Rumah Sehat longhouse

While the visitors from Camp Trinil were outside on the *ruai*, Urs and the Penan had entered the longhouse through Ding Ajang's kitchen. It was a risk, but Urs did not expect any problem as long as he stayed quietly in Ding Ajang's quarters.

It was vital, Urs felt, to make sure that the logistics were right for the next morning. Although he viewed it as primarily a Penan exercise, the Kayan were helping with logistics. It was a big breakthrough having the Kayan help out and he wanted to make sure that everything went well.

As usual, the Penan looked around the room with quiet, wide eyes. Avalon, Urs' foster brother, whispered in the Swiss man's ear. "I didn't know Ding Ajang has the same totem as our family."

"How do you know that?" Urs asked.

"On his shirt. Look," Avalon said, his eyes picking out a small crocodile on Ding Ajang's new fire-engine red knit.

Having been scolded for playing on the *ruai* while white people visited, Robert Anyi screeched his Ferrari into his uncle Ding Ajang's room. The Penan were startled by the intrusion, then laughed nervously when they saw that it was a city-toy. How did it work? Urs asked the boy if he could play with it. Reluctantly, the boy surrendered the controls. Urs stood and piloted the car back and forth, not nearly as expertly as Robert, but with a modicum of facility that improved rapidly. Urs manoeuvered the Ferrari underneath the TV, around the dinner dishes, straight at the cat and, finally, directly into a tumbler of *tuak*, which rolled across the

157

linoleum. The boy was nervous that this crazy foreigner would use up his expensive batteries and gestured that he would like the toy back, please. Urs reluctantly gave up the controls.

By this time, the Camp Trinil group had departed, but the *sapeh* player continued his simple melodies. He was joined by his friends with guitars and another young man with a cassette player. Soon, centuries-old rhythms alternated with the Beatles and Jim Reeves. Men and a few women, having finished dinner, sat around the musicians, chatting, smoking, laughing at B.B.'s tumble into the mud. After an hour, the men decided it was time for them to engage in a classic bit of displacement behavior.

Headhunting used to be the sole means by which a young man in Borneo could prove himself a man – bring back a head and get the girl. Never mind if the head is that of a defenseless old woman or an innocent man ambushed while going to weed his rice field. These days the male psyche is in a bad state. Most of the day-to-day chores are done by the women and although the men do most of the hunting, there are few, real tests of their masculinity now that headhunting has been deemed unsocial by the British colonial powers and, more recently, the Islamic, Manusian Sultans. The ultimate blood sport had been replaced by well-educated and, generally, unemployable men who wear animal skins and wave a *parang* through the air.

Night had fallen and the dancing had been going on for an hour, when Urs and the Penan walked quietly out to the *ruai*. The Kayans nodded to Urs and shifted to make room for the visitors.

One man was just finishing his dance when he spotted the unexpected dignitary. He strode up to the Swiss and welcomed him in English. "Please. You will dance for us. It will be our honor."

Urs nodded and donned the clouded leopard skin cape, which was studded with black and white tail feathers from the helmeted hornbill. He placed on his head a woven helmet decorated with the grey and white patterned feathers of the argus pheasant. He accepted the ceremonial *parang,* the blade of which had been hand-wrought by a Penan artisan and the hilt of which was carved out of deer horn. Urs recognized the motifs of the Tree of Life, with the animals of the world living in cautious harmony with each other.

The *sapeh* player strummed patiently, waiting for the performer.

Urs bent down, as if praying. Then, with a shout, he leapt over the seated *sapeh* player and into the center of the dance area. Urs was big and awkward, but he knew his audience. He slowly twirled, eyes on the horizon like a hawk, studying the enemy's encampment. He sighted his prey. Urs walked in a circle, as if stalking a deer, and then he crept up on his opponent, waddling duck-like until he was within swooping range. He held his breath and looked up at the stars, imploringly, then turned to the crowd. He saw Mimes and his eyes asked for her approval to kill the enemy. She nodded. He gave a wink, and he whirled and leaped, screamed and flew. The sturdy porch swayed and bounced underfoot. Dogs and little children scattered. The men laughed, the vibrations unsettling the quarts of *tuak* in their guts. Pigs squealed below the longhouse as Urs waved his *parang*, lopped off the head of his enemy and, in a moment of inspired improvisation, grabbed a hapless black and white puppy by the tail and brought back the yelping head/dog to Mimes, as a souvenir. It was not the head of John the Baptist – but, then, Mimes was not Salomé. Urs sat down to howls and cheers.

In the lantern light, Mimes' face had a soft, red glow. At the urging of her girl friends, Mimes walked to where the men sat, poured a large glass of *tuak* and stood in front of Urs. She then began to sing a *pantun*, a lyric, poem-like chant that the woman would improvise to suit the occasion. She sang of Urs' success in battle, of his powerful physique, of his friendship with the Kayans. She looked into his eyes and held the glass to his lips. He took a sip. Not satisfied, she pulled his head back by his ponytail and poured the rice wine down his throat. Urs did not realize he could have saved himself by singing a *pantun* to Mimes, forcing her to drink, but nobody was about to help him. The people of Rumah Sehat watched, fascinated, as he drained the glass to their cheers.

Fifteen minutes later, Urs walked to the other end of the *ruai* for some air. He was soon joined by Mimes. "Meet me at the first upriver bend of the river?" he half ordered, half asked. "There's a clearing there. Half an hour after I leave?" Mimes nodded.

Urs shared several more glasses of rice wine before gathering Liebchen, who had been tormenting a kitten, and excusing himself to return to the forest. The Penan, feeling uncomfortable in the longhouse, had left an hour earlier, carrying a large bundle. Urs walked through Ding Ajang's rooms, into the kitchen and down the back, tree-trunk ladder. He walked around the longhouse, guided by the light of the half moon, and headed for the river, where the longhouse's boats were tied. He had some time before Mimes came down, so he took off his loincloth, carefully placed his glasses on the fabric and jumped into the water. He swam upriver for ten minutes and, by swimming hard, he just managed to avoid being swept downriver by the current. As he waded ashore, a powerful flashlight caught him in its beam. The naked Swiss, in water up to his thighs, sinking slowly into the muck, said nothing.

"We have you, Mister Urs," the voice said. "Maybe you can't see us, but there are four of us, with shotguns. We are not like the idiots on that timber truck. You won't escape this time. Put your hands up."

Liebchen, who detested the water and preferred to stay on the shore, did not recognize that her master was in danger. However, she did recognize that he did not have his glasses, which she fetched. She went to the edge of the water to hand them to Urs, expecting him to come forward.

The security police were startled by the unexpected movement by their feet. The man with the flashlight shone the light on Liebchen and the frightened animal scurried through his legs, flinging the glasses back over her shoulder, towards Urs. Urs quickly fell backwards into the water, which released his feet from the mud.

"Stop, you idiot!" one of the security men shouted, as he wildly fired his shotgun in Urs' direction. A few pellets grazed the Swiss man's shoulder, but most missed him by a foot and, instead, shattered his glasses that were in mid-flight.

Desperately, Urs stayed underwater and swam into the middle of the river. He drifted downriver for half a mile, before swimming for the near shore and stumbling back to the Penan encampment. The security men cursed all manner of gods and ran thirty yards along the river bank to where their motorboat was tied. They drifted downriver in search of the man and saw nothing.

Mimes had just been leaving the longhouse when she heard the shot. She reached the river bank minutes later and saw the footprints of three men – one with no shoes and two men with boots. She picked up a two-yard long piece of soft, blue cloth that was on the shore and watched the moonglow on the water for several moments. She was soon joined by others who had heard the shots. Some of them thought they saw a speedboat pass out of view as it turned the downriver bend. None of them saw Urs' granny glasses, diopters minus 6, sink into the mud.

CHAPTER 17

28 July. 02:00.

Penan encampment

Urs woke four hours before dawn. Maya knew better than to ask where he was going. He never replied when he left long before dawn and sauntered off into the forest. Even Liebchen stayed curled up by the still-warm embers of the cooking fire.

Early each morning, Urs would pick a tree, by some instinct that he couldn't explain if he had been asked, sit against it and hum a Swiss lullaby. "*Schlaaf Chindli schlaaf,*" he hummed. It was his form of meditation and it helped him get in touch with the forest life around him and center him for another day.

Usually, his half hour of meditation would relax him and help him focus on the reasons why he was stuck in the middle of Earth's oldest rainforest, so far from everything he had taken for granted prior to arriving in Manusia. As he meditated, he would hear the rustle of small forest animals, the whistling of the birds and watch bats swoop up flying insects. He sat against a hardwood tree and made it his cathedral.

On this morning, he did not have any feeling that this was the holiest place on earth, that he was fighting an ecological *jihad*. Leave that to the real radicals. What he felt was a combination of peace and of fatigue, the feeling that everything here was right and it was about to go so wrong. He had done what he could. He couldn't fight everyone else's fight for them. His parents – his biological parents – were aging – surely they needed him as much as Laki and his adopted family in the wilderness. He hadn't spoken Swiss-German for years, yet he could identify several dozen medicinal plants. He could make a fishing line from vine, he could build a branch shelter in minutes and he could endure long nights of mosquito-generated insomnia – yet he had no idea whether the Swiss had made it into the World Cup qualifiers. He could survive on land snails and grilled python, but he yearned for a glass of Goron and a *rösti*. Where was the balance in this equation?

* * * * *

Urs and the Penans moved silently into the timber camp.

Avalon had scouted the area for the past two weeks. "Three armed watchmen," he had reported. "Sometimes they walk around, usually they sleep."

"Anything else?" Urs had asked.

"Seven dogs. Three bitches – one in heat and one with puppies."

Armed with blowpipe darts encrusted with diluted poison, the Penan circled the timber camp and sensed the location of the dogs. The dogs smelled the Penan and came to investigate. Urs had seen the Penan steal through the forest and creep up on seemingly hypnotized deer. Domestic dogs, even those that are expected to be aggressive watch dogs, were no problem. The men whispered softly to the mongrels to approach and when the animals came within range, whooft, a quick series of blowpipe darts sank into their hindquarters and sent them to sleep for a few hours.

This morning, the timber camp guards were together in a shack on the outskirts of the timber camp complex. One of the guards was napping and the other two were playing cards when the Penan quickly came up behind them, clamped a wodge of leaves into each man's mouth and trussed each of them like a wounded, wild pig. Gathering the oily rags that lay on the ground, the Penan blindfolded and gagged the men and hung them upside down from the beams of the wooden building. The men were unharmed, but not happy.

Urs joined his friends as they silently leapt from shadow to shadow to enter the sprawling motor pool, a partly-covered area housing six timber trucks, eight Caterpillars, assorted forklifts, Land Cruisers and an off-the-road, Yamaha motorcycle. A single, bare, 60-watt light bulb swung on a cable in the pre-dawn breeze, generating gently waving shapes. Once inside, the Penan stood motionless, hiding in the shadows of trucks and pillars, waiting to sense if danger was present. Engine parts littered the hard-packed, dirt floor. Engine blocks sat rusting, welder's masks and propylene tanks lay in the dirt. Urs glanced at his friends. For them, he imagined, this heavy machinery was alien and inexplicable, products of a civilization that they knew existed, but chose not to join. Urs, however, saw the trucks as agents of destruction. He stepped gingerly, avoiding wrenches and oil cans scattered on the floor. He breathed deeply to calm himself. In his family's work shed, every tool had a place, nothing was left lying about, your daily chores were not completed until you tidied up after yourself.

One group of guerillas stayed in the motor pool area and set about cutting wires, clogging exhausts, slashing tires – all the usual, schoolboy eco-tricks Urs had taught them. They were finished in twenty minutes and, on their way out, they stopped on the bridge that spanned the Manusia River to make one last point.

The second group, led by Bujang, silently entered Jong Il Kim's quarters.

* * * * *

Jong Il Kim woke, as was his custom, just before dawn this morning. He was startled to find a letter on the pillow, a foot from his head.

"We mean you no personal harm," the letter began. "Perhaps you do not even understand why we are angry," it continued in English, written by Robin Nawan Bala. "The forests are our homes. From them we get food, clothing and pleasures. We do this without harming to anyone. We have done so for thousands of years. We can continue to do this if we are left alone. This is our land. We have been lived here since before Manusia existed. We bury our ancestors in the forest where your timber trucks work. We pray to the gods in the trees that your machines cut down. We get fish and turtles from the rivers that now run dirty and which are rooned. We, not you, are the sons and daughters and children of the soil. We ask you to please STOP. This is not your country. We would not go to your country and cut down your homes. Please do not do it to ours." It was signed: "The people of Mount Malu".

Urs had asked the author to write out the text two additional times. These copies he had carefully folded, with short letters he had written – one addressed to a journalist in Singapore and another to a rainforest campaigner in London. Hopefully, one of them would get through.

Jong Il Kim read the letter several times. He was not a man to be easily intimidated. Who the fuck did those people think they were? How did they get into his bedroom? He wanted to face them himself, man to man.

Jong stormed out of bed and jumped into the simple, attached bathroom. He peed, brushed his teeth and took a cold shower. It all took no more than three minutes. He went to the dresser for a clean pair of underwear and gasped as he opened the drawer. His first reaction was a visceral shiver, which was soon replaced by fury. Seeping blood into his boxer shorts lay Manja – a poison dart through her eye.

* * * * *

Jong Il Kim rummaged through the hamper for the previous day's underwear, dressed and walked outside as a gray dawn approached. At this time of the morning, it always looked like it was going to be a rainy, miserable day, but you couldn't tell in the tropics. Sometimes it rained. Sometimes the gray disappeared and the sun beamed down like a cosmic microwave. It did not take long for Ramsay Wong, the security chief, to fill him in on the morning's events. He ended it by asking the boss to walk with him down to the river.

Jong and Wong joined a group of men who had gathered on the rickety dock that provided both mooring and toilet facilities. All turned a communal gaze upriver. A large banner hung from a 50-yard long, modern, steel bridge that spanned the upper reaches of the Hotut River. It fluttered lightly in the gentle, dawn breeze.

Urs had gotten the idea from one of his correspondents in Denmark, who was an activist in Greenpeace. "Make a sign and display it prominently. Show them that you can be anywhere, do anything," he had advised. "Hold off on the violence as long as you can. That will backfire on you. Just make sure that everybody sees what you do. Go for the big gimmick."

Urs hadn't been too sure what a gimmick was until Bujang had explained the concept. However, the idea for this specific gimmick came from Mimes, who was proving to be a valuable member of the brain-trust. She had organized the women of Rumah Sehat to purchase the cloth and sew it using an old, foot-powered Singer. Three high school students, home on vacation, wrote and painted the message.

Urs and his colleagues watched quietly, invisibly, from a similar vantage point across the river. They, too, had a good view of the home-made banner, on which was written in English: 'Leave us our Forests'. When the light became brighter, Urs snapped off six quick photos and silently disappeared into the jungle.

CHAPTER 18

28 July. 07:00.

Camp Trinil

Stanford Business School had taught B.B. to tackle one situation at a time, to think rationally, to see things through. However, those professors, she thought, had never gone through what I've just gone through. This place is off the wall.

B.B. brushed her teeth using the bottle of water that Gilda had sworn had been boiled.

She tried to list the pluses and minuses. The people here are flakes, but the forest is important (but not as beautiful as I had imagined it would be). The longhouse people, even if I discount what they said by 50%, told a convincing story about why they need the forest. On the other hand, Gilda and her orangutan fixation is doing zip to save it. Urs is fighting the fight of the century, but what chance does he really have? Bujang is an interesting man (with great shoulders) and I think he knows more than he lets on. Everybody hates me. The bottom line: who the hell knows what's going on? Which put B.B. in a very strong position – since she was the one person to whom people would turn to make it all clear.

B.B. had asked Gilda to make another appointment to see Gerry so she could get more information on the sign language project. B.B. found Gilda at the end of the dock, squatting on her haunches as she chatted to the women who washed the clothes in the cola-colored river.

B.B. concluded that the tension between her and Gilda served no purpose and she might as well get the most out of her visit. On the sartorial side, B.B. had learned something about dressing in the tropics. She wore a T-shirt and a thin, batik skirt wrapped over her bathing suit. She ran into Gilda and they fell into step on the way to the dining hall for breakfast.

"Thanks again for organizing the longhouse visit yesterday," B.B. said, as she nibbled a fresh papaya.

"My pleasure," Gilda answered. "How's your head?"

"A bit soft. That stuff has a kick."

"Not as bad as the *arak*. That's their moonshine."

"I think I'll pass."

"Have some cereal. Don't worry about the milk, it's powdered and we mix it with boiled water. So, what did you think about all of it?"

"All of what?"

"You know, life in the longhouse."

"Well, I got the feeling that the daily life you showed me was somehow exaggerated and that the explanations gained a bit in translation."

Gilda said nothing for five seconds. The two women continued walking. "I'm sorry you think that," she said bitterly.

"Damnit, Gilda. Tell me if I'm wrong."

"You *are* wrong, but you don't want to admit it. The people in that longhouse need the forest and that's the truth."

"God, I get the feeling we're speaking six different languages. Let's change the subject. What about this sign language business?" B.B. asked as they walked. "I mean, what does it prove?"

Gilda thought for a moment. Gilda's thinking drove B.B. crazy. It drove most people crazy. Gilda had developed the useful trait of going quiet whenever a question of greater magnitude than 'what did you have for breakfast' was asked. She would purse her lips, half of her mouth would frown, the other side would smile. Her hesitation before replying was so intense that, in bad light, the person with whom she was talking might think she had fallen asleep.

Gilda mulled over the question. What does the sign language project prove? "It tries to integrate the theories of dexterity as a measure of intelligence with standard measures that rely on social communication skills," Gilda answered after ten seconds.

Come on, Gilda, B.B. thought. Here I am trying to be civilized and you start playing head games. "Could you say that in English, please?"

"Pardon me?" Gilda asked, as she turned to the pale woman.

"You heard me, Gilda. Cut it. What the fuck does all this orangutan sign language stuff mean? Why do you bother? More to the point, why should my donors bother? What are we collecting money for?"

"Oh, you and your donors," Gilda said testily, then apparently changed her mind and lightened her tone. "That's what I was trying to explain," she said. "We know the orangutan is among the most dexterous of animals. We had an animal in camp once, what *was* his name – Morgan was it, or Oliver – anyway, he picked two locks on his cage to escape, another who was a whiz at putting square pegs into square holes. Another who could play frisbee like a college student in San Diego. That surely is a sign of intelligence, but how much? So we decided to test it.

"This was all before Gerry came, of course, but I did a bit of psychology in college. We used a test which gauges intelligence based on manual dexterity, not language skills. Do you know that a few of the orangutans – three, I think – scored in the normal range of human intelligence?"

This is better. B.B. pressed the microphone of the Sony Professional Walkman tape recorder closer to Gilda, having found that the ambient noise of the rainforest, not to mention the generator from Camp Trinil, which was two hundred yards away, played havoc with recording quality.

"No other animal had ever tested that high on manual problems. Not the chimpanzee, not the gorilla. Although, in all honesty, if they tried it with porpoises, I'm sure they would be absolutely brilliant – if only they could get their flippers to work properly.

"When I was in the States during my last lecture tour, you know I stopped by the Foundation and met Penny Paterson, who was working with Koko – she, too, was writing an article for *Nature's World* and we just kind of got together," Gilda said. "Funny how it works. She told me what she was doing and said that Koko had learned more than 375 Ameslan words and scored between 85 and 95 on the Stanford-Binet.

"Well, I *know* that my orangutans are smarter than her gorillas. Gorillas might be better signers, because they live communally and are more used to talking with each other than orangs, which live alone, usually. Gilda decided to dare a joke. "You know, the Javanese used to say that orangutans could talk, but didn't – for fear of being put to work."

"Anecdotal, Gilda," B.B. said sternly, wondering how she was every going to get through to this woman. "Facts. Just facts."

Gilda scroonched her lips together while she seemed to ponder the question. For added inspiration, she looked up towards the treetops. Almost without thinking, she flicked a metallic-blue colored beetle from her arm. This tiny action was enough to break her from her pout and stimulate her to rejoin the human race.

"Well, Darwin claimed that animals show wonder, curiosity, reasoning and a sense of beauty. He even thought that animals can believe in spiritual agencies which, taken to its logical conclusion, means they could believe in God."

B.B. saw that she was going to have to spoon-feed this interview. "What about the search for food? What does that tell us about orangutan intelligence?"

"I was coming to that," Gilda said with annoyance, for she had been thinking about raising that point herself. "You know how much they eat. Well, how do they find enough food? There aren't *that* many fruit trees out here and they're far apart. Well, what happens is that they remember which trees were in flower and return to them a few weeks later when the fruit is ripe. I've even seen orangs remember the location of durian trees that last fruited several years earlier. During their daily strolls, they invariably choose a route that takes them past the greatest number of fruit trees, as if they had a mental map. Say, can you use that?"

"Uh, use what, Gilda?"

"Mental map. It's a nice phrase, isn't it?"

"Great. And then you wanted to try to talk with the animals yourself."

"Right. I arranged for Gerry to come out to test just how smart these animals are – particularly the ones that started off life as people."

B.B. was astounded – this was the longest conversation she had ever had with Gilda. She didn't want to break the flow, but there was one question she had to ask.

"Gilda, there have been some, uh, disturbing stories that Gerry

170

is falsifying data, that he's pretending the animals are smarter than they actually are. Do you think ..."

"Who told you that?" Gilda demanded.

"No one. It's a story going around the office. And yesterday, during the class, Gerry's scientific method seemed a bit slipshod."

A four breath pause. B.B. knew that Gilda was the independent observer who regularly confirmed that Gerry's apes had actually learned the signs he claimed they had learned. She had to authenticate his data. "Let me tell you something. Gerry Schwartz is a true scientist, a scholar about on a level with Wallace or Darwin. He's doing important work with important subjects. He's an equal among equals."

* * * * *

After breakfast, they walked the short distance to the feeding platform. Class was in session. Ringo was working on sentence construction. Gerry would perform an action – eating a banana by himself on the corner of the platform, for example – and Ringo would sign the appropriate gestures to describe what was happening. Gerry thought he noticed Ringo sign: 'Gerry - eat - selfish - Ringo - no - banana', although the psychologist knew that, in all likelihood, the ape was signing his favorite sentence: 'Ringo - hungry - banana.'

Gerry then grabbed a rope hanging over the platform and swung in large circles, screaming like a gibbon and waving one arm. That time, Ringo did sign something different: 'Gerry - play - funny' – a phrase he had learned after several weeks of tedious practice and which he called up from his memory whenever Gerry yelled and carried on like an animal.

Gerry returned to earth, slightly winded, his frizzy, auburn hair wet with sweat, which smelled of the rice he had been eating for countless months.

"Well, maybe we should continue what we were talking about before. It would be interesting to hear Gerry's viewpoint on orangutan intelligence."

Gerry pretended he had just noticed the two women. "Good morning," he said. "Did you see that sign?"

B.B. invited herself onto the platform. Looking over his shoulder at his notebook, she asked, "How do you write down those signs?

What do all those squiggles mean?"

"They're shorthand for each student's gestures."

"Such as?"

"I'll show you. Ringo, *apa ini?*" Gerry asked, holding up a banana. The ape made the banana sign – an extended, left forefinger and a peeling motion with the thumb and forefinger of the right hand. "See, B.B. That's the shorthand for banana," he said, scribbling a triangular ideogram that looked like a refugee from the Rosetta stone.

"That's fascinating. Do you mind if I take a picture of your notebook entries? That's science at work."

"Uh, yes, I'm afraid I do mind," Gerry said. "I've developed my own special code and I don't want anyone else to steal it."

"I promise not to use the pictures until you publish your paper. You'll surely have to explain your system then in any case," B.B. said.

"Sure, but it's more than that. I know what the notes mean. But in the wrong hands, someone might misinterpret them."

"The only thing I see in your notes is an abundance of little triangle shapes. But then, I'm not a trained observer. You mean someone might look at the raw data and conclude that the apes didn't really learn everything you say they've learned?"

Gerry was caught in a corner. "Look, everybody has his own way of working. I have mine, you have yours. The graduate review council of the University of North Carolina is happy – I might say, very happy – with my preliminary results. Surely that should be good enough for you, too."

"Gerry, what are you trying to accomplish here?" B.B. said, getting out her tape recorder and placing the powerful microphone on the platform between them.

On seeing that B.B. was getting her camera ready, Gerry fluffed up his red beard so it covered his acne scars, put on his mirrored aviator sunglasses and launched into a detailed history of theories about orangutan intelligence.

"Why can't you just teach them to speak?" B.B. asked abruptly.

B.B.'s questioning of Gerry's scientific method had shifted his self-confidence to the pit of his stomach, where it was being eaten away by green acid that turns carrots into food but which lets beer go by virtually unscathed – one of life's conundrums he would have to address in Nirvana some afternoon. Nonetheless, he plodded on. "Right. Speech. Why they can't speak." He explained that the problem is anatomical. Apes have differently shaped lips, tongues and palates to man, and some of the apes' natural cries are made as they breathe in, unlike humans – who speak as they exhale. "There was this American researcher named William H. Furness," Gerry explained in a low voice, as if he was lecturing a particularly slow group of students. "This Furness dude was one frustrated researcher. He decided that his pet orangutan should learn to say the word 'cup'. So, Furness took a spatula and pushed the animal's tongue to the back of her throat. When she took a deep breath and exhaled through her mouth he let go of the spatula. This produced a sort of 'ka' sound. To complete the word, he snapped her lips shut when she completed the exhalation. This produced the 'p' vocalization."

B.B. laughed like she hadn't heard a joke for weeks. "Can't you imagine this guy playing with the monkey's mouth?" she asked no one in particular.

Gilda scowled. "Orangutans are apes. Not monkeys."

"Then what happened?"

"Well, that's the point. Nothing much happened. The orangutan only said the word when old Furness was around playing with her mouth. But, he *was* vindicated years later."

"What happened?" B.B. asked.

Gerry's voice became deep and dramatic. This was one of his party stories. "The ape was dying of fever and was thirsty. Since, during most of her life, she had always drunk water from a cup, she naturally whimpered her only spoken word – 'khapp, khapp,'" Gerry mimicked the thirsty ape in a screechy, throaty voice. "Furness took this as a 'glimmering of hope for proper word usage.'"

"Okay," B.B. continued. "So they can't speak. But what will you prove by teaching Ringo to sign frying pan – which, you'll admit, is something he's unlikely to use much in his daily life? Is that going to tell you how smart he is?" B.B. asked.

"We have other ways of testing his intelligence. He understands human speech and sometimes responds by signing. Where is that blasted ape?"

"Ringo, get down here you ragamuffin," Gilda called to an

orange shape in the treetops.

"Is this relevant to anything in real life?" B.B. pursued.

"Sure it is. This kind of study helps us understand the evolution of the brain. And, just maybe, if we can learn how an orangutan's mind works, perhaps we can help human children with learning difficulties. Maybe we can learn what causes autism and how to treat it. We're pioneering new concepts of communications here."

Gerry's well-rehearsed, self-congratulatory lecture was disturbed as Ringo clambored down to the platform. He saluted on arrival, a trick which usually elicited food.

B.B., who was sitting lotus position with her tape recorder at her side, found this vaguely amusing. She saluted back, dug a wide-angle lens out of her bag and stood. "Gerry, can I have one of you and Ringo saluting each other?"

Just as Gerry was moving into position, Ringo decided to explore the newcomer. He hunkered over to B.B., knuckles rubbing along the wooden platform. He went straight for her crotch and began sniffing. "Not again," she said.

Gerry and Gilda giggled nervously. "Typically, adolescent orangutan, pre-rape behavior," Gilda said, not making a move to help.

B.B. tried to push the ape away and appeared surprised at the tension and strength in his shoulder muscles. Ringo uttered four loud, rhythmic squeaks, grasped her hand and held it immobile. With his other hand he ripped off her sarong and stuck his face between her legs. B.B. was too startled to move. Then, she tried to back away. Ringo twisted her hand hard, forcing her to fall on her ass. He began confusedly clawing at her bathing suit, unable to understand lycra.

Alarmed, Gilda and Gerry shouted "Ringo, get off her. Ringo, let go. Ringo, come here."

B.B. screamed: "Get off me, you fucking ape!" and swung her camera onto Ringo's temple.

In spite of the F3's mass, she had little leverage and the Nikon merely bounced off his skull and grazed his ear. Ringo reacted as most animals do when physically attacked. He attacked back, first screaming, then biting B.B. on the stomach. Blood seeped through the pink, Gortex one piece.

Gerry finally had the presence of mind to go to the grappling pair and try to wrench Ringo away from the terrified woman. Not happy at being thwarted, Ringo turned and bit Gerry hard on the left forearm. Gerry cried out: "You motherfucker!", grabbed the frying pan, which represented the second sign Ringo had learned, and bashed the ape on the head and neck. After the third swing, Ringo backed off and turned to Gerry.

One doesn't know what would have happened if Gilda hadn't been by Gerry's side. Perhaps the ape would have savaged Gerry, perhaps not. But seeing Gilda, who had helped raise him during his formative years and who was one of the leading role models for the human side of his behavior, calmed the animal. "Ringo, go get durians," she commanded and the ape slunk off the platform.

* * * * *

Gilda, who had taken an extensive first aid course at Jaap Van der Kamp's insistence before going to Manusia, used her living room as an impromptu infirmary. B.B.'s wound was not serious. She cleaned the slash and sent B.B. off to bed with a double dose of Valium.

Gerry's wound was serious. It required ten stitches and a tetanus shot. Gilda was just finishing her next-to-last suture when she was distracted by a shadow in the doorway. "Christ, I don't believe it," she sighed. Standing on the front porch was Ringo, gingerly holding a wild durian. He had the forlorn look of a naughty child who realizes he has misbehaved, who has been punished and who wants to be taken back into his mother's arms and told that she still loves him.

"Thank you, Ringo," Gilda said carefully, not sure how the volatile animal would act. "Drop the durian." Ringo did as he was told. "Ringo go." The animal made no move.

Ringo made a face that Gilda had never seen. He tensed his mouth and jammed his lips together. The effect was that his eyes narrowed and his mouth became a thin slit. He relaxed enough to make a gentle 'grumph' noise, then pouted – while signing to Gerry, imploringly: "Ringo stay. Banana."

Unsmiling, Gerry got up and walked into the pantry, the surgical needle and thread dangling from his arm. He returned with a banana and threw it across the room to Ringo, who caught it one-handed, like a pitcher taking the throw back from the catcher. Gerry signed back "Ringo bad. Ringo go."

Again, Ringo stood his ground. It was only when Gilda spoke again, "Ringo go," that the ape turned into the approaching night.

"That bastard ruined everything for us. I should have bashed in his head," Gerry said.

Gilda said: "Hold on. He's an ape, not a person. He's not responsible for what he does."

"He's not a person?" Gerry was incredulous. "You treat these apes like people, you raise them like people, then you say they're not people. You yourself have said they are as smart as children. Gilda, people with IQs of 60 and 70, idiots by most definitions, are considered to be responsible for their actions. They've been tried for murder. Don't tell me Ringo's not responsible."

"Oh, Christ! I don't know anymore who's responsible for what," Gilda sniffled.

The two were quiet for a moment. "Why do you think he attacked her?" Gerry finally asked.

"I've seen it with wild orangutans," Gilda replied. "Young, male orangutans just entering adulthood are often rapists. It's the only way they can get a female."

"How's that?"

"Quite interesting. I've observed it about a dozen times in the wild," she said. "You see, the big males control individual territories, which means they control all the females that live there. The younger males, who are fully mature sexually but not powerful enough to establish territories of their own, skulk quietly around the forest by themselves, generally trying to avoid the dominant males," she explained with as much emotion as a home economics teacher giving the class a recipe for cherry pie. "When they come across a female, they might rape her – it's the only way they can get any action."

"But that's animal sex. Ringo attacked B.B.. A woman," Gerry argued. "How do you explain that?"

"I'm not sure I really understand it," Gilda ventured, after a long pause. "I think Ringo was having an identity crisis." The ends of her mouth went in opposite directions. She finished the last stitch. "You see," she said, biting off the cotton thread, "Ringo was raised as a human child. So one part of him feels he is human – attracted to women, but also in awe of humans as disciplinarians and parent figures. The other part of him is ape – and rape is normal ape behavior."

"Gilda," Gerry said enthusiastically. "I think this might be the break we're looking for."

"What break? What are you talking about?"

"Look. You're long overdue for a scientific paper. And, if we're honest with ourselves, it might be a while before I get enough data to prove that the orangutans have learned sign language. So why don't we write a paper about orangutan psychoses. We could start a new field – primate behavior disturbances. We could be the academic equivalent of Freud meets Robert Louis Stevenson."

"Who?"

"Stevenson. He wrote *Dr. Jekyl and Mr. Hyde.*"

"I'm not Dr. Jekyl."

"Nobody said you were. But you're the one who knows these apes best. You know orangutan behavior. I know the psychological terminology. Just think about it, okay?"

"Listen, Gilda, I don't feel so great. I'm going to lie down for a while."

"Good idea. You've got shock and you've lost some blood. I can give you a tranquilizer if you want."

"No, I'll be okay."

"Then, at least let me make you some tea."

CHAPTER 19

29 July. 08:00.

Dorchester Hotel, London

"S crambled eggs and bacon, please." the reporter requested.

"Eggs benedict and cappuccino," Mustafa bin Kayu instructed the Dorchester waiter.

"Very good, sir."

The British, Mustafa bin Kayu reflected, can't even distinguish between the good American habits and the bad. Big, American breakfasts were good. American breakfast meetings, however, were perverse. How could anyone possibly discuss anything of substance when his mind is fully engaged in trying to manipulate a dab of butter onto his toast?

The breakfast interview was the first of six hurriedly put-together, press briefings which Mustafa bin Kayu was scheduled to have with journalists in London, followed by four in Paris (with one evening free to discuss Sartre with Mimi in his suite at the George V), two in Germany, two in Switzerland, six in Rome (with a break for a dinner in Trastevere with Loredana) and eight in the United States. Damn those embassy blokes for being so efficient, the Manusian Minister of the Environment thought, as he sipped his pineapple juice.

His whirlwind schedule reminded him more of a BeeGees tour than a dignified series of diplomatic briefings. Mustafa bin Kayu had been lucky to get the last, business-class seat on the previous day's flight from Singapore and he was so nervous he didn't even chat up the sultry, Eurasian stewardess who kept him plied with

178

Dom Perignon. The Sultan's fury at Urs' escape immediately became the Minister's dilemma. Solve it and he just might keep his job. Screw it up and he might become the assistant, commercial attaché to Libya.

The solution: Go on the counter-offensive.

"You must understand that I want to speak frankly with you, but I ask that you do not quote me directly or mention my name or position. Is that all right?"

The reporter from *The Guardian* nodded.

"I can't hear you."

"All right."

"Now," Mustafa bin Kayu said, "you can ask me anything you want about the situation in Manusia. Politics, the economy, the upcoming, local elections."

"Let's talk about the environment," the young man said.

Just my luck, Mustafa reflected. First interview I give in years and those bastards in the embassy line me up with somebody who might know something.

The two men talked about rainforest destruction, about how the trees form the lungs of the earth, about climate change and the greenhouse effect. The Minister challenged the young man's assumption that timber operations were destroying the forest. "The indigenous people are doing it to themselves," he argued, "with their slash and burn techniques everywhere you look. We commissioned an independent study that found that 85 percent of the forest loss in Manusia is due to shifting cultivation." They intellectually danced a tango and a few cha-chas before getting down to the reason they were both there.

"What about Urs Gerhard?" the long-haired reporter in the rumpled suit asked. "Any news?"

"I suppose you fellows hear more from him than I do," the Minister joked. "But seriously, Urs is no longer just a fugitive who evaded our immigration laws. He is, at the very least, an accomplice to murder. I don't want to pre-judge the man, but it is possible he is himself a murderer."

The reporter looked up, deadpan. "How's that?"

"You are familiar with the illegal Penan blockades of the timber operations. In fact, I believe your newspaper has run stories on that subject. Last week, Urs Gerhard led another of his guerrilla strikes

– but, this time, someone was killed." He reached into his crocodile-skin, attaché case from J. Press (sustainably-produced, ranch-bred crocs he would have explained, had he been asked) and gave the reporter a school photo of a serious-looking, Malay youth. On the back was printed: Taib bin Susah, Kampong Jodoh, near Bohong, Manusia. "This young man was a security guard on the timber truck. Urs Gerhard and his friends murdered him."

The two men spoke about this violence for ten minutes, before the Minister played his next card.

"We are angry that the Penan have refused to negotiate with us like gentlemen. But we are magnanimous. We turn the other cheek. The real reason I wanted to meet you this morning was to advise you that we have instituted a national development scheme, worth some 50 million pounds sterling, to provide a better quality of life for all the upriver people – including, of course, the Penan. This will be in the form of modern villages, employment opportunities in light industries that we will establish, schools, medical clinics and improved transportation facilities."

"I can't help but feel you're not telling me the whole story," the reporter said, putting down his coffee cup. "What's the catch?"

Mustafa bin Kayu laughed. "Catch? Come on, how could I tell you all this if there was a catch? There are, however, one or two *quid pro quos*. The first is that the Penan may have to move to new areas. But that shouldn't be objectionable, once they see what they are being offered in terms of improvement in their lifestyles."

"The other *quid pro quo*?"

The Minister had thought of singing out, in his best Liza Doolittle, cockney, voice: "All I want is Urs Gerhard's head". Instead, he said, in his most continental accent: "Just this. That the Penan realize that they are Manusians. Like me. Like two million other Manusians. That their larger family wants to take them in. But that cannot happen as long as a foreigner – a murder suspect, mind you – continues to put bad thoughts in their heads."

Ten minutes later, the reporter got up to leave.

"Oh, I almost forgot," the Minister said, digging again into his briefcase. He handed the reporter a long, narrow, cardboard box that looked as if it might contain a tie. "It's a little memento of our conversation. Please be careful as you open it," the Minister cautioned. The reporter lifted the lid to see a foot-long, blowpipe dart, nestled in cottonwool. "This is similar to the poison dart that murdered Taib bin Susah. That's the kind of people we're up against."

PART V

PLAYING THE CARDS YOU ARE DEALT

CHAPTER 20

29 July. 09:00.

Camp Trinil

The morning after Ringo's attack, a Hong Neiyi speedboat abruptly stopped at the Camp Trinil dock. A swaggering, Chinese youth, dressed in 501s, a cowboy shirt, Ray Bans and flip-flops, asked the first person he saw where he could find Gerry Schwartz. He was directed to Gerry's modest cabin and knocked on the screen door.

"Who the fuck is that?" Gerry said.

"Special delivery."

Gerry tightened his sleeping sarong around his waist and went to the door.

"Letter for you, Mister Gerry," the delivery boy said. "Just sign here."

* * * * *

Gilda went to B.B.'s cabin with a cup of tea. *I've got to mend this fence,* Gilda thought.

"Feeling better?"

"Still pretty shaken up," B.B. answered.

"You had a bit of a scare."

"You've got to have more control over these animals."

"What do you mean?"

"You can't have wannabe rapists like that ape roaming around ready to attack visitors. Don't you know anything about liability? Shit, he could have killed me."

"Ringo was just acting naturally," Gilda said, defending her

185

almost-son.

"I don't believe this. Hello? That animal almost killed me. That ape should be put down."

For Gilda, criticizing Ringo was like criticizing her son. "You don't belong in the forest. There are different rules here. Natural laws. Genetic codes."

"You wouldn't know what natural meant if it hit you on the head. You want natural? Go see Urs Gerhard and learn his version of natural."

At the mention of Urs Gerhard, Gilda began to lose it. "Who do you think you are, coming into our world and turning it upside down? I don't have to take your threats."

"You call this circus nature conservation? You're nuts. All of you. If I were you, I'd start to learn some secretarial skills, Gilda, because your conservation days are finished, if I have anything to do about it. Get me a boat out of this place."

Gilda had reacted as a cornered, male orangutan might. "You try to bust me and you'll be sorry."

"Trust me on one thing, Gilda. You're toast."

"I'll tell that Rod Lawrence of yours the true story."

"I know the true story. About how you and Gerry are falsifying data. About how you haven't done a stitch of scientific research for over a decade. That you deliberately get in the way of Urs Gerhard, who's fighting the real conservation fight. That you have a bunch of psychotic apes brushing their teeth with Colgate."

"Wait till I tell your boss that you were having an affair with Bujang."

B.B. opened her eyes wide. "You're crazy."

"And that wasn't enough for you, Miss East Coast Thrill Seeker. Wait till I tell your boss that you were having an affair with Ringo. You brought the whole thing on yourself. Ringo was just doing what any teenage boy would do when his date wears a too-tight tank top and short shorts," Gilda screamed. "The jungle is no place for a cockteaser."

Penan encampment

Urs' mail came via many routes and he was never sure when he was going to get a delivery. He sat cross-legged in front of the campfire, reading the most recent correspondence, which arrived through what he had termed the 'sugar and spice' route. This particular, convoluted trail began with his correspondents sending letters to him care of Hans-Peter Fritz, a high school buddy now resident in Basel, Switzerland. Fritz then re-packed the letters into an envelope which bore the return address of "University of Strasbourg, France, Department of Linguistics and Modern Philosophy". Fritz personally drove across the border to France and mailed the letter to the headmaster of the Methodist Boy's Junior College in Anjing, a respected community leader and member of the board of the prestigious Manusia National Museum, named George Wee. It was not unusual for Wee, a reasonably well-known scholar of languages and European history, to receive letters from abroad. Also, because Manusian officials probably wouldn't realize that France was next to Switzerland, the postal authorities at the Central Post Office in Anjing had no reason to suspect the middle-aged, bespectacled teacher.

George Wee was not, by nature, a political animal. However, he did have a reason to support Urs. Two reasons, actually. The more important reason was that he harbored a strong, but unrealistic, desire to see the government of Sultan Ibrahim bin Akbar Harrods fall. Mr. Wee, some twenty years earlier, had wanted to apply for a Rhodes scholarship to Oxford and had learned that the then Assistant Deputy Minister of Education, an ambitious young man named Mustafa bin Kayu, had refused to process George Wee's application and had, instead, pushed through the papers of his cousin. It was a clear case of nepotism, rationalized by the fact that the Deputy Assistant Minister's relative was a Malay – and Malays deserved more chances than Chinese Manusians, such as George Wee.

Although George Wee never forgot that incident, he rarely spoke about it to strangers. However, his reticence had fallen one night several years earlier, when he had been particularly indiscreet with three of his second year, upriver students – an Iban, a Kayan and a Kelabit. After too many beers in a dive called the Tokyo Bar in Anjing, George Wee had spilled out his heart and made an awkward pass at the very attractive, Kayan boy in the group, a lad named Bujang Bungan.

When George Wee received a letter from Switzerland, he re-

187

packaged the contents, yet again, in a large envelope that appeared to be a personal packet and sent them to his cousin, Goh Teck Leong, a provision merchant in the town of Bohong. Part of Mr. Goh's business involved running a series of provision boats that plied the Hotut River. When Mr. Goh had such a special-delivery letter from cousin George, he would pack it in a sack of rice or flour or sugar and stick a label on it that told the boat driver it was destined for Miss Mimes Bungan of Rumah Sehat. Mimes then collected the delivery and passed the letter to her brother Bujang, who, in turn, relayed it to her Urs. It was a cumbersome, difficult system – and just one of several, but it worked. For now.

Urs knew it was too early to hear anything from B.B. Derek. However, he was curious, even anxious, about whether she would keep her promise. She had power, that woman, but he wondered whether she had the common sense to use it wisely.

Instead, there was other news.

"Greetings from Byron Bay," the letter began. "I've been here for a few days hols with my girlfriend, Heather. You'd like her, she's just like me. I thought you might like some photos of sun and sea. I bet you don't see too much of that – I mean the sea – where you are. So here they are. Sun, sea. And me. Sorry to ruin the view, but I come with the territory. I'm the one in the pink bikini.

"Now, down to business. We've been busy. Was in Canberra last week and managed to convince (I hope, keep your fingers crossed) three Labor MPs to introduce a bill condemning Manusian genocide of its native peoples and recommending a boycott of Manusian rubber, tin and palm oil. If this resolution takes off, we might even get a ban on direct flights (that's a pun, Urs. You have puns in Switzerland, don't you?) from Oz to Anjing. Anyway, here are some press clippings that might be interesting. As you can see, we've made good use of your "at home" pictures. And your drawings are *fabulous*. Just great. If you can send some more, we can produce a special book.

"A suggestion. I think it would be useful if we could get a television crew in to interview you and your friends, record daily life, see how you live – you know the kind of thing I have in mind. I know we would never get official permission to see you, but maybe we could enter under the pretext of making a tourist film and then run up and see you. No? Sounds too crazy, huh? Maybe *one* person? I'm pretty handy with a camera and these new camcorders have built in mikes, so even a clutz like me can pretend she's Fellini.

"I know it isn't easy for you to write, Urs, but it is important for the cause to know how you are doing. And it's important for me to know, too.

"Yours, with affection, Jennifer."

Maya came and sat next to him, just as Urs finished re-reading the letter. Before he could place it back in its envelope, she held out her hand, innocently, to look at the photos. He handed them to her. Photos were a big event in a Penan community, but this time, besides Maya, only old Laki was on hand to examine them – soiling the images with dirty thumbs, turning them over to see if there was an image on the back. Urs calmly explained to his wife and father-in-law that the woman in the pictures (with the pink bathing suit) was responsible for the terrific articles in *The Sydney Morning Herald* and *The* (Melbourne) *Age*, the clippings of which he carefully unfolded. Maya and Laki looked at the incomprehensible (to them) newspaper clippings for several moments.

Urs opened another envelope. "This article is from the largest newspaper in Germany," he explained to Maya. Her eyes widened as she saw a picture of her husband and four close friends and relatives captured in newsprint. She had never had her photo taken, but often hoped that someday Urs would take her to the Chinese photo studio that she had heard about in Bohong. A Penan girl from their group, the only girl she knew who had gone to school, had once had her photo taken. She had looked very strange in the photo, dressed in a blouse, a skirt and shoes. She sat on a white bench, in front of a backdrop that showed a dark mountain with white on the top.

That girl had returned just once to the Penan community. After she had gone back to school for the second term, she had disappeared. The family had no news of her, just her well-worn photo. Someone said that someone in Rumah Sehat had said he had seen her in a bar in Bohong.

"The man who wrote this article says that all the people in the world support the Penan and are against the government in Anjing," Urs said. "Maya, do you have any idea how many people there are in the world?"

189

"There are twenty in our group," she said, trying to do well. "And there are other groups in the forest. And in Rumah Sehat there are many. And there are big cities, like Bohong. So yes, Tuan Urs. There are many people."

"That's good, Maya. And do you know where this place called Germany is?"

"I don't know, Tuan Urs. Is it further than Bohong?"

"Much, much further."

"More than eight days walk? That is the furthest I have been from this area."

"Much more. Much more." Urs took off his wire-rimmed glasses, carefully placed them by his side and rubbed the bridge of his nose. His eyes hurt. He wasn't sure if it was a dietary deficiency or because his eyesight had changed. He was down to his last pair of glasses.

While Urs massaged his temples, Liebchen grabbed his glasses and dragged them over the rough ground, scampering in front of Urs, screeching. Like a dog that enjoys chasing a stick, but doesn't want to give it back, Liebchen enjoyed this game of keep-away until something in her master's voice told her to quit fooling around. "Liebchen, *du blöder Penanaffe*, if you don't give me those glasses right now, I vill roast your little ass for dinner." The monkey gently placed the glasses at his feet before scampering off. Urs picked them up. One lens was cracked. He wanted to cry, something he had not done for many years. He wished that Penan custom did not prohibit a woman from touching a man in public – he would have given almost anything for Maya to bend down and rub his neck and his shoulders and whisper that she was glad he was there and that she was proud of him. Instead, she walked to the kitchen area of their hut and returned several minutes later. She knelt and offered him a soup of boiled ferns, slugs and minnow-sized fish.

* * * * *

Gerry ripped open the letter.

"Dear Mr. Schwartz,

1. It has come to our attention that you are attempting to teach Manusian orangutans a form of language called American Sign Language.

2. You will recall that, before commencing your research, you were asked to complete the 'Official Sultanate of Manusia Form 136B for Foreign Research Activities of a Scientific Nature.'

3. On your application for a visa, a photocopy of which is herewith attached, you agreed that your experiment would not promulgate a specific foreign state or encourage cultural values that are alien to Manusian society.

4. That you have done so, we consider a grievous insult to our national sovereignty.

5. We therefore inform you that your work permit will not be renewed after it expires on 31 August of this year and that you are expected to quit Manusia before that date. Failure to do so will be a most serious breach of Manusian law and you will be suitably punished if you do not heed this notice.

Yours sincerely,

Mustafa bin Kayu
Minister of the Environment"

PART VI

WHEN THE GOING GETS TOUGH, THE TOUGH RE-GROUP

CHAPTER 21

15 August. 09:00.

Anjing

The Sultan of Manusia held his cabinet meetings in the grand ballroom of the royal palace, an Arabian Nights-inspired structure, the minarets of which gleamed with gold flake.

Although Mustafa bin Kayu was dressed in a lightweight, wool, Christian Dior suit, he felt cold and had to stop his teeth from chattering. He sipped a cup of Earl Grey from a Sevres service and wondered how could the Sultan wear just a silk, batik shirt and not die of hypothermia?

Sultan Ibrahim bin Akbar Harrods liked to keep up-to-date on what all his Ministers were doing. This didn't stop him from meeting each Minister privately, Mustafa bin Kayu knew, where the old man could play one Minister off against another with the skill of Machiavelli.

The Minister of Overseas Development Cooperation outlined his presentation to an upcoming, World Bank conference, by floating the theme of 'enlightened development for a contemporary world.' The Minister of Foreign Affairs explained his role in seemingly-endless, ASEAN negotiations on the future on Cambodia, where he argued that stability would only come to that troubled land with a return to hereditary, royal rule. The Minister of Trade reported on his attendance at an important WTO meeting on European quotas of third world, textile production. The Minister of Industry presented the finishing touches to his 'Action Plan for the Next Decade', which proposed luring South Korean, semiconductor industries to set up manufacturing facilities in Manusia.

The Manusian Minister of Sports was absent, having been encouraged to take early retirement after the national athletics team tied with Trinidad and Tobago for 56th place in the Fourth Non-Aligned Nations' Sports Championships held in Costa Rica.

The Sultan turned to Mustafa bin Kayu. It was the Minister of the Environment's turn to justify his existence in the Manusian food chain.

Mustafa bin Kayu realized that this was the only agenda point in the cabinet meeting that the other Ministers looked forward to. A real controversy in Manusia. Piranhas. They were waiting to see if his head would roll.

He planned to put a positive spin on his just-completed, whirlwind, western, media tour. Truthfully, he admitted that it hadn't been a huge success and he had left a trail of bewildered reporters in his wake, men and women who wondered what was the connection between the fine wines they had just drunk and tribal rights and rural development half a world away.

Meanwhile, the increasingly embarrassing, anti-timber operations had become contagious and had spread to other parts of the country. The Minister, of course, had been kept advised of the increasingly desperate security situation and was surprised that, in spite of security crackdowns and restrictions on foreigners going to rural areas, the news leaks continued. Just that morning, he stopped eating his scrambled eggs when he read in the morning's *Singapore Straits Times* (air-expressed before dawn and untouched by the censors), an article that declared:

"The Sultanate appears to be fighting for control of the interior. Although few observers claim the situation is serious enough to be identified as a civil war, it is becoming increasingly clear that Manusian security forces are unable to contain the situation. One high-ranking Manusian official, who asked not to be identified, compared the security effort as 'about as effective in stopping those naked natives as a used condom would be in stopping AIDS.' Recent reports indicate that the disturbances have expanded to other remote parts of the country from the region around the Mount Malu National Park, where the protests began. Perhaps more important, no longer is this simply a fight between the shy, nomadic Penan and the government. A wide variety of native peoples are now engaged in blatant, anti-timber activity. A Roman Catholic Bishop, Father John Galvin, was reportedly deported for encouraging a group of Kenyah tribesman to lay siege to a timber camp on the Marab River, isolating workers in the camp without outside supplies for three weeks. A large contingent of Land Dayaks reportedly control traffic on the trunk road between the capital of Anjing and the second division capital of Kota Besar and an Iban group near the mouth of the Hotut River has kidnapped a foreman of the Sen Yat Timber Company and are reported to be holding him hostage. The ransom they demand: irrevocable title to their traditional lands."

"Well, well," Mustafa bin Kayu had said to himself, as he buttered another slice of toast. "I wonder what the Harvard case-history method says about taking management decisions in a time of crisis?" He remembered an aphorism from his student days. When you're up to your ass in crocodiles it's bloody difficult to remind yourself that your initial objective was to drain the swamp. He then recalled a second maxim that had always seen him through difficult times. When the going gets tough, nibble on something warm, white and round dressed in red silk. You'll think more clearly afterwards.

Mustafa bin Kayu's reverie was interrupted by an angry Sultan. He, too, had read that morning's *Straits Times* and he knew, better than the other cabinet members, that the rich façade of his reign was as artificial as a stage set. The Sultanate was going broke, fast. Soon the world would stop buying tropical timber from virgin rainforests. Manusia had no gas or oil reserves. The Sultan certainly didn't feel like digging into his own pocket to save the country.

Unlike Mustafa bin Kayu, the Sultan had a plan. Further, because his cabinet meetings didn't pretend to run on Robert's Rules of Order or Jeffersonian principles of one person, one vote, he explained what needed to be done. Increase the effort to find Urs and capture his white ass, damnit. Take a big chunk of money and build luxurious, resettlement camps for the Penan, who would be ordered to move out of their jungle home. Accept the generous offers of the Malaysian, Korean, Japanese and Chinese timber companies, who had new and efficient methods of clear-felling the forest. Then, enter into joint ventures with those clever, Indonesian, agro-technical folks to convert the newly-cleared land into palm oil plantations.

"Anyone think this isn't a good idea?" the Sultan asked.

The room was quiet.

"Good. Meeting is adjourned. Oh, Mustafa, could you come into my private office for a moment?"

CHAPTER 22

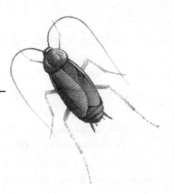

15 August. 09:00.

Nirvana

Less than two weeks left. Two weeks to finish his research and get enough data to convince his committee that he had earned his doctorate. It was raining. Pouring. Rationally, Gerry knew that the reason they called it a rainforest was because it rained. However, he always felt annoyed when the skies opened up, as they had every day for the past week. For one thing, he usually managed to get soaking wet, which generally led to a noisy bout of sneezing and misery. If that discomfort wasn't enough, there was the emotional depression of not seeing the sun. Rainy days reminded him of those aimless, inclement days at camp, when the counselors desperately tried to amuse the kids with billfold-making and lanyard-twisting.

Gerry had no handicrafts at Nirvana, but he did have Queenie. The orangutan was terrified of the rain and refused to leave Gerry's side.

"Now, whisten to me, Queenie," Gerry sniffled above the storm, setting the ape in front of him, as he squatted on the floor. "I carried you all the way up that wretched mountain to give you an accelerated course." He held up a Playboy magazine. "*Apa ini?*"

Queenie made the sign for magazine.

"Terrific. Now, let's try ..."

Queenie reached for Gerry's arm and motioned that he was supposed to give her two peanuts.

"Queenie, sorry, I forgot the treats. They're back in camp. Be patient and you'll get rewarded. I promise." To prove it, Gerry signed 'peanut'.

Queenie responded by licking the snot dripping from his nose and signing back: "Queenie peanut."

Gerry signed: "Gerry give Queenie peanut."

Queenie began to get frustrated. She had made the right signs for food. Yet, there was no food. She tried once again: "Gerry peanut Queenie." Then, to add her own accent to the conversation, she punctuated her demand by slapping his thigh.

"That is absolutely incredible, Queenie," Gerry said, scribbling in his notebook. "Let me just make sure I've got the sequence right. A few more weeks like that and we'll have cracked it." But I don't have a few more weeks, he thought ruefully. I've got six days. Six days to accumulate enough data to write a dissertation. Six days before he had to get on a plane or get arrested

For Queenie, time did not exist. Her mind focused on things she could understand. Like rewards. She knew that it had been several minutes since her last peanut. She sulked by grabbing the magazine, rolling it into a cylinder and chewing on the end.

Gerry began to regret his rigorous, scientific method. In order to protect his data from paper-eating bats and mildew-monsters, he had carefully copied the contents of his notebooks every three days. He had sent these duplicate notebooks to Professor Pong at the university for safekeeping. Professor Pong, in turn, passed the notebooks to one of his Masters' degree candidates, who entered the data on a computer program designed specifically for Pong.

Gerry began to play the 'if' game. If he hadn't have sent the data home, he could have pre-dated some of his results, accelerated the learning curve and concluded his research before he was forced out. However, now he was stuck, a prisoner of his own self-discipline and foresight. Further, the photo feature 'Girls of the Southwest Conference' was being crunched, chewed and torn apart by a mischievous student. He sneezed into space, sending droplets into the mist. He wiped his nose on his sleeve.

Queenie, perhaps sensing that her master was upset, whimpered and climbed into his arms. Gerry walked to the edge of the shelter and shouted into the storm: "Are you coming, Herr Urs?" He adjusted the canvas cover over his shelter to partly stop a drip. Nearby, his yellow INF koala T-shirt flapped in the wet wind – the marker to signal Urs that Gerry needed to see him.

The rain died down after half an hour, leaving the forest steamy and sticky. The insects started their calls, as if they had been re-hydrated and brought back to life by the rain. It was muggy and Gerry debated whether a cold shower was good for a cold. He decided that a brisk bath was the manly thing to do – so he stripped, put on his rubber flip-flops and stood under the waterfall for ten minutes.

When he returned, he found Urs sitting on his chair, glancing through the *Playboy*, seemingly oblivious to the fact that the magazine had a slippery coating of orangutan saliva covering some of the best parts.

"Hello, Urs. I was hoping you would come."

"Yes? You have mail for me?"

"No. No mail."

"Then why do you fly the flag?" Urs asked, pointing to the soggy T-shirt.

"We need to talk."

"Yes?"

"I've got problems. Serious problems. I need your help."

"*You* have problems?" Urs asked incredulously.

"That's right. Me."

"Are there people trying to kill you?"

"No."

"Do you have malaria?"

"No. But I do have a bad cold."

"Then you have no problems. Unless, of course, you've been talking to people you should not talk to, about me. Then you would have problems."

"I don't get this. I'm your friend. Why so hostile, guy? It sounds like you're threatening me." Gerry cursed his dripping nose. It probably looked like he was afraid of Urs.

"First, I ask you a question," Urs said. "Are you cheating on me?"

"What does *that* mean?"

"It means I was almost killed the other day. Again. I'm, how you say, feeded up with almost being killed. Somebody tells the police where to find me. Is it you?"

"You insane idiot. Is *that* what you think? Why should I tell anybody about you, even if I knew anything, which I don't? *I'm* the one who's in the shit because of *you*. You probably haven't heard, but I've been thrown out of this wretched country." Gerry reached into his backpack and withdrew the letter from the Minister. "Read this." He threw the envelope at the Swiss.

Urs thought for a moment, before handing the letter back. "Who will open your mail when you leave?"

"How the fuck do I know?"

"You must leave instructions at the Bohong post office to forward all your mail to you in the States. Then someone will contact you with instructions."

"Will you stop thinking about yourself for a second? I want to help you. I want to stay."

"You want to stay? Why?"

"To help you."

"Any other reason?"

Gerry realized he had nothing to gain by lying. "Actually, there is. I haven't finished my research. I need another two months. Maybe one, if I work fast."

Urs deliberately turned away from Gerry and read two letters in the *Playboy* Advisor column. One asked for advice on selecting a video disc system, the other was from a 16-year-old boy who was having an affair with his younger sister's piano teacher.

Like a child who is bored with the grownups' conversation, Queenie grabbed Gerry's survival pack and climbed a tree. Inside, she found a mirror. She licked it. Not great. She held it so that the sun reflected off it into her eyes. She waved it in front of her face several times, at first enjoying the new effect, but soon getting bored. She shifted her position and noticed something odd in the glass. A face. She brought the mirror to her mouth and licked it again. Nothing. She held it at arm's length and saw an orangutan. Queenie reached out to touch the other ape and instead touched glass. She scratched her eyebrow and the mirror-image repeated the gesture.

"You want to help me," Urs said finally. "What can you do?"

"I can sneak into Bohong, get supplies. I can help you write reports for the outside. I can take photos. Lots of things."

"And you will live where?"

"In the forest. Like you."

Urs was skeptical. He massaged his temples. "What about your work?"

202

"I will stay near the Camp. I can stay here. The orangutans will find me. Actually, I just need to stay in contact with two or three who speak well enough to get me my Ph.D.."

"Even if I thought you could live in the forest – which I don't – why should I take the risk? You could be a *doppel*-agent and tell the police where I am. Or you could just be innocent but dumb and people would find me because you were careless."

"Urs. You owe me."

"*Bitte?*"

"You owe me. For all these weeks I've risked my career in Manusia to get your mail. Now I'm being kicked out, because *you're* still running around free. I'm a scapegoat because of you. The way I see it, you owe me a chance."

Urs took off his glasses and rubbed his eyes. Without looking up, he asked: "Do you have any more of that dry fruit?"

"Finished. How about a Snickers?"

"*Danke.*" Urs chewed noisily. He let Liebchen lick his fingers. After two minutes, he spoke. "My trust comes easily. But the trust of the Penan, it has to be earned. Listen and tell me if you are enough of a man to help them." He outlined his plan. It took four minutes. When he finished he looked at Gerry, who nodded. Urs smiled and walked away.

"Hey, you've got my magazine," Gerry called after him. However, it had started raining again and Urs did not hear.

203

CHAPTER 23

---

15 August. 11:00.

Camp Trinil

"S quark."

Gilda had come to despise the field radio.

"The Honorable Minister has asked me to convey to you a message of 'Red Alert'," Tusau Padan said. "He wants you to meet him in Bohong tomorrow afternoon."

CHAPTER 24

16 August. 07:00.

Bohong

Gilda and Bujang left early. She was in such a hurry to see the Minister that she and Bujang raced the Camp Trinil longboat downriver as fast as it would travel. Several times they narrowly avoided collisions with huge logs floating downriver to the sawmills where they would be cut into timber or chopped to make plywood.

"Bujang, *pergi kepada kantor pos dan ambil seurat seurat-nya,*" she said when they reached Bohong in the early afternoon, ordering him to fetch the mail at the post office. She gave Bujang 50 Manusian dollars to amuse himself with and left him in the shopping district of Bohong, a central square lined with Chinese shop-houses that surrounded an open market. She would meet him that evening near Mama Cheng's fried noodle stall in the hawkers' center.

* * * * *

"Ah, Gilda, my dear," Mustafa bin Kayu said in his sing-song voice. "How delightful you could come."

Gilda accepted a cold beer. The Minister drank Glenfiddich on the rocks.

"There are a few things you might be able to help me with," he said amicably. "A few pesky issues you might know something about."

Gilda was nervous. She had been alone with the Minister for two minutes now and he had not nuzzled her neck or stroked her breast. He sat harmlessly on a sofa six feet away.

"And I have some questions for you, too," she said.

"Really? Such as?"

"Such as what is going on? Why did you kick out Gerry? You promised me."

"I promised you? Think again. I said that there was pressure, at the very highest levels, to get rid of all foreigners. Especially those that caused trouble."

"Gerry never caused trouble."

"Didn't he? Don't be too sure. In any case, he was a pawn. A warning."

"To me?"

"I'm afraid so. I told you I wanted to protect you. I told you I would protect you, as long as you worked with me, not against me."

"What do you mean? I haven't done anything against you."

"If I am not incorrect – and I am certain I am not – you get the majority of your funding from the International Nature Federation. Said organization publishes a popular journal called *Nature's World*. The latest issue was pouched to me by our embassy in Washington." He reached into his briefcase and passed her the familiar, yellow-bordered magazine.

The photograph on the cover was a close-up of Urs Gerhard, seated cross-legged in front of a fire, applying black poison to the tip of a blowpipe dart. A wide-eyed, naked child, with one hand on Urs' shoulder, stared wistfully into the camera. The headline screamed: 'INF Launches Battle to Save Manusia's Forests'. A sub-head added: 'Inside: Exclusive interview with Urs Gerhard, the Swiss Robin Hood fighting for tribal rights against corrupt officials'.

Gilda, usually at a loss for words when discussing things as mundane as recipes for chocolate cake, was speechless when she considered B.B.'s coup. She opened the magazine. Five cards fell out. On the side of one was a pre-printed message: "I deplore the actions taken by your government that disrupt the life-styles of the tribal people of your country. I will urge my legislators, who *do* respond to the will of their electorate, to ban Manusian products and commodities from the United States. I beg you to stop the genocide. Leave the forests for the people." It was pre-addressed to

Sultan Ibrahim bin Akbar Harrods, Prime Minister of Manusia, c/o the Embassy of Manusia, Massachusetts Avenue, Washington, D.C. A similar card, but with a modified message, was addressed to the President of the United States. Three others had just the admonition "To be sent to your Senator or Congressperson – see our website for names and addresses".

Gilda shivered in the airconditioned room. She did not look up during the fifteen minutes it took her to read the piece. She was furious. There was no mention of her work. Just Urs this and Urs that. Penan plant medicine. Penan hunting methods. Penan black-smithing. With photo after photo of the idyllic life in Rumah Sehat, a "typical, nature-friendly, Kayan tribe longhouse set in the middle of the threatened, Borneo rainforest." Gilda was so mad that she didn't know what to say, so she re-read it. As she did, she added a second, grudging emotion to her fury. It was admiration, an appreciation that a few words and a few pictures could have such an impact.

As Taffy got up to refill his glass, he remarked: "You can see that the author is a Ms. Derek. Who was your houseguest a few weeks ago."

"Yes, but I didn't know she met with Urs. Honest. I swear. I didn't know she would write this," Gilda said.

"How could you not know?"

"I don't see how she could have … I wasn't with her all the time?"

"Who was?"

"I don't know."

"Gilda, this is what is called strong, circumstantial evidence. She was *your* guest, in your camp. She represented *your* funding agency. *Ipso facto*, you were involved in this article."

"You don't understand, Taffy. We fought. She almost got raped by Ringo. She hated me. She wants to cut off my funding."

As soon as she said it, Gilda wanted to retract the statement. Shouldn't give away your vulnerability like that, she thought. Oh, what the hell. He'll find out sooner or later. "That Derek woman is a menace, Taffy. And so is that Urs. I hope you catch him."

"You're the one closest to him. What are you doing to help us catch him?"

"That isn't my job."

"Yes, I know. Studying orangutans fornicating in the forest is your job. But, in this case I'm afraid you're either part of the solution or part of the problem. If it's the latter, as I told you before, I can't protect you."

Gilda forgot about pleading for Gerry. She finished her Tuborg. Taffy handed her another. She felt the beginning of a sore throat.

"And if I can't help you?" she asked.

"If you can't help, or you don't help, it comes to the same thing. 'All *orang putih* out.' Direct quote from the Prime Minister. All foreigners out. Right away. You may not have heard, but you're one of just six or so who haven't gotten their marching orders yet."

"And all those six are helping you to find Urs."

"All those six have shown a commitment to maintaining stability in the Sultanate of Manusia."

"But, Taffy, I don't know this guy. I swear. How can I help you?"

"Damnit, think, woman. He is in your neighborhood. He must be getting help from *someone*. Tell people you've decided to help him. Say you'd like to set up a meeting. When you hear something, mention during the morning 'tomtom' broadcast that an orangutan has died. Then leave a letter with instructions tacked to the bottom of your landing pier at Camp Trinil. Better wrap it in plastic. Someone will fetch it."

"Taffy, I just want to stay here. That's all I want. I don't want to be a Mata Hari. I don't want to get people in trouble."

"Well, then it seems like all the more reason to do a little work. Now come here."

"No, Taffy. Not today. I can't."

"Period?"

"No, I just don't feel like it. This has been so stressful, these last few weeks."

"And for me? Don't I deserve a bit of sympathy? My career is as secure as a hangnail. I have three children in the States – do you know how much those American universities cost? My reputation is on the line. I get vilified in the foreign press. I haven't slept for three days. My blood pressure is skyrocketing." He closed his eyes and shuddered.

Gilda did what she had told herself she wouldn't do. She walked over to Taffy, stood behind him and let him lean his head back against her breasts. She took off his gold, Christian Dior glasses, laid them on the side table, and massaged his temples. She bent over and kissed him on the forehead. He reached back and took her head in his hands. He pulled her mouth to his and kissed her. She tumbled over the sofa. Taffy stroked Gilda's neck, working his way down as far as the dress buttons would allow. He opened them urgently, anxious to undress her. He only got two buttons down before he stopped.

"What's wrong, Taffy?" she whispered.

The Minister said nothing. He grabbed the bottom of her dress and yanked it up. Gilda was exposed to the airconditioning, protected only by a white cotton bra and white cotton panties. "Where's your underwear?" Taffy asked, annoyed.

"Oh, the red ones? I told you I didn't expect to make love with you. They're back in camp." She yanked at his belt. "What's the matter, Taffy? I'm more than my underwear."

Taffy patted her on the head. "Of course, you're right, Gilda. Go take a shower first. There's a silk robe in the bathroom. You'll look good in it."

CHAPTER 25

16 August. 18:00.

Hong Neiyi timber camp

Gerry held Queenie's hand as they approached the rear of the Hong Neiyi timber camp office, a tin Quonset hut that stood by itself fifty yards from the motor pool. Gerry hadn't figured out any specific plan, but thought that the late afternoon break between the end of office hours and dinner would be as good a time as any. He also had a startling bit of good luck. Today was the weekly Hong Neiyi internal soccer match and virtually the entire camp was half a mile away, either playing or cheering. The office area was deserted.

Gerry went to the side window. It was shut around a Carrier air-conditioner powered by the camp's noisy generator. He tried to pry the window open. Sealed. Gerry peered through the window for some hint of how to gain access. He was surprised to see Queenie staring back at him. She had simply walked to the front door, found it open and strolled in.

Gerry's treasure-hunt shopping list was short. He was to collect documentary evidence that Hong Neiyi was operating within the national park. A bonus would be correspondence that implicated specific government officials.

Bingo. Sitting on the largest desk was a black binder titled "Mount Malu Timber Operations. Projections and cost estimates." He glanced at a few pages and quickly placed the file in his daypack. He grabbed a few rolled-up maps, a few construction reports and an attractive calendar for a Japanese ball-bearing manufacturer that featured a redhead writhing in a bed of small, stainless-steel balls.

"Hot damn, Queenie. We've done it," he whispered to the ape. She had stopped to examine a family photo on one of the desks. There was a husband and wife, two children and a dog. Queenie nibbled on the wooden frame.

"Let's go, Queenie," Gerry said, grabbing her arm. She reached up to take his pack, as she often did at Camp Trinil when she carried Gerry's teaching props. "Okay, you want to carry this thing like you do back in camp? Here you go," he said, as he strapped it onto her shoulders.

* * * * *

"I'll join you fellows later," Ramsay Wong told his colleagues at half-time during the match. He was sweating and pumped up from scoring two goals, but his voice was soft. "It's my son's birthday. I'm going to give him a call," he said, heading towards the office and the radiophone.

Holding hands, Gerry and Queenie ran across the open space between the timber camp office and the forest edge. They had crossed half of the 300 yards when they were spotted by Ramsay Wong. He saw the two odd figures running from the office toward the cover of the jungle. If they reached the forest, they would disappear quickly in the dim light of sundown.

Wong sprinted after the intruders. He ran silently, low to the ground, combining his army training with his experience as hooker for the Manusian Armed Forces Rugby Team, which had won the Asian seven-a-side championship in Hong Kong two years earlier.

Gerry never knew what hit him as Wong tackled him from behind. This resulted in three surprised creatures. Gerry, certainly, who had, at the time of the tackle, been congratulating himself on a successful commando raid. Wong, who found that he had captured, not a native thief, but a red-bearded American. Also Queenie, who scampered the remaining thirty yards to the forest and climbed the nearest tree. From there, it was an arduous, but not impossible, trip back to Nirvana. Surely, Gerry would meet her there.

* * * * *

In Bohong, Gilda and Bujang had taken two rooms at the New World Hotel, a simple establishment run by the Kwok family and situated over a sprawling, noisy coffee house. The towels were so thin as to be virtually useless, the walls not much thicker, but there was a telephone in each room, which Gilda used for about an hour as she worked her way through three layers of marines and duty officers in order to leave an urgent message for Ambassador Richard Fangar.

Gilda remembered the advice Maria-Angeles Guzman, the famous gorilla researcher, had once offered. "When things are really tough, go see the American Ambassador. They're all jackoffs, but they hold power that these woggiepoo countries respect."

The Ambassador was her last card.

My fame is worth something, Gilda thought, when the Ambassador had phoned her back half an hour later. Yes, he would see her the next morning. Gilda would take the morning flight to Anjing. Bujang, too. She needed him with her in the capital. Good thing he had brought along his 'city' clothes – crumpled, brown slacks and a yellow and green, batik shirt. No shoes, though. Flip-flops forever.

She hadn't planned on the flights from Bohong to Anjing being fully booked. At the Manusian Airlines System office, her fame was worth zip and she was told by the complacent bookings clerk to take the coastal express boat. Instead of an hour's comfortable flight, Gilda and Bujang would have to spend ten, miserable hours in a noisy and hot express boat.

CHAPTER 26

17 August. 09:00.

Rumah Sehat longhouse

Urs vowed never to go into Rumah Sehat again. Someone in the longhouse wanted him out of the way.

This meant problems for Urs. No longer could he enjoy a good, home-cooked Kayan meal. No longer could he watch international soccer games on television. No longer could he discuss anti-timber strategy with the Kayans. Further, it made it damn difficult for him to see Mimes.

Urs waited on the edge of the vegetable gardens and small rubber plantations that the Kayans had hacked out of the forest. He kept out of sight until he spotted someone he thought he could trust – Charley, the twelve-year-old, younger brother of Mimes and Bujang. Urs waited until the boy wandered off by himself to shoot birds with his homemade slingshot, constructed of a small, forked branch, dozens of interlinked rubber bands and a bit of old inner-tube.

"Hey, Charley," Urs whispered. "Over here."

"Uncle Urs. We were so afraid for you."

"I'm okay. Here, this is where they almost got me." Urs showed the boy the superficial wounds from the shotgun blast.

"Wow," Charley said. "Can I come with you next time you … you know … go up to the timber camp?"

"I've told you before – you can't. Maybe in a few years."

"But I want to help you."

"Charley, somebody in the longhouse wants for me to get captured. Who is it?"

As soon as Urs asked the question, he realized he had no right to get the boy involved in grownup problems.

"Gee, Uncle Urs. I don't know," Charley said, dejected because he couldn't help his friend. "But, I'll find out. Honest, I will."

"Look, it's not important," Urs said. "What else is new?"

"Nothing."

"Nobody going downriver?"

"Uncle Ding went down to Bohong last week with Bunga."

"*Ja*. Why?"

"Remember, Uncle Urs, how she cut her foot in the river? It didn't get better and Uncle Ding took her to see the doctor. She has to stay in the hospital. Maybe for a long time. They said she cut her ak-lee-lees tendon or something."

"Charley, listen, there is something you can do for me," he said, in a conspiratorial whisper.

"Sure, Uncle Urs."

"Could you give this note to your sister? And please, don't tell anybody you saw me. Deal?"

"Deal." Charley put up his hand, wanting to slap Urs' hand. The Swiss didn't understand.

"Uncle Urs. You put up your hand like this and we slap each other. That's a high five. The basketball players on TV do it."

"Okay, Charley. Five high." Slap. Urs turned to go. He stopped and called after Charley. "Have you seen my monkey?"

"Mimes is looking after it. I'll tell her."

Nirvana

"Ooph. Ooph." Queenie softly exhaled at Ringo near the feeding platform at Camp Trinil. She made her message more precise by signing: "Come. Hurry." Ringo grunted and signed: "Here. Banana." Queenie repeated her request, oophing with more urgency. Ringo pouted and accepted Queenie's outstretched arm.

The two apes swung lethargically through the trees towards Nirvana. Queenie's nervous energy excited Ringo and he followed the younger ape. Maybe she had found a fruiting fig tree.

There was no food to be had at Nirvana. Just Gerry's backpack, which Queenie threw in the air like a beach ball. It grazed Ringo's head on the way down, eliciting an annoyed grunt. Queenie opened the pack and pulled out the Hong Neiyi documents.

Ringo touched the binder. He put the edge of one plastic cover into his mouth and, during the process, smelled Gerry. These papers were Gerry's papers. He also smelled Queenie. Also strange, unidentifiable, unpleasant smells. He ripped out one looseleaf sheet and stuffed it in his mouth, then spat it out. Ringo made a sharp cry, then another, followed by a raspberry flubbering of his lips. He tore out three more pages, chewed on the edges, spat them out and defecated on them.

He found Gerry's T-shirt and rubbed it into his face. He chewed the bottom half, ripping a saucer-sized hole in the yellow fabric. He wanted to throw it away, to destroy it, but he was attracted to it. It was power. It was power over Queenie and, in a sense, over himself. Ringo jerked the shirt over his head, as he had seen humans do, forcing his head through one of the arm holes. It hung down his back like a cape, the koala symbol appearing to hang onto Ringo's neck. Ringo made no attempt to rip it off.

He walked over to Queenie and smelled her genitals. She whimpered and did not move. He placed a finger in her vagina, not urgently, but casually, as if he had all the time in the world. Queenie was too young for all this. She shrieked and scampered to the edge of the platform. Part of her wanted to stay and wait for Gerry. Part of her wanted to get out of there and return to the security of Camp Trinil. She tensed her mouth, slightly expanding her cheeks. "Camp. Food," she signed, turning to go. Ringo shrugged, sniffed his finger and followed the younger ape.

CHAPTER 27

17 August. 19:00.

Anjing

Gilda had never met Richard Fangar. Luckily, she had had the foresight to write him a personal note when he arrived, welcoming him to the country and inviting him to visit Camp Trinil. He had written back saying that he admired her work and hoped, one day, to be able to accept her invitation. Then he had become heavily involved in meetings and briefings, often held on the manicured grounds of the Royal Manusia Golf and Tennis Club. Camp Trinil remained on his 'pending' list.

The embassy was in the finest residential section of Anjing, a wide, tree-lined, colonial street with fine, white villas and yards framed with blue and orange bougainvillea.

Manusia was a posting for Foreign Service officers whose careers were either beginning or ending. Ambassador Fangar was a young man on the way up. About 35, Gilda estimated. Wavy, brown hair like a Kennedy. Thin. Strong. Glasses with round, bright red frames. A yellow bow-tie with red doo-dads.

The office of an experienced diplomat often has framed photos on the wall featuring the Ambassador with Heads of State and several US Presidents. Richard Fangar, whose collection of political memorabilia was still in the embryonic stage, decorated his office with his BA parchment from Wesleyan, his law school degree from George Washington University, and his gilt-edged membership certificate in the *International Societé de Amateur Chefs de Cuisine* – a Boston-based group in which overseas members promised to prepare a gourmet-standard, home-cooked meal for visitors who were also members.

The first ten minutes of the interview with the Ambassador were pleasant and inconsequential.

"I really am sorry, Mr. Ambassador, for being late. Thanks so much for seeing me after office hours. Those people at the MAS office just wouldn't get me on the plane." She paused, not sure how to continue. "I suppose that never happens to you."

"You'd be surprised at how casually we ambassadors get treated," Fangar said, smiling. "So how are things out in the jungle?"

Gilda scrunched her cheeks. "Oh, really good. Every day it seems we're pushing the envelope on orangutan research. We've got six mother-child groups under regular observation and the rehabilitation program is continuing very successfully."

"How interesting. Can I offer you some tea?"

After ten seconds of silence, the Ambassador asked again. "Tea?"

"Please."

He walked out of his office and spoke with his secretary. Moments later a uniformed, Manusian maid, a Malay, Gilda guessed, served refreshments. Limoges china, she observed, glancing at the bottom of the saucer.

"Ms. Korda-Breckenridge. I believe you called me on urgent business," the Ambassador said finally. "Perhaps you could explain your problem and we'll try to find a solution."

It took Gilda fifteen minutes to tell her story. She had never been so nervous. She had written notes the night before and rehearsed in the bathroom of the hotel. She had wished Bujang was more proficient in English so she could bounce ideas off of him. But, still, his presence was reassuring, even if he couldn't help with her logic. She smiled, remembering how he had met her the previous evening with eyes aflame, like a little boy. In his basic Malay, which, she admitted, was almost as bad as hers, he had told her that he had seen something strange and wonderful. An off-the-road, Yamaha, trail bike, with a raised frame, a reinforced suspension, knobby tires, reinforced gas tank and, best of all, painted bright yellow – her favorite color. She had been surprised at her reaction. She was happy when he was happy.

The Ambassador was a good listener, asking a few pertinent

questions along the way, taking notes on a yellow legal pad, nodding where appropriate, grimacing when Gilda told of the attack on B.B..

"So you see, Mr. Ambassador, I am an American." She stopped, not sure what direction to go. "The work I do is proof that America supports nature conservation," she said finally. Gilda reached into her head for buzz words. "Mount Malu is one of the most biologically-diverse forests in the world," she said quickly. "It is essential for sustainable development. Without an independent, scientific, rational foreign presence to keep an eye on things, the entire National Park could be cut down in a year. The United States owes it to the people of Manusia, not to mention to the people of the world, to protect that rainforest."

"Which it would do by suggesting to the Government that you remain in place?"

"Exactly."

"Let me ask you something, Ms. Korda-Breckenridge."

"You can call me Gilda. Everybody else does."

"Fine. Do you think that this Government is good for conservation?"

Double breath pause. "Well, it says all the right things."

"Yes, but on a scale of one to ten, with ten being the highest, where would you place this Government in terms of environmental sensitivity?"

Gilda thought about the variance between Taffy's public pronouncements and his actions. She considered the conservation successes and disasters of neighboring Malaysia and Indonesia, and further afield, of Thailand and China, India and Nepal. She thought of which answer he wanted to hear, couldn't decide and tried to fudge it.

"I guess Manusia is no better than the rest," she ventured, "but not much worse."

"Very diplomatic, Gilda."

"Thank you," she said, then immediately felt stupid for not recognizing when a big chunk of irony slapped her in the face.

He nodded. "You haven't mentioned Gerry Schwartz very much."

"Oh, Gerry. A sweet kid. Doing some interesting work."

"What's his involvement with Urs Gerhard?"

"Involvement with Urs?" She was genuinely surprised. "Nothing. Zip. He's just stuck trying to get his Ph.D.."

The Ambassador sipped his tea and offered Gilda a biscuit. "It's not quite that simple. Right now, Gerry Schwartz is babbling like a young girl in a Manusian jail for breaking into the office at the Hong Neiyi timber camp and stealing confidential documents."

Gilda's eyebrows scurried towards each other. She exhaled loudly. "No. I don't believe it. Gerry isn't a political animal. No, it just doesn't make sense."

"I'm afraid people often do things that are not sensible." The Ambassador explained the bits of the story that he knew. He concluded: "It just happened yesterday, so it's too early to see where this messy business is headed. But it wouldn't surprise me if the Manusians put him on trial and make a big publicity stunt out of his case."

"Can't you do something?"

"They're very sensitive about your friend, Gerry. But I spoke to the Manusian Attorney General today and I got the feeling he might agree to drop the charges and simply expel him from the country."

"I should hope so. After all, he's an American."

"An American, or a Lithuanian, or a Martian. Doesn't matter. He's a foreigner who broke the laws of a sovereign state. Having gone to the well for a favor for Schwartz, it makes it more difficult for us to come back the next day and ask for help for you."

"But, if what you say is true, Gerry broke the law. I haven't broken any law. There's a big difference."

"You're both foreigners living in a very touchy corner of the country and dealing with sensitive issues of national security."

"It sounds like you're on *their* side."

"I'm on the side of the United States. Listen, Gilda. I have a few favors left in this government. And they rely on us for foreign aid. So we have *some* leverage. I'll see what I can do. But I promise you *nothing*. Things are volatile across town at the State House. Who knows what the Sultan might do? He could dissolve the government tomorrow and install a new cabinet. He could even declare martial law. Take my word for it. It's touchy."

Gilda remembered Taffy's fears. "Does the United States support this Government or do you want to see it fall?"

"Gilda, you know that we are not empowered to meddle in the

internal affairs of a sovereign state. I can't answer that question."

"I see." Gilda thought. "You will help me, then?"

"Let me turn that question around. Will you help us?"

* * * * *

While Gilda chatted with the Ambassador, Bujang spent the evening visiting an old teacher. He showed George Wee the latest edition of *Nature's World*, which he had nicked from Gilda's mail, and told the portly man how grateful the upriver people were for his help. He hugged the older man when it was time to go. Bujang didn't turn, but he knew there were tears in the teacher's eyes.

It was time for a celebration. He went to one of his favorite haunts from his student days – the Roseland Coffee Shop. It stood on a busy corner of Anjing, open on both sides – at closing, the Chinese owner would tediously replace three dozen, numbered planks to form a wall. Bujang sat at a small, round, marble table near the street. He sipped thick coffee, sweetened with condensed milk, from a quarter-inch-thick, white, ceramic coffee cup. He munched on a *kueh kelapa*, a treat he had been looking forward to for ever-so-long. It was still warm from the oven, a round bun filled with sweetened, chopped coconut. Bujang read, for the third time, the cover story in *Nature's World*. Madame Doctor Gilda would probably be interested in it, but it would be of more interest to Urs. What a break that she had asked him to collect the mail the day before. He had another pastry to go with his second cup of coffee. He thumbed through the magazine and read about the difficulty of saving elephants in Zambia, of the politics of saving whales. One article he found particularly interesting. It was a memorial to people who had died fighting for nature and tribal rights. He stared at the photo of Chico Mendez, who had been murdered by powerful land-owners because he had defended the rights of Brazilian rubber tappers to live and work in the rainforest that the rich people wanted to cut down for cattle pasture. He looked at other "eco-martyrs". Barbara d'Archille. Joy and George Adamson. Dian Fossey. Mostly white, he noticed, but he found their situations recognizable. He wondered if his photo would one day appear in those columns. He turned the page and learned how he could support nature worldwide by buying gifts from the INF *Natural World Gift Catalog*, which was inserted into the magazine. He looked at the bedsheets with pictures of lions, at the wind-breakers with the INF koala symbol on the chest, at wine glasses and note-pads, pen and pencil sets and bird houses. He looked particularly hard at the Swiss army knife, all fifteen blades and gadgets exposed. Bujang caught the eye of the owner, a skinny, chain-smoking man that everyone had always called Joe. "Joe, old friend. I haven't seen you for ages," he said in English. "Is it too early for you to share a drink with me?"

"It's never too early, young man," Joe said. "Headhunter brandy?"

"No. I think something big is going to happen today. Let's pre-celebrate." Bujang wanted to ask for Courvoisier. That was the brandy that he had heard the rich, Chinese merchants drank at their ten-course meals. It was also the brandy of Napoleon, one of Bujang's few role models. A small guy, but a tough guy. But Bujang wasn't too sure how to pronounce the name and didn't want to be thought of as an upcountry hick. "Something good," he told Joe. "Hennessy Three Star."

* * * * *

Gilda's head felt like a durian – spiky on the outside, mushy and rotten on the inside. Taffy wanted her to catch Urs. The Ambas-sador wanted her to protect Urs. Bujang wanted an all-weather Walkman he had seen in the Anjing Electronics Emporium.

Time for Plan B. She was going to make Bujang an offer he couldn't refuse.

Rumah Sehat longhouse

Mimes dressed carefully for her rendezvous. A green, red and blue batik sarong from Java. A blue T-shirt purchased in the Bohong bazaar that said Yankees. Red flip-flops. Slipping away from a community of dozens of families was difficult enough without having to carry a screeching monkey, she thought. Still… She calmed the pet and placed Liebchen inside her T-shirt.

Mimes waited for Urs at the edge of her family's rice field, a half hour walk from the longhouse. When he was certain that she was alone, he called to her. She followed him into the forest for ten minutes. Two Penan guards were hidden near the edge of the cleared hills, ready to signal Urs if danger approached. Urs motioned Mimes to sit and remain quiet. For another ten minutes, they listened for the 'took-took-took', the first stage of the complex cry of the helmeted hornbill that would have indicated that Mimes had been followed. Instead, as dusk approached, the couple heard the calls of gibbons, the singing of a hundred different birds, the scrattering jangle of cicadas that foretold of night.

Urs lopped off several leafy branches from a nearby tree and built a nest, not too dissimilar from the tree-nests orangutans make each night. He wanted the first time with Mimes to be as good as he could make it. They lay down on the springy leaves, using Mimes' sarong as a bottom sheet.

"Why won't you kiss me?" Urs asked.

"I am kissing you."

"That's not a real kiss, with your mouth closed."

"Don't ask me to do it the other way. It feels dirty."

So they nuzzled. They smelled each other – Mimes was treated to the aroma of old burlap, Urs enjoyed Mimes' combination of essence of Hotut River and coconut-oil soap, which smelled like train engine oil. They came together quickly and made love, urgent and hard.

The second time, Urs and Mimes took their time.

"How can you do that?" Urs asked.

"This?" Mimes teased, squeezing her vaginal muscles.

"Oh God, I've never felt anything like that."

She squeezed again. "You've lived such a sheltered life, my strange, foreign friend."

Urs gently moved her black hair from her face. She wore it like the young girls did – cut in bangs and hanging down to her shoulders. She had eyes the color of the night sky.

"Tell me, who is trying to kill me? Who's talking to the police?"

"I have no proof," Mimes said. "But, I think it's Uncle Joseph."

"Why?"

"You *are* silly, aren't you? Because of you and me."

"Why, that's ridiculous. This is ..." He wanted to say the year, but wasn't too sure what year it was. "We're both adults. There's nothing wrong."

"There's a lot wrong. You're a criminal white man who is living with savages, is wanted for murder and God knows what else. I'm

222

an innocent Kayan girl from a good family who should marry a Kayan warrior and have many babies."

"You should marry me."

"You have the fever. You don't know what you mean."

"I know what I mean. I want to marry you."

"You are married. To that Penan girl."

"I mean really married. A love marriage. Like you read about in those novels you longhouse girls are always reading."

A tear dropped down her cheek. It ran against her broad nose and slid towards her mouth. "I am not worthy of you."

Urs grabbed her shoulders and shook her. "Don't you never say that. Ever." She continued to cry.

They lay for fifteen minutes, until the insects became too overpowering. "Let's walk," Urs said.

"I have to return to the longhouse," Mimes said.

"I know. I'll take you back."

"It's too dangerous. I can go back by myself."

"No. We'll be careful."

They walked through the garden paths towards Rumah Sehat. Urs asked Mimes when her brother was going to return.

"I never know. A few days, a week."

Urs had no choice but to trust the woman. The timber people were out to make as much money as quickly as they could in case the government collapsed. It was all in those reports that Gerry had somehow managed to steal. How? Who knows? Urs had found the young orangutan waiting at Gerry's hideaway with the files, but no Gerry. Stupid bastard must have been captured. They'll throw away the key. Never thought he'd have the balls to even attempt it.

"Listen to me. The kampeni has helicopters now. They are planning to cut trees everywhere in the National Park, including places just half an hour from here. We need to stop them."

"But, you are stopping them, I thought. Bujang told me about the mail you get …"

"No, not yet. This is a fight that is bigger than the Penan can handle. It's a Kayan fight. We need Kayan help. Tell Bujang that. Tell him I need six good men. In ten days. He knows where to reach me."

They were near the longhouse. It was the time of parting that young lovers like to prolong in order to maximize their pain.

"Mister Urs. I worry for you," Mimes said, squeezing his hand. As she spoke, she heard voices coming up the path. She released her grip and turned to the sound. When she turned again, Urs was gone.

CHAPTER 28

19 August. 10:00.

Anjing

Gilda and Bujang were married in a simple, civil ceremony in Anjing. It was quick, neat and soulless, which suited the participants perfectly.

Gilda had few illusions about marriage and didn't expect it to change her life. She was surprised that Bujang had agreed so quickly. She wondered if it was the pre-nuptial gift. Or was it because she had told him that she was pregnant and that he wouldn't be able to see his child if she left the country?

The bottom line was that Gilda would become Manusian. Hopefully, Bujang would stick around camp a little bit more. She was content. However, Bujang seemed, somehow, pensive. The thrill of being in Anjing? No, it must be the marriage. Gilda promised him that he could organize a party in Rumah Sehat, where he could drink Headhunter brandy until dawn, when they got back to Camp Trinil.

After the ceremony, Gilda told Bujang about the custom of *"bulan madu"*, a honeymoon. She wanted to go deep into the rain-forest and look for orangutans. Sleep in shelters that Bujang would construct. Eat provisions that Bujang would carry. Roast wild game that Bujang would kill with his shotgun. It was the best break from the dramas of camp life that Gilda could think of. Bujang suggested a real honeymoon would be Singapore, but Gilda was determined.

Rumah Sehat

The papers Gerry had stolen confirmed Urs' fears. All the signs indicated that international, public pressure would sooner or later force a reduction in logging operations. It made sense therefore, at least to the owners of Manusia's timber concessions, to maximize their income while they still could – by cutting vast swathes of tropical forest, the Southeast Asian equivalent of making hay while the sun shines. Greed feeds on desperation, Urs realized. The Manusian officials were encouraging their Korean, Malaysian and Filipino contractors to bring in extra men and equipment. Part of that influx included expatriate expertise to establish 'heli-rigging' services – a procedure in which heavy-duty choppers airlift components of tractors, earthmovers and backhoes to the middle of nowhere. The ground vehicles are then re-assembled so that they can eat their way out of the forest by digging roads that run towards the nearest other road or river. First perfected by oil companies exploring in Irian Jaya, the method is an expensive, but quick, way to construct roads where none existed previously. Once the roads were in, the logs could come out.

On his return from Anjing, Bujang had gathered a group of Kayans he trusted. Urs knew them all and he introduced them to the Penan, who offered limp hands to shake. "I have sent pages from the Hong Neiyi program to my correspondents overseas," Urs told the Kayans. "This afternoon, when the helicopters return like swifts return to the nest, we take photos of them to prove they exist."

"And then?" asked Avalon.

Urs remained quiet, hoping that somebody else would complete the sentence. It was Ding Ajang who spoke: "Then we get rid of the problem."

Finally, the aristocratic Kayans were going to be full partners in this escapade.

The plan had been worked out by Bujang and Ding. An advance party would set fire to the office building and, if possible, the ramshackle longhouse where the laborers slept. During the commotion, the Kayans figured, the Hong Neiyi men who guarded the equipment would rush to fight the fire, leaving the tractors and helicopters exposed. The second guerrilla group would then burn the equipment and get the hell out of there. The plan required guts, coordination and fifteen jerry cans of gasoline.

"And when will we do this?" Avalon asked.

"I say tomorrow," Ding Ajang answered.

"No, let's wait for Bujang," Urs cautioned.

"But we don't know when he and Gilda will return," Ding Ajang said. "They could be away for weeks."

"Let's give him another few days," Urs said. "I don't think he'd want to miss this."

CHAPTER 29

23 August. 10:00.

Mount Malu National Park

It took the couple four days hard slog to march from Camp Trinil, at the southern end, to the northern boundary of the park, near the international border with the Malaysian state of Sarawak. Gilda had never been in this part of the forest and Bujang could see that she was entranced by the different vegetation in the higher altitude of Borneo's central plateau. "It's so much more pleasant than the soggy, lowland part of the park," she said. "Amazing I haven't been up here."

They saw tracks of clouded leopard, deer, wild pig and foot-prints of the rare Sumatran rhino.

There were plenty of orangutans as well – not on the 5,000-foot-high plateau, but in the untamed, river valleys.

"Buji," Gilda had said to her new husband the night before, as they shivered together in two sleeping bags that had been zipped together, "*di sini ada banyak baik.*" This is a great place. Let's stay a while.

"*Banyak baik*, Madame Doctor Gilda," he agreed, half-heartedly. Bujang was getting restless. During the few hours they had stayed at Camp Trinil after their marriage in Anjing, Mimes had sent him a message that there was a big operation coming up and that he was needed. Bujang didn't want to be out in the middle of nowhere when there was work to be done.

Gilda snuggled closer to Bujang for warmth. She nestled in the crook of his arm and pushed herself against him. Wife or not, Bujang didn't like screwing in a communal sleeping bag – since he would have to smell Gilda's juices throughout the night. Funny, with the longhouse girls the *jamu* usually takes care of those things, he thought.

Bujang was no match for Gilda. She rolled on her back, pulling him on top of her. She had a million dollar view of the Milky Way. In the moonlight, Bujang had a view of Gilda's lips, mouthing the words: "Fuck me, Taffy."

Bujang woke before dawn and stoked the fire, warming some of the roast boar he had cooked the evening before. Gilda awoke half an hour after dawn, crawled out of the sleeping bag, walked five paces from the fire, had her morning pee, washed her face in the stream, pulled on her soggy jungle pants and sat down next to her husband. Still sleepy, she laid her head on his shoulder. She heard the melodic love songs of Indonesian torch-singer Budi (Silver Queen) Sutanto leaking through the earphones of Bujang's bright yellow Walkman. "You're going to use up all your batteries," she had warned him more than once. He did not hear.

The sound that jarred Gilda from her early morning stupor was a faint rumbling in the distance.

The noise became louder. A helicopter. Within thirty seconds, it passed directly overhead and continued out of sight over a ridge to the east.

"We're going to look for them and see what they're up to," Gilda announced.

Of course, looking for a landed helicopter in tropical rainforest is a hit or miss proposition. They stumbled up ridges and slid down gulleys. At least three times during the first two hours, Bujang complained to his employer and wife that this journey would have been a lot easier if they had only waited a few weeks for his motorcycle to arrive. Gilda thought this was cute and did her best to be romantic by calling the younger man *anak nakal*. My naughty boy.

After walking half a day towards the headwaters of the Marab River, Gilda and Bujang heard a shot. A minute or two later, they heard another. The noise was soft, maybe half a mile away. Northeast.

The terrain was relatively flat and they arrived half an hour later. Bujang saw the reason for the shooting before Gilda. "*Jangan tengoh, jangan tengoh*," he said, protecting her. However, of course she came closer and looked. She gasped when she saw the body of an adult, female orangutan crumpled on the jungle floor. The flies had already discovered her, as had a weasel-like civet and several dozen dung beetles.

They examined the carcass. Her left hip had been blown away, probably with the first shot, which had knocked her and her infant from the fig tree. Although crippled, she had apparently tried to run after the attackers, who killed her with a blast that ripped her open. One side of her chest was a mass of blood and muscle. Her one visible nipple was elongated and dark brown. It oozed milk.

Bujang had no trouble in tracking the group. Three men, he explained, as they walked.

Gilda and Bujang walked another twenty minutes and came to a natural clearing, hardly larger than the rotor span of the helicopter. One man was down by the river, soaking his feet while he punched numbers into a laptop computer. Another was nearby, packing up the team's surveying equipment. A third, probably the pilot, sat on a rock near the river holding a very frightened and exhausted orangutan baby. The tiny ape sucked on his index finger.

Gilda rushed out from the forest. "Who the hell are you?" she said from fifty yards. "You fucking murderers. You killed one of my orangutans."

"Madame Doctor Gilda," Bujang called, chasing his wife. "*Hati hati. Dia orang gila. Biaran, lah.*" Watch out for these crazy guys. Leave it alone. Stupid woman, he thought in English. This could be trouble.

Gilda shouted back for him to leave this to her, explaining that this was a fight between white people.

Gilda pulled out her *parang*. The startled helicopter pilot froze. His passengers, dressed similarly in worn, short-sleeve, white shirts and tan shorts, stayed where they were for several seconds – then, almost on signal, they began backing towards the helicopter.

"Stop, you bastards. I want to know who you are and what you're doing in my Park."

"We're just out for an innocent picnic, ma'am," the pilot said. "Don't mean to disturb nobody."

"Disturb? Disturb, you cocksuckers? You just killed an orangutan. Who the hell do you think you are, Alfred Russel Wallace?"

The allusion to the co-developer of the theory of natural

selection, who, coincidentally, was one of the all-time, greatest orangutan hunters, was lost on the men. They couldn't tell what this crazy woman was up to.

"Do you know who I am?"

"Yes, ma'am. I believe you're Gilda Korda-Breckenridge."

"My name is Gilda Korda-Breckenridge-Bungan. This is my husband."

The men weren't sure if they should shake hands and congratulate the half-naked Kayan. They decided to nod their greeting from a distance. They inched closer to the chopper.

"Give me that orangutan."

"Sorry, ma'am. Can't do that."

"What do you mean? You've broken about eighty Manusian laws. You've killed one animal, orphaned another and now you're kidnapping her on top of it. I demand to know your names and who you work for."

"Come on, guys, let's get out of here," the pilot said to the others. Casually, trying to pretend that they were not being threatened by a mad, henna-haired Amazon flailing a *parang*, they climbed into the helicopter.

"Give me that orangutan," Gilda shouted.

"Sorry, ma'am. This is my pet. Her name's, uh, Princess. You wouldn't want me to give up my pet, would you? Think how sad she'd be. Wouldn't ya, darlin?"

The pilot slammed the cockpit door, started the engine and lifted off. Gilda threw her *parang* at the helicopter. It bounced impotently off the door.

From the ground, Gilda and Bujang could clearly see the painted notice on the bottom of the helicopter as it whirred above them. "Hong Neiyi Timber. Wood for modern living." Gilda sat in the sun, staring up at the spot in the sky where the helicopter had disappeared. For fifteen minutes, she sat motionless. Bujang decided to leave her be, but finally he approached and sat down next to her. He saw something he had never seen before in Gilda. There were tears running down her cheeks. *"Pulang,"* he said gently. Let's go back.

CHAPTER 30

30 August. 04:00.

Hong Neiyi timber camp

At four a.m., the Penan group, by virtue of their greater stealth and night vision, advanced on the metal-walled timber camp office building, leaving in their wake the carcasses of ten watchdogs which had been blowpiped an hour earlier. The subtlety of the previous operation was missing. This was a scorched earth campaign. The office building was unguarded and two Penan poured two jerry cans of gasoline around the building.

A second Penan group poured gasoline on the wooden stilts of the rough barracks. They poured enough to burn the buildings, but not enough, they hoped, to create a fire so great that anyone would be killed.

When the Penan were finished, they gave the 'kwankwit-kwankwit-kek-kek-kek' call of the bay owl, called the 'ghost bird' in Malay because bad luck usually befalls anyone who sees the nocturnal omen. Urs, who was with the Kayan group at the river below the motor pool, replied with a higher pitched 'kwankwit' response. The Penan confirmed the message with one, last owl call and lit their fire.

Within seconds, the camp was in turmoil. Sirens sounded, men shouted and, amidst the confusion, Urs and six Kayans, including Bujang, started their early morning's labor. Two Kayans torched the six speedboats docked in the simple, wooden harbor. The other guerillas moved up to the motor pool, now empty since the guards had run off to help fight the fire in the residential area 200 yards away. The natives worked quickly, not bothering to slash tires but

232

simply pouring gasoline over anything that resembled an engine. When all three terrorist groups – the boat terrorists, the tractor terrorists and the helicopter terrorists – had retreated to relative safety at the outskirts of the motor pool, one man in each group gave out his best rooster cock-a-doodle-doo. One. Two. Three. Everything was ready. One man from each group lit a match.

The men then had a choice of two escape routes. One was to slide down the mud bank below the motor pool to the river, jump in and then drift downstream with the current.

The other route, taken by Urs, Bujang, Ding Ajang and Robin Nawan Bala, was riskier – but offered the satisfaction of having a final look at the carnage. It meant backtracking towards the workers' quarters and, at the last minute, turning left towards the forest, passing directly behind the sturdier structures housing Jong and the other managers.

"Looks like Apocalypse Now," Bujang said.

"No, more like Gone with the Wind," observed Robin.

"Let's just get the hell out of here," Urs said.

Urs stopped at the forest's edge for one last photo of the conflagration. During the pause, Bujang spotted something odd, about 40 yards away, in front of the 'executive housing' where Jong had his quarters. It was a wooden cage, measuring about one yard on each side, covered with wire. It was hard to tell in the combination of dark night and blazing flames, but Bujang thought he saw something small and orange inside. He went to have a closer look.

"Bujang, come back," Urs urged in a stage whisper. Either Bujang did not hear or chose not to hear the command. He ran towards the cage in a zig-zag duck waddle, something he had seen in World War II movies.

Urs had no choice but to shout. "Bujang. Get your ass out of there. Let's go."

While Urs' intention to save his friend was noble, his timing was awful. Two people heard the warning above the turmoil. One was Bujang, who simply zig-zagged towards the cage in faster, jerkier movements. The other was Jong Il Kim. He was a hundred yards away and armed with a shotgun.

Bujang reached the cage and confirmed his fear. Cowering inside was the orangutan infant that he and Gilda had seen captured by

233

the helicopter crew. He ripped open the flimsy door, yelling: "Run. Get your ass out of there," at the tiny animal.

Just before Bujang could reach into the cage to grab the orangutan, Urs tackled him. It was timed so that Jong Il Kim's shotgun blast, taken on the run from fifty yards and aimed at Bujang, missed the Kayan and hit Urs in the side instead. The two men tumbled on the hard dirt for three yards, rolling over twice. Although not planned, this action saved their lives, since it denied Jong another clear shot. It also cost Urs his glasses, which were ripped off during the tumult.

The two friends stumbled into the shadows and, soon thereafter, into the sanctuary of the jungle. The tiny orangutan crawled to the open door of the cage, took a look around and retreated to the corner of the enclosure. She cowered in her sleeping blanket, wondering where her mother was.

CHAPTER 31

30 August. 10:00.

Penan encampment

Following the attack on Hong Neiyi, Bujang had half-carried Urs back to the encampment. The Swiss had cursed every step. He was virtually blind without his glasses and it seemed to him that during that adrenalin-filled march he trod upon every exposed tree root in all of Borneo. He was paying the price today, he thought, as his sprained ankle swelled to the point where each step required every bit of his Swiss mountain courage.

But still, he was alive. Crippled, old Laki, wounded by a shotgun blast during one of the earliest anti-timber skirmishes, reached out to his son-in-law as Bujang helped Urs into the camp. Laki was the most experienced Penan medic in the group and gingerly tried to extract the pellets from Urs' side. He was picking away with his *parang* tip until Urs told Maya to get his Swiss army knife from their shelter. He handed the knife to the old man and showed him how to sterilize it in the fire. It was a quick and nasty operation, during which Urs bit on a stick to keep from screaming with pain. The old man covered the wound with a leaf poultice to prevent infection.

Urs seemed to recover quickly. His side hurt, but surely that was due to old Laki's gouging and scraping. Urs spent the afternoon stumbling around, joking with his group and writing in his journal about the extraordinary events of the past twelve hours.

"You seem to be okay, brother Urs," Bujang had said. "I will call back in a couple of days."

"Bujang, please do me a favor," Urs said.

Bujang understood. "I'll send your regards to my sister."

That night, Urs experienced severe abdominal pain, coupled with nausea. It was a normal reaction to a colon that had been perforated by two lead pellets, leaking stool into the peritoneal cavity and infecting the normally-sterile internal organs with the nastiest bacteria the body produces.

"I'm worried about Brother Urs," Maya told Laki during the night. They had both been awake for hours, ever since it became clear that his groaning was not his usual, high-decibel snoring.

That night, his stomach became as stiff as an ironwood tree. Peritonitis had set in, accompanied by vomiting. His temperature rose to 104 degrees.

Urs lay semi-comatose. Maya dabbed his head with water from a gourd. She offered him jungle fowl soup. He babbled and dribbled and shivered in response.

Maya pleaded with her husband. "For the love of God, Brother Urs, take some water. You're burning up." He was sufficiently conscious to sip some of the water. Ten seconds later, he vomited with a dry, racking cough that had long ago cleared his stomach.

"Look at his tongue, Father Laki," Maya said. They stared at it – bone dry, hanging out like a dog's, coated yellow with dried saliva and bile.

"Go get Bujang," Laki ordered Avalon.

"*Wo ist meine Liebchen?*" Urs babbled.

"She is here," Maya said, recognizing the name. She handed him the little monkey, which he clutched like a rag doll. Liebchen chattered and scampered away.

"*Wo ist meine Liebchen?*" Urs cried through the fever. "*Wasser*. No, you can't do that to us Penan. *Mami, ich gehe nur nach Zurich, nicht aus Ende der Welt*. Marry me. *Schreibt den Politikern und helft uns!*"

Avalon had first looked for Bujang at Rumah Sehat. There he was told Bujang was probably at Camp Trinil. Like the original marathon runner, Avalon finally tracked him down and accompanied the Kayan back to the Penan camp.

During the six hours Avalon had taken to return with Bujang, Urs' fever had begun to wildly soar and plummet, and he suffered malarial extremes of hot and cold in five minute intervals.

Bujang saw how serious the situation was. He slapped his friend across his face. "Answer me," he shouted. Urs replied by babbling in German about the Zurich Grasshopper soccer team.

"Urs. Talk to me. It's Bujang."

Bujang had hit on a moment of clarity. "Hello," Urs said, sounding like a child.

"Urs. Listen to me. You are very sick. You need a doctor. If you stay here, you will die. We have to take you to Bohong."

From somewhere, Urs got strength. He reached out and grabbed Bujang's arm. "*Nein. Kein doctor.* If I die, I die. I die here. *Ich werde hier sterben.*" The effort of that little speech exhausted him and he fell back on his mat with a shiver.

Bujang, Laki and Avalon discussed the options. Carry Urs to Rumah Sehat, which would take four hours, and then put him in a longboat to Bohong. There, he might be cured, after which he would be arrested, along with Bujang and half of Rumah Sehat. Or leave him here to die as a Penan. "There's just one other option," Bujang said to his Penan friends before he ran back to Camp Trinil.

A military hospital outside Anjing

Taib bin Susah strolled restlessly around the military hospital outside Anjing. He was desperate to get out and return to his family. He swore never again to work in the timber camp. Never, ever again, he repeated to himself. He set it to music. Never, ever again, he hummed. Next time the doctor came, he would insist that he be allowed to leave. However, he had insisted last week – and the week before. Never, ever again, he whistled, as he smashed his tin, eating plate against the wall.

Anjing

"Beer?"

"Yes, please."

"Have some popcorn."

Gerry took a handful. Mustafa bin Kayu placed a cold Tuborg in front of the visitor. He sat down on the opposite end of the sofa and sipped a Bloody Mary.

"Thank you for getting me out of that prison," Gerry said. "It *was* you, wasn't it?"

It was really the American Ambassador, but the Minister of the Environment kept silent, willing to take credit from wherever it came.

"Don't get too relaxed, my friend. Technically, you are still under arrest, Mr. Schwartz. You have been released in my custody for questioning. That's all."

Gerry said nothing. Mustafa bin Kayu saw that Gerry felt terribly uncomfortable. The Minister's house was luxurious and immaculate – and Gerry wore the same clothes that he had worn when he was arrested at the Hong Neiyi timber camp. Mustafa bin Kayu was not accustomed to having malodorous people in his home. He would have to disinfect the living room. Such was the price of being a senior, government official.

"Now, I know you've told the police a dozen times, but would you tell me as well – exactly what you were doing at that timber camp."

The questioning by the Manusian security forces and the nights he had spent in jail had worn down Gerry's powers of fabrication. He told the Minister the truth.

"It seems to me like you've been had, Mr. Schwartz."

"What's going to happen to me?"

Mustafa bin Kayu didn't like this man. He was wimpy. He didn't look you straight in the eye. He had dirty fingernails. However, those characteristics, as loathsome as they were to the Manusian official, didn't account for all of his distaste of Gerry. He chewed on a carrot stick, wondering what it could be.

"What's going to happen to you? Good question," Mustafa bin Kayu answered. "Who knows what is going to happen to any of us?"

"Why don't you get to the point?" Gerry said, emboldened by fatigue and beer.

Mustafa bin Kayu smiled. He had figured out why he found Gerry Schwartz so galling. It was because the young American was of so little strategic use.

"The point. The point is that you are stuck between a rock and a hard place," the Minister said. "Tell me, Mr. Schwartz, what do you want most in life?"

"Oh, I don't know."

"Come on, now," Mustafa bin Kayu said, urging him on like a

child. "Think."

"I really would like my Ph.D.."

"I have one. They're nothing special, you know. They merely prove that you can put up with the whims of pig-headed professors for three years. It's more of an endurance test than an intellectual achievement."

"I didn't know that you had a doctorate."

"Does that surprise you? That a brown man from a tiny country can earn a graduate degree? Global, macro-economic theory as it applies to resource-rich but cash-poor, developing countries. London School of Economics. Then a post-grad at the Sorbonne. Fat lot of good it did me."

Mustafa bin Kayu hadn't decided whether he would or wouldn't make Gerry Schwartz a martyr by publicly prosecuting him for a string of criminal acts. Stealing private documents from Hong Neiyi was the least important crime for which Gerry could be tried. Mustafa bin Kayu was tempted to throw the book at the American and implicate him in every act of sabotage, arson, civil disobedience and public riot that had been committed by the natives during the last few months.

"Tell me everything you know about Urs Gerhard."

Gerry's exposé of the Swiss was mild. The Minister was experienced enough to realize that Gerry really didn't know very much.

"Well then, tell me about Gilda Breckenridge."

"What do you want to know?"

"Oh, whatever you think might help us in our investigations. She's been out there a long time and she is ... was ... your boss. How does she spend her time?"

Gerry wasn't sure whether it was a good thing to be a friend of Gilda's or not. "She spends most of her time studying orangutans. She's accumulated books and books of data. She's one of the world's experts on the animals. She ..."

"Yes, I've heard all that. But what is she like as a person?"

"Oh, quite friendly. Supportive."

"Come on, Mr. Schwartz. Don't treat me like a child. Does she ever engage in behavior that might be, how shall I say it, somehow unusual?"

"I'm not sure what you mean."

"I can assure you that what you say will remain between us. I think it is unlikely that you will see her for quite some time in any case. So humor me. We have to know about everything that goes on at Camp Trinil. Help us with our investigation and we might be able to help you. I heard, for example, that whenever she goes away from camp for more than a day she engages in a certain ceremony."

"You know about that?"

Mustafa bin Kayu had baited his hook with a bit of Gilda's pillow talk. He nodded sagely.

"Well, it works something like this. Whenever she ..."

Gerry's narrative was interrupted by the phone. The Minister walked to the other side of the room to answer it. "Mustafa bin Kayu," he said into the elegant apparatus that looked as if it might have been designed for Louis XIV. The Minister listened for two minutes, alternately nodding, scowling and rubbing the back of his neck. "Yes, I'll be right over."

"Mister Schwartz," the Minister said, after he had hung up, "as much as it pains me to tell you I'm afraid I have good news for you. You have been expelled from Manusia, effective immediately."

Gerry thought it was a trap. "I don't understand. Why? How?"

"You obviously have friends in high places. A car is coming to take you to the police station and then to the airport."

Gerry let out a shriek of joy that he had not uttered since Queenie had learned her first sign. He gulped down the last of the beer, pumped Mustafa bin Kayu's hand and rushed out of the house, his fist punching the air.

Mustafa bin Kayu was less sanguine. The phone call was from the Sultan's uncle, who was also Chef de Cabinet. In addition to the good news for Gerry, the caller had told Mustafa bin Kayu that the Sultan wanted to see him. Within the hour. Mustafa bin Kayu went into his bedroom to put on a suit.

Camp Trinil

"*Tapi, Madame Doctor Gilda. Dia sakit benar benar.*" Bujang begged Gilda to go and help Urs. "Urs is dying," he said. She had refused and was planning to refuse again. "That man is trouble. He wants to get us thrown out," she explained to her husband in Malay. "There's no way I'll help him. And you still haven't explained to me how you know him and how you're involved in all this," she scolded.

Bujang was forced to play his last card. "Madame Doctor Gilda," he pleaded and then explained quietly, in simple Malay, that Urs had saved his life.

Gilda looked at her thin husband. Her left eyebrow scrooched down and her mouth formed a perfect O. "*Kamu kenal dia?*"

Bujang nodded. He knew Urs.

Gilda needed a while to consider this. You know him and he saved your life? "*Kamu tidak bilang.*" You never told me, she scolded.

"Enough of this," Bujang erupted. "I never asked you for anything. But now I'm begging you to help this man," Bujang said, wanting to add, but holding back: "I married you when you were stuck. Now do something for me."

Gilda paused just three seconds before replying, a decisiveness record for the woman. "*Ayo. Berangkat,*" she said, as she began gathering her meager medical supplies. Let's go.

During the forced march to the Penan camp, Bujang told Gilda almost all. He told her about his involvement with the anti-timber blockade. He told her about Urs and Mimes. He provided details of the raid on the Hong Neiyi timber camp, how he had gone back to save the orangutan and how Urs had taken the shotgun pellets meant for him. He told her all of this in Malay. He couldn't bring himself to reveal his facility in English. Some skeletons must remain, he and Urs had decided at the beginning of their partnership. The less Gilda knew about Bujang's affiliation with the Swiss, the easier things would be for everyone.

When Gilda arrived at the Penan camp, Urs was wracked with pain and delirious. It was clear, she explained, that Urs could only be saved by immediate surgery, intravenous fluids, steroids and antibiotics, and a big favor from God. He was not quite in a coma, but close, his mind roaming in a netherworld that flitted between coherence and dreams.

"Urs. Do you know who I am?" she asked the man in English.

He opened his right eye and tried to focus. His tongue sagged against his upper lip. Gilda bent closer.

"My name is Gilda. I am married to Bujang."

"*Ja, Gilda. Ich kenne dich,*" he managed to sputter.

"*Du bist sehr krank,*" she said, switching to German. "You need help. We must get you to Bohong. To a doctor."

If Urs had been unconscious during that exchange, chances are that the group would have tried to carry him out of the forest, risking their own security. However, he was coherent enough to repeat what he had said to Bujang. "I will die here." Gilda reached into her medicine case and extracted the closest thing she had to a sedative. It was antihistamine, used to combat bee stings. She injected it into Urs' muscular hip. He shuddered at the jab, then relaxed.

The injection seemed to give him a few moments of strength. "Gilda. I have heard of you," he said in English. "You have your work. I have my work. Your work will continue. Forever. My work is finished, unless you can help."

Christ, someone else who wants me to help, Gilda thought.

"These people are good people," he continued. "They have a good fight. But they cannot fight by themselves. They are too small. They need someone big. Someone from the outside."

The injection began to take effect and Urs' eyes started to close. By the time he awoke, it was night and only Maya was awake to hear him mumble: "Marry me." She did as she thought he requested and placed a few drops of water on his tongue. Penan rarely cry, but Maya was as close as she had ever come. "Brother Urs. Don't die," she whispered in his ear. "Your son will need a father."

PART VII

THE
LIVING
LEGEND

244

CHAPTER 32

2 September. 16:00.

Mount Malu National Park

The Penan band, accompanied by Bujang and Gilda, buried Urs deep in the forest. As Urs was lowered in the ground, Laki had gently placed the Swiss's blowpipe alongside, so Urs would have good hunting in the next life. On Urs' other side, Gilda had placed her ritual *parang*. The Penan erected a hand-carved, burial pole. Everyone's unspoken hope was that the burial site they had selected was so far into the interior of the forest that it wouldn't be desecrated by timber trucks.

"*Kenapa kamu akan tolong*, Madame Doctor Gilda?" How are you going to help?" Bujang had asked Gilda, as they walked back to Camp Trinil.

CHAPTER 33

2 September. 22:00.

Camp Trinil

Bujang repeated his question after dinner that evening.

Gilda didn't have a glib answer. The man had saved her husband's life. Then he had asked her to help fight for the forest.

"Nevertheless, he died before he told me what he wanted me to do," Gilda had argued with Bujang. "His fight's over. Urs is dead. Gone. *Kaput*. All bets are off."

"*Dia tidak mati*," Bujang had said after a while.

"*Apa kamu bilang?*" Gilda asked sarcastically, adding in English: "What do you mean, he's not dead? He's as dead as Hitler."

Bujang then took a deep breath. "Who says Hitler's dead?" he said in not-bad, vaguely British-accented English. "They never found his body. He might still be in Argentina or someplace."

Gilda had not been this startled since Jaap Van der Kamp had demonstrated the usefulness of the *palang*. She looked at her husband, dressed (or undressed), as usual, in faded, blue basketball shorts and a smile.

"Bujang. Run that one by me again," she said in English.

"Simple. Nobody knows Urs is dead. Therefore ..."

"Hold it. Hold it. Do you know what you just said?"

"Yes, Madame Doctor Gilda. I was proposing that ..."

"Since when have you spoken English?"

"Since I was a boy."

"And you never told me?" she scolded.

"I never had anything this important to tell you."

Gilda ignored the non-sequitur. "I can't believe this. Who else knows you speak English?"

"Just a few people in the longhouse. Urs knows. Knew. My sister. Some school friends in Anjing. Not many."

"You tricked me. My own husband. He tricked me," she cried to an unseen God. "I don't believe this."

"Madame Doctor Gilda. I am sorry if I have brought you pain. I thought it was better you did not know I spoke English. Now I think it is better."

"Why? What's changed?"

"Brother Urs is dead. And my people are in trouble."

"So?"

"So … you and I can help them."

Gilda and Bujang decided that it served nobody's interest for the outside world to know that Urs had died. Bujang would spread the message that Urs had been injured and that the Penan had carried him deep into the forest to recuperate quietly. Mimes would be distraught, Bujang realized, but maybe it was better if she thought the European had forgotten about her. Those inter-racial affairs rarely work out.

Bujang would take over as field commander. He looked forward to directing the rebellion. He would create strategies to keep the pressure on the timber companies, saying he was acting on behalf of Urs.

Gilda would keep the pressure on the outside world. She was a good symbol for the west, so was Urs. With two good symbols, one working to save the orangutans, the other working to save the people, they could together keep the forest more or less intact.

CHAPTER 34

7 September. 15:00.

Camp Trinil

Gilda tried holding the pen in her teeth. That produced a scrawl that *no* one could understand. She then held the pen in her right hand, but without using her thumb. Not too bad. However, a scientist has to try different approaches, so she tried writing with her left hand. Maybe.

"Dear Ms. B.B. Bitch" Gilda began.

No, seriously, how would he phrase a sentence? she said to herself.

"Dear Ms. B.B. I wish to thank you from all of us for …"

No, too formal. B.B.'s letter, which Bujang had found in Urs' meager personal effects, had been more personal.

"Dear B.B. We are thrilled to see the latest issue of …"

No, he wouldn't have used the word 'thrilled'.

How about "Dear Fraulein B.B." That sounds about right. "My Penan family and I are very happy that you were able to help us get our message across to INF members in the United States. My friends say that they have never seen such good photos of themselves. What is the news of the lobbying effort? Please send details, through the normal channels."

I can't do this, Gilda screamed inside herself. B.B.'s not so dumb. And I'm not that good. But you promised …

"Life here continues to be busy. Several weeks ago, we were able to dismantle …" no, 'dismantle' isn't right … "destroy six helicopters owned by Hong Neiyi. Here are some unprocessed films. Could you please make pictures and send extra sets to our mutual friend in Europe? Thank you." Thank you? Thank you for what, you silly, spoiled woman? Thank you for getting me killed?

"During the action against the timber company, my right hand was badly wounded by a shotgun blast. It is quite painful to write, but I hope you can read the writing anyway. I wanted to write to you quickly to tell you our success and to tell you we also still need your help."

Gilda was beginning to get into the swing of things. She continued: "I still have not met Doctor Gilda Korda-Breckenridge. I hear she got married to a wonderful man and her name is now Gilda Korda-Breckenridge-Bungan. I understand from mutual *freunde*, that she is making spectacular achievements in her studies of orangutan behavior."

She'll never buy this. Never mind, finish it.

"I will close the letter now. It is time for me to hunt the wild pig. This is a bad year for wild pig, because of all the timber cutting – but we must eat.

"Your friend, Urs Gerhard."

Gilda folded the letter around a dried, jungle orchid she had picked out of the Camp Trinil herbarium. Might as well keep the old flame alive, Gilda thought.

One down, six to go. Maybe I should take a break and see what the orangutans are up to? Haven't been in the forest for days. And I have to write that blasted, six-monthly report. I knew they wouldn't have the guts to cut off my funding. But, shit, I don't have the time to write reports.

That letter you just wrote is shit, Gilda, the scientist said to herself. Just awful. She scrunched it up and threw it into a corner, where Ringo picked it up, chewed open the envelope and placed the dried flower in his protruding, lower lip. He balanced it there, like a waiter carrying a tray of drinks, as he wandered outside. You promised that Swiss you'd help. You didn't promise you'd be his ghostwriter.

* * * * *

God, this guy got a lot of mail. "Lieber Hans-Peter," she began to Urs' best friend in Switzerland. No, better not risk it. He knew Urs too well. What's next in the pile?

Gilda couldn't resist one, last letter. "Dear Minister Mustafa bin

Kayu," it began. "Please be careful when you go out to the golf course. There are dangers in the rough. Your humble servant, Urs".

"Squarwk."

The noise jolted Gilda as she was licking the envelope. She cut her tongue.

"Screerch. Urgent for Doctor Gilda. Come in Camp Trinil."

"Camp Trinil, here. Identify yourself."

"I am James Ong, personal assistant to Minister of the Environment Tusau Padan. Do you scrorch me?"

Minister Tusau Padan? "Yes, I scrorch you," she said.

"The Minister has declared a red alert and requests your presence in Bohong in two days' time to discuss urgent, environmental reforms."

Gilda started to giggle, then she started to laugh and, finally, she guffawed. Great wales of laughter ran through the sticky afternoon.

"Camp Trinil. Come in. Do you read me?"

Gilda switched off the radio.

Queenie, who had been watching this scene, scurried over to Gilda. The radio frightened the orangutan. The lonely ape, confused and abandoned since Gerry's disappearance, clasped Gilda's hand.

Gilda heard the faint noise of a motor. Too low-pitched to be Bujang's trail bike. It was a speedboat. Gilda walked outside and headed slowly to the river. She arrived at the end of the dock's walkway just as a tall, sun-burnt young lady with straight, auburn hair climbed out of the boat forty yards away. The stranger thanked the smiling, Chinese driver, who sped away upstream. She wore pink, satin basketball shorts which hugged her not-very-large ass and a loose-fitting tank top bearing the inscription: 'Rainforests Don't Grow on Trees'. She hoisted onto her back a well-used Kelty pack, shouldered a brand-new, aluminum camera case with tripod strapped to the side and firmly grasped a jet-black Sony camcorder. As she walked up the dock, she confronted Ringo, who stood in her way and saluted. The visitor saluted back. Ringo grabbed hold of the bottom of her shorts, fascinated by the slippery texture of the material. He held the material in his fingers as the woman-ape couple continued up the dock until they met Gilda and Queenie. The visitor spoke first.

"G'dye. My name's Jennifer. From Australia?" she said with a rise at the end of the sentence – making it sound as if Australians aren't really sure that what they say is correct. "I thought you might be able to help me find Urs. Urs Gerhard?"

Ringo licked the sweat-stained, pink material. It was an odd taste, but not unpleasant.

EARTHLOVE
By: Paul Spencer Sochaczewski
Publication: Summer 2001

ROD LAWRENCE, ex-college basketball star and ex-United States senator struggles not to become the ex-director of the world's largest nature conservation organization. While Rod's sex-performance-rating sinks as low as a developing country's credit rating, his luscious turncoat Swedish secretary plans a conservation marketing coup that promises to radically change the way people relate to nature.

Meanwhile, a perky but pesky Italian reporter has her own methods of getting to the root cause of Rod's dilemma, provided that the scheming exiled Queen of Romania doesn't crush him first with her plans for pelicans and glory. Can anyone save this planet? Can Rod regain his manhood with a tropical herbal concoction? And while we're looking for miracles, what about curing those yips on the green?

* * * * *

Paul Spencer Sochaczewski's next major work of non-fiction:
An Inordinate Fondness for Beetles

An Inordinate Fondness for Beetles is a personal nature-travel book, based on imagined campfire conversations with the Victorian-era British naturalist/explorer/philosopher Alfred Russel Wallace.

* * * * *

For an authoritative view of how people and nature influence each other in Southeast Asia, look at
Soul of the Tiger
by Jeffrey McNeely and Paul Spencer Sochaczewski.

University of Hawaii Press
ISBN: 0-8248-1669-2

Soul of the Tiger takes us to an exotic world where human life is intimately linked with rhinos and cobras, crocodiles, elephants and man-eating tigers.

During two decades, the authors, American conservationists and adventurers, lived and learned in Southeast Asia – from Thailand and Burma, to Cambodia and Vietnam, to Malaysia and Indonesia. Their fascinating, bizarre, and often hilarious accounts reveal the vital connection between these people and their animal neighbors. To villagers, animals are omens, deities, meat, leather, jungle tractors, competitors, and even ancestors. To senior government officials and kings, the same animals are powerful symbols of power and order.

* * * * *

Become an instant environmental expert with
Eco Bluff Your Way to Greenism – The Guide to Instant Environmental Credibility
by Paul Spencer Wachtel and Jeffrey McNeely.

Bonus Books, Chicago. 1991.
ISBN: 0-929387-22-8

G REEN is the world's trendiest color. Everybody wants to be seen as caring about the environment, but few people have the time or energy needed to get past rudimentary exclamations about the greenhouse effect or the loss of tropical forests.
   Eco-Bluff Your Way to Greenism provides quick and painless eco-credibility.

* * * * *

Check the publisher's websites
http://www.sidharta.com.au for our best-selling titles
http://publisher-guidelines.com.au for manuscript submission guidelines

Other best-selling Sid Harta titles:

The Timor Man (book of the month, Singapore, Hong Kong, Australia)
The Asian Trilogy
Jakarta
Freedom Square
Merdeka Square (book of the month, Singapore)
The Fifth Season (book of the month, New Zealand, Singapore, Australia)
(All of the above titles by: Kerry B. Collison)

* * * * *

Northaven – Sally Graham
And So To Court – Jeanine Lloyd
Falkenhayn Park – Tineke van Houdt
Human Stock – Vaughan Whitlock
Rig Ship For Ultra Quiet – Andrew Karam